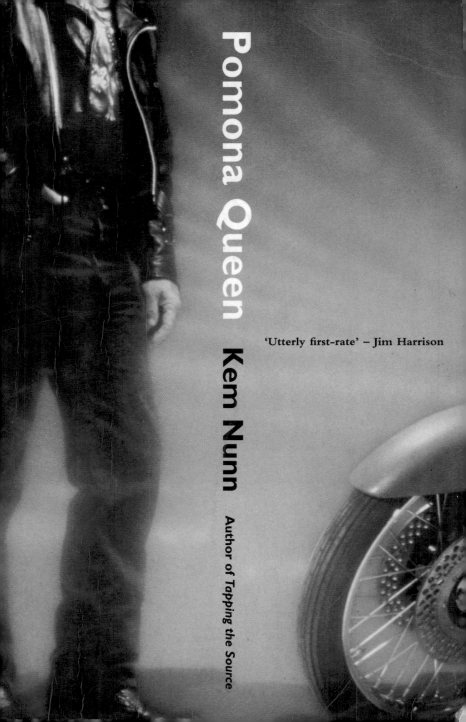

Pomona Queen

Kem Nunn

'Utterly first-rate' – Jim Harrison

Author of *Tapping the Source*

POMONA QUEEN

Kem Nunn

POMONA QUEEN

FOUR WALLS EIGHT WINDOWS NO EXIT PRESS

Published in the United States by
Four Walls Eight Windows/No Exit Press
39 West 14th Street, Room 503
New York, N.Y.10011

www.fourwallseightwindows.com
www.noexit.co.uk

October 2000

ISBN 1-56858-176-9   Pomona Queen

2 4 6 8 10 9 7 5 3 1

Printed and bound in Great Britain

For Jessica

Meet me tonight, love, meet me.
Meet me out in the moonlight alone.
For I have a sad story to tell you,
Must be told in that moonlight alone.

—"The Prisoner's Song"

POMONA QUEEN

ONE

Certainly the natives of Southern California were an inferior race. . . . Physically they were not strong, lithe and active, like the Cheyenne or Sioux, but squat, fat and unattractive. Untrustworthy they were, and ready to kill on provocation or for gain, but not brave or fierce.

—F. P. Brackett

A Brief Early History of the San Jose Rancho and its Subsequent Cities: Pomona, San Dimas, La Verne and Spadra

Earl Dean lost a good deal of hair quickly in his early twenties and the experience had left him in the habit of rubbing his head. In the beginning, he believed, the habit had sprung from curiosity, wondering at a given moment, say, just how many more of the bastards had jumped ship, which was how he thought of it then. He thought of it in terms of desertion and betrayal. When he rubbed his head now it was generally for some other reason. He knew what he looked like. He would sometimes catch himself at it while receiving bad news, listening to Carl upon the subject of Adverse Possession, for instance. The man had unearthed the item in a dog-eared copy of *The Real Estate Handbook*. It was a law by which he hoped to separate his stepson from his inheritance, namely the last acre of citrus in the Pomona Valley, and definitely qualified as bad news. Dean also rubbed his head when something was making him nervous, which was why he rubbed it now. When he became conscious of the act he stopped.

1

It was the part of town he was in that he didn't like, a run-down barrio south of Pomona someone with a sense of humor had thought to call Clear Lake. There were no sidewalks in Clear Lake, no streetlights, practically no roads. The lake, if in fact you wanted to call it that, was nothing more than a large hole dug to accommodate the runoff from a nearby cement factory. The stuff that filled the hole was the color of coffee and stank of rotten eggs.

It was an odor which, on the evening in question, Dean thought unusually strong. It seemed to fill his '62 Falcon station wagon as it humped along in the gathering darkness, a front end in need of a rebuild rattling and shimmying as the car passed over what, in Clear Lake, passed for a street. The rear of the wagon, filled as it was with Dean's equipment, rattled almost as loudly as the front. The equipment was this: a dozen dollhouses and half a dozen vacuum cleaners. Except of course that you weren't supposed to call them vacuum cleaners. Air purifier was the correct title. The dollhouses were the free gifts people got for allowing you to demonstrate the difference.

Dean drew a hand through what was left of his hair and looked once more at the address he had scribbled on a notepad before leaving the office. Not that the thing did him much good here. The place was a maze of cheap, look-alike tract homes and most of the addresses were illegible, though it occurred to him that this was perhaps intentional. It seemed to him the sort of neighborhood in which a good many of the citizens were probably wanted by someone, a collection agency, the law, an estranged mate. . . . Thinking this he paused to marvel that somewhere out there in the foul-smelling night someone really did want to be found by a vacuum-cleaner salesman.

But then that prospect was of course suspect itself,

given the level of telephone soliciting currently going on back at the office. The way it was supposed to work was that the girls at the phones were supposed to do a little preliminary screening. They could, for instance, make sure the prospective buyers were of age. They could make sure the people knew what it was they were being asked to look at. In three weeks on the job, however, Dean had already seen enough wild-goose chases to induce skepticism. The Clear Lake address had made him suspicious when he'd written it down, though Betty, the chain-smoking heifer who had sent him here, seemed to think they had a hot one on the line. Of course Betty had been wrong before, about a number of things, and Dean, lost now in the bowels of Clear Lake, a quarter moon shining slyly above him in a murky sky, was just about ready to bag it and start looking for the exit. He would tell Betty the address was nonexistent. He would tell her someone had been pulling her leg. These things happened and he had just about convinced himself of it when the address suddenly appeared before him—a series of painted wooden numbers tacked to a stucco wall at the end of a narrow, weed-choked driveway. The numbers were illuminated by a light that had been left on in the carport, just as if someone were expecting him.

Dean pulled to the side of the road and looked down the narrow drive. The carport was empty, its grease-spattered floor shining in the light. There were half a dozen yellowed newspapers in the drive and a pair of big chopped scooters parked on what was left of the grass. The scooters were not of the variety to set a man's mind at ease. There were some tools in the yard, near the bikes, and a tire leaned up against the fence, which had been built to screen off the front of the house. Behind the house a pair of ancient palms scratched at the sky, their fronds tipped with silver in the scant moonlight.

Dean slouched behind the wheel, double-checking the address on the card with the wooden numbers at the end of the drive, torn between his gut feelings for the place and Betty's words about a hot one, torn, one might say, between fear and greed. He allowed himself the momentary luxury of imagining it a predicament he no doubt shared with other movers and shakers, those sleek characters he'd observed on his last drive down Santa Monica Boulevard, landsharks behind tinted glass, car phones pressed against sleek, predatory heads. The image, however, was only marginally comforting and he made himself stop. The bad part was, Dean was proving to be something of a salesman. In three weeks he had already sold more Cyclone Air Purifiers than anyone else in the office. Also, there was this: the selling, if in fact he kept at it, was only the beginning. Just last week the office had been visited by a former graduate, a man who had himself begun in sales, just like Dean, then worked his way into management, a position in which he now took a percentage of what everyone beneath him made. Dean had sat in his metal folding chair and watched the figures go up on the blackboard. He'd seen the dollars multiply like rodents. He'd seen the branch manager's fire engine red El Dorado with the white leather interior parked in front of the office, shining like the Star of India between the California Thrift & Loan and the pizza parlor, and it had not been difficult to imagine he was at least as smart as the oily-looking bastard who drove the thing. Nor did he have difficulty imagining the precise look on his stepfather's face at that moment in which Dean would come forward, enough bread in hand to claim his inheritance, claim it as his great-grandfather had claimed it before him—surely a magical moment in which some cosmic arc would come full circle, in which parallel lines at last would meet, in which, at the very least, Earl Dean's stepfather would be given to understand he had just been quite righteously fucked in the ass. The image suited him. It was motivational. Armed with it, he was a salesman. He could stare down fear. It was enough at least to get him out of the car, get him around to the back, and start him toward the house, a dollhouse jingling at the end of one arm, a Cyclone Air Purifier at the end of the other, across the ragged grass where the scooters hunkered like mutant insects, chromed pipes and high-gloss lacquered tanks shining softly in the moonlight, and not until he'd rung the doorbell did he realize that somewhere between the Falcon and the porch, distracted no doubt by the sweet scent of victory, he had stepped in dog shit.

The door was answered by a huge, blond-haired woman. At least her hair was blond on top. The roots were black. She was dressed in a kind of flowered shift beneath which her breasts bounced like a pair of underinflated beach balls. She was barefoot. She had a beer in one hand and the door knob in the other. When she saw Earl Dean, with his dollhouse and Cyclone Air Purifier, she said, "Shit."

"Who is it?" Someone Earl could not see spoke from the interior of the house.

"Looks like a fucking salesman," the woman said. She looked at Dean's shoes. "With a case of the dogshit blues."

"Tell him to go fuck himself," the same voice said.

Dean thought of leaving. But then he had come so far. He had stepped in dog shit. He asked instead if someone had agreed to a demonstration of the Cyclone Air Purifier, thus making themselves eligible for a free gift.

"What?" the woman asked in return.

"Oh, yeah." a second voice, clearly female, issued from the room behind the fat woman.

The man Dean had yet to see responded angrily, "What in the fuck would you do a stupid thing like that for? Tell him to beat it."

The fat woman looked at Dean and shrugged. She moved as if to close the door.

"No, no, wait," the second female voice said.

Dean could hear footsteps and soon a thin brunette appeared in the armpit of the blond. "He's got a free gift," she said. She looked at Dean. "We want our free gift, dude."

Dean took the girl to be in her late teens. Perhaps she was twenty. She was dressed in a pair of black jeans and a sleeveless purple top. She wore a faded red bandanna on her head. A thin golden ring pierced the delicate wing of one nostril.

"The free gift is for watching a demonstration of the unit," Dean said. He was speaking to the girl and he wondered how he had managed to say something as corny as "the unit." One was supposed to refer to said unit as your Cyclone. As in: I've come to demonstrate your Cyclone, Ms. Finkbinder. The power of suggestion. Though in point of fact, Dean attributed his success as a Cyclone salesman thus far to his ability to ignore the rules most of his brother salesmen were trying hard to live by. In his opinion the rules did little more than play the man trusting in them for a fool.

"That's not what the lady on the phone said," the brunette told him. She was leaning forward now, her pale face shining in the light at the side of the house, her eyes warming to the fight.

Dean thought of telling the girl she was mistaken. It quickly occurred to him, however, that Betty may have said exactly that, or something just as bad, and he allowed himself a moment of silent hatred, which he felt, under the circumstances, might be divided evenly between fat Betty and this dark-eyed waif before him. "If the lady told you that," he said, "she was mistaken. I'm suppose to show you the machine. You get the free gift for seeing how it works. You are of course under no obligation to buy."

"Of course," the fat woman said.

"So what's the free gift?" the brunette asked. Her voice was filled with suspicion.

Dean raised the dollhouse. "Odds and ends," he said. "Things you can use around the house, cleaning products, that sort of thing. If you've got kids—"

"For Christ's sake." It was the man who spoke again. He was at the door now too, and Dean took him at once for the owner of at least one of the bikes on the lawn. The man looked to be only slightly taller than the blond, and probably about as heavy, except of course that the weight was distributed differently. It was also made of different stuff. His was bone and muscle. He was bare chested. A leaden pair of jeans hung about his hips. He was sporting a T-shirt tan of the classic variety, arms and neck nearly black with a combination of sun, dirt, and grease, while his torso remained the color of a new baseball. It looked just about as soft as a new baseball too. A long, pink scar wound its way over one hip and disappeared beneath the jeans. He had a couple of tattoos on his forearms, a pair of Harley-Davidson wings on one shoulder and some fancy blood-red letters on the other that read NO GUTS NO GLORY. The man's face, which was large and somewhat triangular in shape, was nearly as white as his torso. Dean found that the face looked like something a pit bull might own. The hair that capped it was thick and black, though streaked here and there about the temples with bits of gray. The man wore it pulled back in a ponytail. He wore a three-day beard and one thick tuft of black hair beneath his lower lip. Without taking his eyes from Dean, the man reached

7

out suddenly and cuffed the brunette on the back of the head, nearly knocking her out on to the porch with Dean. "You greedy little dirtbag," he said to the girl. "You called the dude out here, now you can fucking well see his act. Shit. We can all see it. Is it any good?"

The question, aimed at Dean, took him somewhat by surprise. "The act or the machine?"

"Fuck the machine, pardner. We could use a little entertainment here tonight. Couldn't we?" He reached over and swatted the brunette once more. "Couldn't we?" he asked again.

"A fucking dollhouse," the girl said. She was standing where the man had knocked her, one foot in the house, one on the porch with Dean. She was looking at him in such a way as to suggest that, clearly, whatever happened, from here on in, it was all his fault.

"Well, what did you expect?" the blond asked her. "A trip to Hawaii?"

"Send his ass in here," the biker said. He had already left the door and was somewhere back in the room beyond it.

"He's coming," the blond said. "He's gotta fix his shoes first."

"What's wrong with them?" The man's voice again.

"I told you, he stepped in some of Henry's shit."

"Well, Jesus, tell him to be more careful for Christ's sake."

When Dean had finished with his shoe he gathered his stuff and went inside. He did so with great reluctance. The thought of not doing so at all occurred to him. Scraping the last of Henry's droppings from his wingtip, he had considered making a run for the Falcon. Something kept him from it. He liked to think it was courage rather than greed, a stubborn adherence to the salesman's code, if in fact there was such a thing. If there was it pleased him to imagine it was something like what the marines said, all about how

8

when the going gets tough, the tough get going, so that passing through the door, he was able to see himself, for a moment at least, bathed in a kind of heroic light and it was, he thought, just the sort of thing that got one through the night in the bowels of Clear Lake, probably in a lot of other places too, for that matter. The moment, unhappily, was short lived; it died at about the same time he saw what was in the house.

"What's the matter, pappy?" The biker asked him. "Never seen a stiff before?"

Dean had, by this stage of the game, seen a number of stiffs. Most, however, had appeared in shining coffins, surrounded by freshly cut flowers and bore little resemblance to what the biker had in his house. This body was naked and white, stretched out upon a bed of ice in a large red freezer with the words Coca-Cola, and beneath that the phrase "Things go better with Coke," in white script across the side. The makeshift coffin sat leaking water into a soiled mustard-colored carpet in what Dean supposed was the dining room. A table had been shoved to one side and turned against a wall. There was a chandelier hanging from the ceiling above the freezer. The chandelier had the appearance of something someone had paid a fair price for at one time. But a lot of the glass parts seemed to have been broken and the thing hung at a slightly skewed angle. Still, there was enough glass left to glitter in the light cast by the tiny bulbs, which were shaped like the flames of candles, and the glitter was repeated in the ice that lined the red box. The scene did not look quite real and there was an oddly charged moment in which Dean saw, rejected, and saw some more. When he believed it he turned away.

"You don't have to look at it," the blond told Dean. Then to the biker: "What did you bring him in here for anyway?"

The biker was very drunk. Dean could see that now. He wondered why it hadn't seemed so obvious when the man had appeared at the door. Possibly because he could now see the man on his couch, surrounded by beer cans. The guy had his legs out in front of him and his arms up over the back in a kind of crucifixion pose. His naked chest shone in the yellow light of a small lamp situated on an end table near the couch. He had his head tilted back and was looking at Dean with one eye. "The hell," he said. "Let's see what you got, dude."

"Maybe another time would be more convenient," Dean said. Maybe in another life was what he meant. He was trying to keep his voice from shaking.

"Maybe so," the blond woman said.

"Let's see your fucking dollhouse," the brunette said. She took the thing from Dean's hand and began to open it. She appeared not to notice anything else.

Dean was about to leave. He had in fact already made his turn toward the door when a beer can sailed across the room, missing his head by inches and crashing against the front door. The blond woman said, "Hey." The biker told her to shut the fuck up and when Dean looked at him again the guy was holding a knife. "You ain't goin' nowhere, man," the biker said. He spoke from the couch, staring steadily at Dean. "You think I'm drunk? Question is, how drunk? That right, smart boy? You think you can get out that door before I can get over there? I'll cut your fucking nuts off, man."

Dean felt a sudden flash of moisture on the inside of his thigh and fought to shut it off. He had of course heard about people pissing their pants; it was just that for some reason he had always assumed this would not be his fate. The man on the couch looked to have a good fifty pounds on him. The blade of the knife in his hand was a good ten inches long. The instrument gleamed in the same soft yellow light that lit up the man's chest and stomach. It was hard to know just how crazy the bastard was. Maybe he had killed the other guy. It was a thought.

"Don't fuck with him, honey," the blond offered. "He's gone a little bit nuts." She was speaking softly, just loudly enough for Dean to hear her. "That's his brother," she said.

Dean assumed she was talking about the man in the freezer. He stood where he had stopped, at the edge of the room. No one spoke. They were all looking at him. Dean tried to get his mind to do something. It was like trying to coax speed from the Falcon. He dropped to one knee and began to fumble with the cardboard encasing his machine. Apparently he was going to show them the unit. His body seemed to have made the decision without him, as if some emergency system had kicked in, taken a quick inventory of options, and settled on the line of least resistance. He found, however, that a good deal of the feeling had left his fingers, creating for him the sensation that he too was a spectator, watching as some other meathead tore at the tape that sealed the box, and all the while trying desperately to remember exactly how to begin.

Slowly, he began to come up with something, a very rudimentary plan: show them the unit, as quickly as possible. Then leave. The plan seemed to help. The words began to form. They were the words of the class—all about filters and airflow. He also began to think about which of the parts before him might serve as a weapon in case the part about leaving didn't work out. Perhaps, he thought, the guy will have another beer and pass out. It was the light at the end of the tunnel.

"A vacuum works by suction," Dean heard himself saying.

"Yeah?" the biker said. "I could go for some of that shit my own self. Know what I mean?"

"Suction demands airflow," Dean said.

"Hear that, girls? Best listen to this dude."

Dean had begun a search of the carpet. He was hunting for some bit of trash with which to continue his demonstration: A bit of trash on the palm of the hand. Cover it with the nozzle. Turn on the machine. Turn it off. The trash would still be there. Now turn it on again, this time making sure the nozzle was held above the trash at a slight angle. Zoom. Gone with the trash. Airflow, Ms. Finkbinder. But he was having difficulty. He kept catching glimpses of the corpse. The floor beneath his hand kept doing things, as if it meant to desert him altogether.

He had at last managed to dig a good-sized ball of lint from the carpet. He placed it on the palm of his hand and looked at the man on the couch. The guy had resumed the crucifixion pose, head cocked, one eye open, one closed. The pose suggested, among other things, a certain level of concentration on the man's part and for a moment Dean and the biker faced one another across the gleaming collection of metal and plastic at Dean's knees.

"I know you," the biker said all at once. At least Dean thought this was what he said. It was difficult to be sure. The man had spoken softly, slurring his words, speaking, it would seem, as much to himself as to Dean.

Dean said nothing. He was not interested in any more surprises. He had begun to envision the guy's passing out as if his thinking about it hard enough might make it so. He bent over the machine and was surprised when the man spoke again, his voice having shed the thick, drunken slur of only moments before, sounding suddenly more like the man who had first come to the door. When Dean raised his eyes he found to his great horror that the man had gotten off the couch, knife in hand, and was moving toward him.

"Fuck, man," the biker said. "I said, I know you." There was an attachment in the kit used for lifting dust from corners. Dean felt his fingers, slick with sweat, close around it. He got to his feet and stared into the man's face, the black eyes, the silver front tooth, the whitish scar running through one brow and down across the bridge of his nose. The guy was six inches taller than Dean. He was armed. Dean had a corner duster.

"Hey, give the guy a break, Danny," the woman said.

Dean turned a bit in the direction of the woman. Behind her he could see the thin brunette. She was standing alone in the kitchen, the contents of Dean's dollhouse spread out all around her—a yellow box of SOS pads, a small bottle of 409, a pair of pink latex gloves. . . . It was another world, Dean thought, in the kitchen. He longed to go there, amid those familiar items. He would instruct the girl in their use. Her gratitude would prove undying. In the dining room the corpse seemed to exude a pale white light all its own.

"There's nothing in here but a bunch of shit," the brunette said.

"Fuck a duck," the biker said. He turned to the blonde. "I know this fucker," he said.

"Good, Danny."

"Good, Danny," the biker repeated, making his voice high and whiny. He lurched a step forward and put a hand on Dean. The hand seemed to take up most of the space between Dean's neck and shoulder and he could feel the guy squeezing with it. He could feel the weight of the thing bending him over and he had to work to stay straight beneath it.

"Fuckin' A," Danny said. "Fuckin' Johnny Magic."

He turned Dean with his hand so that Dean was facing the two women. "Johnny Magic," he said once more. The brunette took a step away from the counter and looked at Dean as if she were seeing him for the first time. "Yeah?" she said.

"Yeah," Danny mimicked once more. "Listen to her," he said. "She don't even know what the fuck I'm talking about."

The girl went back to her dollhouse. "So what?" she asked.

The biker turned to Dean "Tell me I'm wrong, dude."

Dean stood looking into the narrowed black eyes, groping for a clue. It had been a long time since he had heard the name.

"Johnny Magic," the biker said. "I used to party to this cat, man."

The biker took a poke at Earl Dean's arm. "Dan Brown, asshole. You look like you just shit your pants."

Slowly Dean began to rearrange the features of the man before him. Get rid of all that hair, chop it down and channel it—a flat top with fenders, just enough in front to get a little roll out over the widow's peak. Shave a good forty, fifty pounds off the body, make it long and lean, skinny almost—kind of skinny that was nothing but cords and cables. . . . The fact was, if he concentrated hard enough he could just about make it all work, turn the clock back—what? Twenty years? Dan Brown? The name did things. He could still hear people whispering at parties, "Watch yourself, asshole, Dan Brown's here."

And he supposed if this really was Dan Brown standing before him, then the body on ice was his little brother, the one they had always called Buddy. For Earl Dean had followed the Brown brothers through the Pomona public-school system. They'd started out three or four years ahead of him, a pair of hardasses in T-shirts and tankers. Kind of guys you'd see in the morning on your way to school, hanging out with their buddies, DAs and jelly rolls slick with grease, cancer sticks spooling out misty threads like pale gray question marks on the damp morning air and if you were on foot you made sure you took the long way around. They said Dan Brown could kick the shit out of his old man by the time he was fifteen, and after that, they said, there was no stopping him. He'd once gone after a shop teacher with a ball-peen hammer, ended his stint at Emerson Junior High School in impressive fashion, amidst a swarm of helmeted cops and flashing red lights. He'd shown up a year later at the high school, where he lasted about six months before stabbing a security guard in the throat with a screwdriver at a football game. He'd done some time behind that one and when he got out he was done with school. You'd still see him around though. He had a panel truck by then and when the beer flowed and the locals got down to serious speculation on the subject of overall, all-time badassery, everyone had at least one Dan Brown story to tell. And when the stories had been told, theories were advanced as to where it would all end, hard time, a padded cell. . . . And then one night in the heart of the sixties Dan Brown had taken a cop's nightstick away from him and beaten him to death with it on the front porch of some shabby tract house in the dead of summer.

The story line blurred after that. There had been a trial of course, local press. Dean, however, had been occupied elsewhere and would have been hard pressed to remember how it had all ended. Forced to guess, he supposed he would have said that the locals had called it, that the man was indeed dead or in prison. It then occurred to him that he had in fact heard of one last item pertaining to the Brown clan. It had to do with the old man. The old man, it seems, had taken his life. He'd driven himself out to a grove one night, this when there were still groves in the valley to drive out to, and shot himself through the head. And that, Dean thought, was the last he had heard of the Browns, certainly the last he had expected to hear, the last, for that matter, he would ever have wanted to hear, had not some guiding star too demented to contemplate led him here tonight, wandering as blindly onto Dan Brown's turf as he had wandered into Henry's shit on a ragged grease-stained lawn. The corner duster fell from Dean's hand, striking the carpeted floor with a barely audible pop.

"What you need to understand," Dan Brown was telling the ladies, "is that Johnny Magic could fuckin' sing like ringin' a bell."

"So what's he doing selling vacuum cleaners?" the brunette asked.

Dan Brown turned Dean back around so that they were facing one another once more. "What are you doing selling vacuum cleaners?" he asked.

Dean could feel the sweat beading up on his forehead where hair used to be. He felt flushed and somewhat feverish. The armpits of his shirt and sport coat were by now well soaked with perspiration.

"You don't look too good," Dan told him. "Perhaps the magic has fled," he said to the women and Dean was once again surprised by how sober he sounded. It was disconcerting really. One second the guy sounded like he was gone, the next he was back, stone sober. When he thought about it, however, it seemed to him that the Dan Brown of old had something of that about him as well, that even then the guy had been about as predictable as a Doberman with a brain tumor. Dean supposed it was what had given him the edge in all those murky encounters across the years, through barrooms and alleys. It wasn't size. Dean had himself once witnessed a fight in which Dan Brown had taken on a local football hero with a scholarship to UCLA, given away fifty pounds, and still sent the guy home unconscious in the back of Ray Estrada's '40 Ford, eyes swollen shut, blood coming out his ears. It was the kind of thing one remembered about Dan Brown. The man could go off. One saw it in the eyes. And it gave one pause.

Dan was still standing with his hand on Dean's shoulder. "Hey lighten up, dude. So you're selling vacuum cleaners. So what? It's not the end of the fucking world. Have a beer, man."

"I'd like to," Dean said. "But I've got these other appointments." He sounded lame enough, even to himself, and he had a fairly good idea about how Dan Brown would respond. Still, he had begun and he figured he might as well see it through. "They set up the appointments for us at the office," he continued. "We have to call in. In fact if I don't leave pretty quick, I'm going to have to call in to let 'em know I'm here. When I call in . . ." Dan Brown was waving a hand.

"Hey I don't even want to hear any of that shit." His eyes met Dean's. "My fucking brother died tonight, man."

The brunette walked from the kitchen and handed Dean a beer. "For Johnny Magic," she said.

Dean took the beer. The can burned like dry ice in his hand and he was granted a sudden image of himself as a young boy, losing a layer of skin out of one palm to a block of dry ice he'd come upon at a wedding reception. He thought of the aftermath as well, the long ride home, the hand wrapped in a bloody towel, and nothing to do but hold the throbbing thing in his lap while Carl lectured him from the front seat. The image came back to him as if it had happened only yesterday and he saw once more the ragged head

liner above his face, the bat-winged shadows of passing cars, the scarred cloth, the headlights shimmering
in the glass.

Dan Brown removed his hand from Dean's shoulder. He took a step toward the kitchen and planted
his knife in the narrow wooden bar separating the two
rooms. He did this in a very nonchalant way, as if he
had suddenly grown bored or preoccupied. There was,
however, Dean noted, a kind of unconscious grace
about the act that one could not quite ignore. "Fuck
it," Dan Brown said. "I won't even cut your balls off.
Sit down and have a beer, man. Have a beer and talk
to your old friend Dan Brown." He waved Dean
toward the couch, then started for it himself.

It was only for a moment that Dean thought of bolt-
ing. The trouble was, he'd seen the speed with which
his host had planted his blade on the bar. He had done
it, Dean thought, much the way a cat might pluck a
moth from the air. He took a long drink of beer and
started across the carpet, stepping as he did so on
the plastic attachment with which he had so recently
thought to save himself. The piece gave beneath him
with an audible crack. Dan Brown turned to look at it,
a ragged smile lighting up his face. "Jesus, Johnny.
Dog shit and vacuum cleaners. You always this clumsy
or you having an off night?"

⚊ TWO ⚊

Don Richardo Vejar and Don Ygnacio Palomares
stopped beneath the willows in what is now
Ganesha Park.... Far to the east the snowy masses
of San Bernardino and San Gorgonio and San
Jacinto glistened in the rising sun.... Yet between
them and the northern foothills lay a great carpet
thousands of acres in extent, whose variegated col-
ors Nature had woven with lavish hand.... How the
hearts of these Spaniards must have thrilled as they
thought, "all this fair land belonged to Spain...." Yet
for nearly three hundred years no one had claimed
this valley as his own.

—F. P. Brackett

When Dean had finished the first beer, the brunette brought him a second. "Johnny must be thirsty,"
she said. In fact, Dean believed the beer might help.
From his seat on the couch he was afforded a view of
the naked corpse. It seemed to him that a dead body
would soon begin to smell but he could detect nothing
coming from the one in the freezer. The room did have
an odor, however, something chemical, the residue of
bug spray perhaps. Dean, seated at the end of the
couch opposite his host, had the feeling that whatever
the substance was, it was making him dizzy. The feeling was distinctly unpleasant and served only to add
to the general confusion of things.

Dean supposed that even under the best of circumstances, Dan Brown was not one of the world's great
conversationalists. He was not a man to linger upon a
single subject, nor was he inclined to go out of his
way for the smooth transition. He expected Dean to
keep up, and when Dean missed something, the man
took it personally.

"So what happened to your band?" Dan Brown asked. They had, up till this point, been talking about the scooters parked on the front lawn.

Dean shook his head. He forced a laugh.

"What's funny?"

Dean had been hoping to make light of his band. He saw now that this was a mistake. He cleared his throat. "Nothing. I was just thinking . . . Nineteen sixty-nine? Who didn't have a band?"

"I didn't," Dan Brown said.

Dean was silent. He couldn't say that he cared for the way the man was looking at him. Dan Brown moved to the edge of the couch and slammed his can of beer down on the coffee table, hard enough to send several ounces of the stuff foaming across the yellowed wood.

"So everybody had a band. What the fuck is that supposed to mean? So every asswipe and his brother has a fucking car. You hear what I'm saying?"

Dean was trying to follow it.

"Pussies," Dan Brown said. "I asked you what happened to them, man."

Dean nodded. "Most of them are married now," Dean said. In fact, with one exception, Dean hadn't the slightest idea of what had happened to his band. "Jobs, families . . ." His voice trailed away from him. He tried to get it back. "Hard to make a living at that sort of thing," he said.

Dan Brown fixed him with a triumphant glare touched with contempt. He retrieved his beer. "Pussies," he said again. The word seemed to make him feel better. He settled back into the couch once more.

The two men stared into the litter of Dean's equipment on the living-room floor. The blonde had disappeared somewhere. The brunette was still in the kitchen. She appeared to be doing something with a frozen pizza while grousing about the dollhouse.

"I don't care if every asswipe in the valley had a band," Dan Brown said at length. "You were good."

Dean nodded. He looked thoughtfully at the equipment spread before him.

"I'm not talking about the music part," Dan Brown said. "Your piano playing and all that shit. You know, that shit all sounds the same to me. I'm talking about your fucking voice, man. I don't care about these other douche bags. You could sing. You hear what I'm saying?"

Dean allowed that he did.

"You were good," Dan said. "If you're good at something you ought to stick with it, right? I mean any asshole could sell this shit."

Dean thought of saying something about the art of salesmanship, something he'd picked up from his class, but decided against it.

"Look at me," Dan said.

Dean looked at him. He wasn't sure what this meant exactly and so took another drink of beer. He assumed that his host was exhibiting himself as an example of something, though perhaps he had missed another transition, in which case silence was no doubt the course of prudent behavior. He was saved, however, from further comment by the brunette, who suddenly walked into the room and turned on the television. She then seated herself on the floor, in front of the two men. Dean half expected Dan to tell her to shut it off, but he didn't. The set came to life in the middle of a Kung Fu rerun. Dan Brown said, "Shit," and took a drink of beer.

Dean had in fact seen the episode before. He recognized the scene. A blond-haired woman was running from a group of men on horseback. The show's star was walking through the woods with a flute. He was about to cross paths with the woman.

"Ass-kickin' time," Dan Brown said.

"I think these guys get off easy," Dean ventured. As he remembered it, the star just shoved the guys around some with his flute and they let the girl go.

"The Kung Fu's jus' tryin' to get himself a little pussy," Dan Brown said.

"The Kung Fu doesn't like pussy," the brunette told them.

"Shit too. It's a fuckin' act, man. You watch. The cat's gonna rail this broad. I can feel it."

"They won't let him rail her on TV, asshole," the girl said. She was seated with her legs crossed beneath her, leaning back on her arms with her hands flat on the floor, her fingers pointing toward Earl Dean and Dan Brown. Dan finished another beer. He flattened the can and flipped it at the girl. It hit her on the back of the head.

The girl told him to cut it out. She reached behind her head to adjust her bandanna, tightening the knot. It was a position in which her shoulders were turned toward the men and Dean noticed for the first time that on her left shoulder there was a scar tattoo. The object was shaped something like a football with a dot in the center, beyond which there were a series of short straight lines, as if the football were giving off rays of light. The lines were raised and slightly mottled, faint shades of purple upon a field of milk white skin.

"So he'll fuckin' rail her during the commercials. Am I right?" Dan Brown reached across the couch and tapped Dean on the shoulder. "He'll be up her ass during the commercial. They try to put it on TV, some citizen'll sue 'em. Am I right?" He poked Dean once more.

"Right," Dean said.

The girl had stopped fiddling with the bandanna. Her arms were now wrapped about her chest. She spoke to Dean without turning her head. "You don't have to say it just because he says so," she said.

Dean thought otherwise. The man's mood seemed to have lightened and Dean was all for it.

Dan Brown laughed. On the screen the Kung Fu had finished with the men. The girl it seems was from an insane asylum. The Kung Fu was telling the men the girl had a journey to make.

"Kung Fu's the one with the journey to make," Dan said. "He's got a journey to make up her ass with his dick."

On the floor the brunette looked over her shoulder, made a face, and then looked back at the set.

Dan Brown cracked a fresh beer. "Whatever happened to that red-haired bitch?" he asked suddenly. "One used to play the fiddle with you guys."

Dean watched the Kung Fu escorting the young woman into the forest. He watched until they were out of sight, swallowed by the trees. Dan Brown had hit upon the exception. If Dean had lost track of the others, he knew very well what had become of the red-haired girl. "She went away," he said. "She went out to New Mexico with this older guy."

"She marry him?"

"She died," Dean heard himself say. He'd heard himself say it before. It never sounded quite right somehow.

"Yeah?" Dan Brown said. "My brother died too. Did I tell you that? That's him over there. I got him on ice. You want to look?"

"I can see him," Dean said, "pretty well from right here."

"You can't see him good enough though," Dan said. "You can't see what killed him now, can you?"

Dean admitted that he could not.

Dan Brown pulled himself from the sofa and crossed

the room. "Come on over here," he said. "I want you to see something."

Dean stood up very slowly. His legs were a bit unsteady. He had never looked closely at anything like this before and he had the idea that if he did so just now he was quite likely to pass out, or puke, or do any number of things, really, that would not create a favorable impression on his host. He had the idea that creating a favorable impression was, under the circumstances, his best shot at survival. It was, in the end, perhaps, this instinct which enabled him to view the body.

Up close there was an odor. Dean guessed the ice helped, for the body was sunk among thousands of tiny cubes, icy prisms to the fractured light of the chandelier, streaked with shades of pink and scarlet. Dean concentrated upon the ice, hoping that by so doing he would view the body only peripherally. It was a ploy that worked fairly well early on. Then Dan Brown elbowed him in the arm and put his finger to the wound, the what, as Dan Brown had said, that had killed him.

Buddy Brown had been knifed in the abdomen. The wound itself was dark and puckered and if one looked closely one could see inside, where bodily fluids still oozed among scarlet folds. It was a situation in which, the more one looked, the more one saw. Dean looked for some time. Once started, it was somehow difficult to stop. He looked until the wound began to move in a slow, undulating fashion, at which point he found it necessary to put out a hand to steady himself. The hand came to rest on the edge of the freezer, his fingers striking the wet metal, the burning ice. It occurred to him that the room at his back had gone quite still, that the television had been silenced. He found himself, in a detached sort of way, wondering if the Kung

Fu had in fact undertaken the journey his host had predicted.

"The little fucker," Dan said. "He never was that good in a fight. Not really. All show and no go. What can I say?"

Dean looked at Dan Brown. It was as if some note of tenderness, or at least some approximation thereof, had crept into the man's voice, demanding Dean's attention.

Dan Brown was staring at his dead brother. Above his head the crippled chandelier spread its dull light. He reached into the freezer once more. "Some bastard did this to my brother, Magic." There was something in his face as he gazed into the sea of bloodstained ice before him, and Dean could not say if the expression had more to do with the loss of his brother or with the simple, incomprehensible fact that Dan Brown himself had been violated in a way he could not quite get a handle on. "I've got my people out right now," Dan said, and when he said it he looked up into Dean's face and there was a light burning back of those dark eyes Dean did not care to bask in for long. He turned instead to the freezer, to the empty, white body on ice, the undulating wound. "I want the fucker's name, Magic. And when I get it, I'm gonna cut his fucking heart out."

Dean looked up once more. Dan Brown was leaning just a bit forward, his broad white brow bathed in perspiration, a huge blue vein trembling slightly along one side of his neck. "Family . . ." he began, then let his voice trail way. The single word, however, had been enough. One didn't fuck with family, and it was as if in that one word, the ferocity with which it had been spoken, was contained a universe and Dean could see them once more, the badasses of his youth, the ones worth being afraid of, the ones born of a long, proud line, full-blown white trash from the purest of stock and if you fucked with the little brother you fucked with them all. They were a tribe, and later Dean had seen something of the same among the Chicano gangs and the blacks come to P town to escape the ravages of south central Los Angeles but managing only to bring the ravages with them. Still, he had seen it first on the playing fields of Kingsley Elementary School, in the likes of the Brown brothers with their ragged clothes, their home-cut hair. Even then they had seemed old beyond their years, all knuckles and Adam's apples, quick and mean, a people not to be trifled with. And now someone had trifled with the Browns in a large way and Dean did not doubt that blood would be spilled before this night was through. "I'm glad you're here," Dan Brown said suddenly. "We go back, man. You're not my blood, but we go back. It's what remains, dude."

Dean was uncertain about how to respond. And yet the man was staring at him as if some sort of response was in order. At which point, a telephone began to ring. Dan Brown did not seem to hear it immediately. He was still staring at Earl Dean with the same unnerving intensity, as if Dean were about to be weighed in the balance and found wanting. For Dean, the sound was a kind of beacon, a signal from the world beyond these yellowed walls.

Soon the brunette appeared. She looked at Dean. "It's for you," she said.

For a moment Dean felt himself quite mute. He simply stared. "It's for you," the girl said again, a bit put out. "It's your stupid office."

Dean turned from the Brown brothers and crossed the floor. The receiver had been placed on the narrow wooden bar in which Dan Brown had planted his knife. The girl followed Dean to it. When he picked up the phone she leaned against him in such a way that the shoulder that bore the scar together with a goodly portion of one small breast were pressed against Dean's arm. It was a position in which she could speak more or less directly into the receiver. "Tell the cheap sons of bitches to get some better gifts," she said. "This one's pissin' me off."

The office Dean worked out of was run by a pair of managers. Bill and Dave. It was Bill and Dave who took turns teaching the one-week training courses you went through to become a Cyclone salesman. Dean had drawn Bill during his week. Bill was a large dumpy-looking guy with a crew cut. He had the soft, well-fed look of someone who had not done an honest day's work in a long time. It was Bill who said hello when Dean took the phone from the girl.

"What gives, tiger?" Bill asked. "Too busy making money to call in?"

Dean was supposed to have called in when the blonde let him through the door. You were supposed to call when you got there, and then call again as you reached the end of your pitch, or rather, when you had made your first close and the people had turned it down. That's when you called. It was best to make sure the potential buyers were within easy listening distance, at which point you said something like: "Hi, Bill. Earl. Just wanted to touch base. That's right. Well, the Finkbinders loved their machine, Bill; they just don't think they can swing it right now. I need to get my next call. Huh, that's right. I can wait." A good idea to pause here, show Ms. Finkbinder your best smile. "By the way, Bill, how am I doing on that sales-promotion contest?" A second pause. "What's that? Just one more? You're kidding. Hold on a second, Bill." Hand over the phone now, addressing the Fink-binders. "You won't believe this, folks. You may be in luck. My manager wants to do us both a favor." And on into the second close. Dean found it difficult to believe that many of his coworkers actually said these things. So far, outside of class, Dean had managed to avoid saying them himself. It brought him in for a certain amount of sermonizing on the part of Bill and Dave. Still, Dean had been selling the things and as long as he was selling they seemed willing to excuse his lapses. Though they did not tire of trying.

"Sorry I'm late," Dean said.

"Never mind that, sport. Where you at, in your pitch, I mean? You killed the vac yet?" It appeared to Dean that either Bill had not heard the girl, which he found difficult to believe, or that for some reason he had chosen to ignore her.

"I've shown them the machine."

"Come on, Dean, *their* machine, remember. So what? They like it? You want help? What gives?"

"Oh, they like their machine." Dean was aware of Dan Brown watching him from the couch. The man had taken a brownish-colored cigarette from a small green bottle and he was sitting there puffing on it. The odor Dean had noted earlier seemed suddenly to have gotten stronger. Dean turned from the scent, back toward the kitchen, which he found suddenly flooded with a harsh fluorescent brilliance that did not seem to him quite natural. The brunette had left him. She had taken up an orange spatula and had moved with it into the midst of the light, the light with which there was something wrong.

"Something wrong?" Bill asked.

"Oh, no," Dean said. "Actually, I'm sort of in the middle of things. I'll get back to you, all right."

There was a moment of silence on the line during which Dean could hear the radio playing in the office. "Okay, tiger. Suit yourself. Just don't go making a career out of one stop. Know what I mean? We got a list of possibilities here. That one's dead, drop it, we'll get you another. And don't forget, things get slow, you can always kill the vac."

Killing the vac was probably Bill's favorite part of the pitch and he seemed never to weary of the phrase, resonant as it so clearly was with military overtones, as if one were planning a campaign. The event itself was a kind of contest one could hold for the benefit of the buyer in which their old vacuum was placed side by side with the Cyclone. The units were connected in some way, then turned on simultaneously. The Cyclone would generally suck all the air out of its opposition, thus proving not only airflow but suction superiority.

"You do remember how to kill the vac," Bill said. The man was obviously a bit put out that Dean was not offering more.

Dean only nodded, saying nothing.

"You sure you're all right?" Bill asked suddenly. "You sound a little weird."

Again Dean was slow in replying. At his back he could hear Dan Brown, growing restless it would appear, shifting his weight on the couch. "It's okay, Bill. Everything's cool. I'll get back to you when I can."

There was no immediate response and Dean hung up. He was on his way back into the living room when he heard a door slam.

There was a long, narrow hallway running what appeared to be the length of the house. Dean was standing at one end of it, at the edge of the kitchen, when he heard the door. He looked up in time to see two men following the blonde along the dirty carpet. When the man closest to the woman caught sight of Dean, he stopped suddenly, forcing his companion to stop as well. "Whoa," he said. "What the fuck is this?" He was looking straight at Dean.

"A friend of Danny's," the woman said. "I told him not to let the guy in."

"Jesus Christ." The guy pushed the woman aside and squeezed past her. He was dressed in a black T-shirt, soiled jeans, and motorcycle boots. He stopped in front of Dean. "Jesus Christ," he said again. "I thought he was a goddamn narc."

The man was as tall as Dan Brown, but thinner. He sported a wild crop of unruly brown hair, which had gone to orange at the ends and hung down far enough to cover his collar. His face was long and deeply tanned. He studied Dean for some time, then said, "Get him the fuck out of here." This was said with no small amount of vehemence. The words, however, did not seem to be directed to anyone in particular. It was, Dean thought, as if the man expected the room itself to expel him.

The tall biker was soon joined by the man who had followed him down the hall. This man was also dressed in a T-shirt and jeans. He was about Dean's height, thicker and with less hair. He was nearly bald up top but wore a beard that reached halfway to his stomach.

"Who are you telling to get out of here?" Dan Brown asked. He had come to the edge of the living room.

"We don't need anybody else in on this," the tall man said. "Least of all this fucking suit."

"The suit happens to be an old friend of mine," Dan Brown said. "We go back. Chuck, Ardath, say hello to Johnny Magic."

The two men looked at Earl Dean. Dean looked at the men. He took the taller of the two to be Ardath.

"You got your brother in your fucking house, man. He's dead. In case you forgot," the tall man said. "You don't need wimps in suits running to the cops about it."

Dan Brown stared at the man who had spoken. "Magic's cool," he said. "I told you, I know the cat. I

30

want him to sing over my brother's grave. That's what I want. I want a righteous ceremony."

Ardath groaned and leaned against the wall. "You're blowin' it, man."

Dan Brown stepped past Dean and lifted his knife from the bar. "I suggest you remember who you're talking too," he said. "I say the dude's gonna sing, the dude's gonna sing."

"Then what? What if the dude gets scared and goes to the cops?"

"The guy may be a suit. He's not a moron. I might decide to kill him anyway. After he sings." Dan Brown smiled at Earl Dean, showing him his silver tooth. He turned back to the men.

Chuck rubbed his beard and looked at the floor. Behind him, Ardath stood looking at the wall. It occurred to Dean that something was amiss. Seconds later it appeared to occur to Dan Brown as well.

"So come on," Dan said. "I want this fucker. You two pussies aren't trying to tell me you can't find him."

Chuck cleared his throat. He continued to look at the floor.

"It wasn't a him," Ardath said. He was staring straight at Earl Dean when he said it.

"Who the fuck you talking to, asshole? Him or me?"

The tall man looked at Dan Brown. "It wasn't a him," he said.

"It was a cunt," the short man said. "A cunt killed your brother, man."

Dan Brown stared into the short man's eyes. "You're not shittin' me, are you?"

"No," the man said. "We're not shittin' you."

The statement was followed by a profound stillness, out of which Dean was treated to the sound of his own blood—echoing among darkened chambers. He watched as the vein pulsed at the side of Dan Brown's

31

neck. Chuck and Ardath were silent, as was the big blonde. Even the brunette seemed to have abandoned her pizza, to hover somewhere at the edge of the carpet, the orange spatula dangling at her side.

"How do you like that," Dan Brown said softly. He turned and looked at Earl Dean. "My little brother gets himself killed by a fucking cunt."

"The Stench was with him," Chuck said. "He was the one who called."

Dan Brown just looked at him. The short man cleared his throat once more and went on. "He thinks he knows who it might be . . ." The man paused to shake his head. "The fucking chick musta been dusted, man, that's all I can say. Stench says Buddy was having an argument with this chick in back of the Mid-Dump. Says he went inside for a beer and when he came back out, that's when he found your brother. That's when he called. He got Kim . . ."

"Yeah, yeah, I know who the fuck he got. So why didn't he tell her about this cunt? Shit, he didn't even say who it was. Kim just gets this call sayin' Buddy's been cut. Next thing we know Buddy's out in the alley, fallin' off his bike. . . . Fucker dies before we can even get him in the house, man. . . . An' all I know is somebody cut him. . . ."

"The cat was scared, man. I think he was afraid to tell you it was a cunt. He was afraid you wouldn't believe him. Like maybe you would think it was him or some such shit."

"Maybe it was him." It was the brunette who spoke. Her voice, issuing from the kitchen, was shrill and birdlike, as if some small, whiskey-throated sparrow had been trapped there in the bad light.

Dan Brown shook his head in disgust. "Give me a break," he said. "That guy wouldn't have the balls even if Buddy wasn't my brother."

The girl made no reply. Dan Brown turned suddenly

and shouldered past the two men. Dean could see the thick, corded muscles of his back, shifting in the light as he walked down the hall and turned in to a room. When he reappeared he had pulled on a black T-shirt and was in the act of pulling a sleeveless Levi jacket on over that.

"I want to talk to this duffus Stench," Dan Brown said. "I want to hear it from him."

"He's gonna tell you it was the bitch," Chuck said. "She's got a band. Pomona Queen, or some such shit."

"He can tell me," Dan Brown said. "I'm gonna hear it from the asshole himself. But I'll tell you one thing. Cunt or no cunt, fucker who killed my brother is gonna pay."

"We takin' the scooters?" Ardath asked.

Brown stopped and looked at him. "You can take your mother for all I care," he said. "Me and Magic here are gonna take the panel. We're gonna take my brother. We're gonna talk to this Stench. We're gonna see about this bitch. And we're gonna bury my brother. We're gonna find a place and fucking Johnny Magic is gonna sing over his fucking grave. Remember?"

The tall man shook his head. The short man gathered his beard into a fist and drew it down into a point. "Gonna be one weird fucking night," he said.

Dan Brown ignored them. He spoke to the girl in the kitchen. "You'd better get Johnny another beer," he said. "He's gonna need it."

Dean took the beer, though by now he barely felt the can in his hand. There were a couple of things on his mind. One was Dan Brown's itinerary, the other was the name of the band, Pomona Queen.

When Dean wasn't out selling vacuum cleaners he was holed up in a tiny, one-room apartment situated off an alley in the heart of Pomona. There wasn't much to look at outside and not much to look at inside either. Dean in fact owned only two items that might pass for decoration. One was a picture of the red-haired girl who had died. The other was a packing-crate label from the days when Pomona Valley was the hub of the nation's citrus industry. The label bore the image of a dark-eyed girl and above her head the words Pomona Queen. Labels such as this were collector's items now. Dean's collection, however, was quite small. He had one and he had it because it was his great-grandfather's. The old man had commissioned the artwork himself from some long-ago lithographer, now forgotten, in the hopes that it would distinguish his produce from that of his neighbors. And Dean had always supposed that it would have, had it ever been used, had it not been left instead to the dust and the moth, to the wood ant of a barn that had begun to decay even before the wasting of the valley, or the quick decline of the McCauly line. That the name should come back to him now, in just this way, on an evening when the fates were already so clearly fucking with him, was enough to flat take a man's breath away. Dean's was. He swayed in the fetid air of the room. He tried for a moment to envision himself some-where in the bowels of the valley, above the open grave of Buddy Brown, his throat clogged with impris-oned words. He saw, in his mind's eye, a girl some-where in the night, a knife in her hand, fair and yet terrible, and suddenly, without apparent awareness or conscious intent, he found that he had moved the hand with the beer away from his body, as if in a toast. "To weirdness," he said. There followed a strange silence, in which Dean could not be immedi-ately certain he had spoken these words aloud. All he knew for sure was that everyone was looking at him. "I think Johnny's drunk already," the brunette said. The short man tugged at his beard. "Drunk or he's been whiffin' fumes." He looked at Dan Brown. "You gotta watch it with that shit," he said.

They had just about gotten out the door when the telephone began to ring once more. The brunette got it but before she could say much Dan Brown had knocked her out of the way and grabbed the receiver himself. "Yeah," he said. "What is it?"

He listened for several seconds, then spoke again. "Listen, you dumb fuck, your fucking salesman's not here anymore. That's right. He said he didn't want to call in because he doesn't want to work for you any-more. That's right. The motherfucker quit. Said there was nothing down there at the office but a fucking bunch of faggots all the time reaming each other's ass-holes, said it was making him physically ill. Know what I mean?"

Earl Dean stood sweating in the entry, the tall man on one side of him, the short man on the other. He was somewhere on that thorny ground between laughter and tears.

"Let me tell you something about that," Dan Brown said into the receiver, his voice a hoarse whisper. "I know right where you are, dickhead. You're in that little plaza off Central. Next door to the pizza joint. So maybe callin' the cops isn't such a good idea, is it? Because if I ever thought you were trying to fuck with me I might have to come down there." Dan Brown paused. "You wouldn't want me to come down there." Dan Brown replaced the receiver. "Your ex-boss, Johnny," he said. "I take it the man's something of a douche bag."

Earl Dean followed Dan Brown into the night. He started on to the grass and felt Dan Brown take him by the arm. "For Christ's sake, Magic," he said. "You track dog shit into my car and I'll put you out of your fucking misery."

"Shit." It was Ardath who spoke. "I'd put him out of his fucking misery anyway."

As Dean allowed himself to be guided back on to the narrow concrete walkway that skirted the lawn, he found that in a completely half-assed sort of way he was actually worried about his job. It was of course, in light of everything else, a ridiculous concern. He next wondered, as a kind of exercise in hope, if in fact Bill's going to the cops was anything he might count on. Somehow this seemed no less absurd. Dan Brown was right of course, the man was something of a douche bag. He had been threatened with bodily harm and Dean could almost see him wilting amid the stale cigarette smoke and fluorescent lighting of the office as the words of Dan Brown came down on him like an unwelcome rain. What in fact the guy would probably do—Dean could just about see it—would be to leave. He'd go across the street for a drink, just to get himself out of the office for a while; just in case, you understand, leave the girls at the switchboard to deal with any psychopaths might show up with funny ideas. The course of prudent behavior. The problem, Dean supposed, was that even an aging bullshit artist like Bill Frank could still recognize the real thing when he flat came up against it.

THREE

In due time the petition of Palomares and Vejar was granted. . . . Their dream was to come true. . . . They would build their homes in the beautiful valley south of the great mountains. . . . So a day was selected and the little party rode out, first to the Mission San Gabriel, where Padre Zalvideo joined them, and then on to the valley of promise.

—F. P. Brackett

The last blush of evening was gone, replaced by an inky blackness. A few faint stars lay strewn across the sky. Their light, however, appeared quite feeble in comparison to the blackness so that Dean, stumbling along the narrow walkway that skirted the front of the house, believed the darkness to be something more than the absence of light. It had substance, he thought, like water. It was something you could drown in.

The carport was no longer empty. Dan Brown's 1950 Chevrolet panel truck sat on the concrete floor, a dozen coats of hand-rubbed black lacquer shining softly beneath a single overhead light.

Dean remembered the car. Like the name of its owner, it did things. The date might have been 1969. Earl Dean might have been eighteen years old, on his way to a party, a girl on his arm, a fifth of apricot brandy in his hip pocket. The night might have been filled with mystery and promise, as if it were something that could never end. For a moment he could almost see it, could almost hear the music spilling out of the party house at his back, could almost smell the scent of orange blossom on warm spring air. And yet even as he toyed with the image it occurred to him that the scent, like the car, was not entirely a figment of his imagination. It was really there, the faintest trace of orange blossom amid the stench of polluted waters, adding in its own subtle way to the unreality of the moment, as if the aging Falcon really had carried him much further than the length of the valley.

Dean followed the scent of the blossoms. He passed through the carport and stood at its edge while Dan Brown unlocked the rear door of his panel truck. The trees were in a neighboring yard, a pair of them, shaggy and unkempt, ringed by ankle-high grass. There was a time when they had done that sort of thing, left a few of the trees in a few of the yards, a little something to speak of what had gone before, the golden age of citrus as it were, before the burning of the groves, the relentless march of the tract homes, from the hills of the Phillips ranch to the foot of the mountains, until the citrus industry was a memory and Pomona Valley was no longer the hub of anything, unless maybe you counted the smog.

Dean stood staring into the dark clutter of limbs, the swirl of white blossom, more vivid than starlight before the blackness of the leaves. The branches were dark and full. No sign of the virus there, he thought, no yellowing foliage, no wilting of the lower branches. Though of course it was possible the trees were symptomless carriers and he found himself rather absently trying to date the Clear Lake tract. It must, he thought, have been built in the mid fifties. He could remember it as a boy. He could remember his grandmother complaining about it at the time. "Houses look like those little things you play Monopoly with," she had said. Later there was that song about little houses made of ticky-tacky. On the streets of Clear Lake, of course,

the little houses had long ago gone to seed; at which
point it occurred to Dean that he'd best stop ruminat-
ing on the past and start looking for a way out.

He could hear Chuck and Ardath behind him now.
They were lurching across a corner of the yard with
the freezer between them. "Jesus Christ," Chuck said.
Both men were breathing hard. As they started into
the carport they banged against one of the wooden
four-by-fours that supported the roof. The wood
cracked and groaned from the weight of the chest. The
men, thrown off stride, were forced to put the freezer
down.

Dan Brown looked up from the rear of his truck. He
had his back to Dean. He told Chuck and Ardath to
watch the fuck out. Ardath was bent at the waist, his
hands on his knees. It was the position from which he
spoke. "What the fuck you got in here, man? I know
this little shit can't be that heavy." The man didn't
bother to raise his eyes. Chuck stood with his hands
on his hips. He was looking into the street. Dan Brown
swore softly beneath his breath and started toward the
freezer. The object was perhaps twenty feet from
where Dean stood, alone, on the far side of the
carport.

Dean watched as the three men began an inspection
of the cargo. He watched for someone to at least glance
in his direction. Oddly enough, this did not happen.
Dan Brown had begun to talk, about something. Dean
could not quite make it out. The man's back was to
Dean. Ardath had opened the freezer and Chuck was
still looking into the street. Dean took a tentative step
to his right. Still no one looked. He had begun to cal-
culate the time it would take him to reach the redwood
fence that surrounded the neighbor's backyard. A
large section of the fence had been broken down near
the front of the house, allowing for an easy entrance.
It was at the side of the house nearest Dan Brown's.

If he could get back there before they knew he was gone. . . . There would be other fences. Other yards. It would be quite dark. There would, Dean thought, be places to hide. He glanced once more at the men. Their positions remained unchanged. He stepped onto the neighbor's grass. He was aware of his pulse as he did so, in the hollow of his throat. He studied the ground he would have to cross. It was true of course that something better might come along later. It was equally true that it might not. A crapshoot, as they said. The trouble was, the stakes were rather high. They appeared, at any rate, to be high to Earl Dean. Ahead of him lay the broken fence—a scant twenty yards through the ankle-deep grass. Beyond it lay the darkness, the sheltering night. Dean went.

He sprinted toward the hole. His tie flipped up and floated back to drape across his shoulder. The tails of the sport coat flapped behind him. His shoes, however, striking the grass, made almost no sound at all so that, later, he would imagine he had in fact gained the rear of the neighboring house before the three men in front even knew he was gone. Also, later, he would remember the line of a song: "I made a good run but a little too slow." The thing was, Dean did make a good run. It was, he thought, for a man in his condition, a damn good run, and if it hadn't been for the dog, it might have gotten him somewhere.

Standing at the edge of the carport, he had considered the possibility of dogs. But if the people had a dog, he had asked himself, why hadn't they rigged something to patch the fence? Another crapshoot. The hole had suggested an empty yard and it was what he had gone with.

He was past the house when he met the animal. The beast gave him no warning. It simply emerged, materializing out of the darkness into which he had plunged. And even then, it made no sound. It was as if the night itself had suddenly sprouted fangs, a slavering tongue. Believing there would be a collision, Dean lunged wildly to his left, tripped over a sprinkler head, and belly flopped on the dank grass. He thought the dog would have him then and it was only when it didn't happen that the situation became clear to him. The animal was attached to the house by way of a rope. The rope was looped around one of the four-by-four posts that supported the roof covering a cement patio, and if the dog had had its way, it would have brought the house down. For the beast continued to lunge, savagely, silently, so that for the moment the only sounds were those of the big paws fighting for traction on the wet grass, the crack of the rope as the dog pulled it tight, the labored breathing of the beast mixing with Dean's own.

Dean struggled to his feet. He put a hand to the fence to steady himself. He might as well have flipped a switch. For even as his hand was pulling away he felt the wooden plank shudder beneath it, felt the rake of claws through a good half inch of redwood. At the same instant the night erupted in sound. It was as if every other dog in Clear Lake had, through the magic of some primordial animal magnetism, gotten wind of their neighbor's blood lust and cut loose in unison. Nor was the eruption limited to noise. There was a light show as well, most of it emanating from the house before him, and voices, human as well as animal. Dean was suddenly beginning to feel very sober.

Without really thinking much about why, he began to run, in a crouched position, hugging the shadows at the base of the fence. A spotlight blossomed suddenly at the rear of the house whose yard he had invaded. It took what was left of the shadow and Dean was given to understand that he was damn short on time, enough perhaps for one shot at the fence separating him from the alley. He grabbed for the top and pulled, swung one leg high enough to hook it with the heel of his shoe. A running shoe might have held. The cheap black dress shoe slipped and swung back to the ground. And that was about it. Earl Dean dropped to his feet as Dan Brown reached him.

Dean saw about as much of Dan Brown as he had of the dog. He saw a white face and dark hair. He saw the arms and the sleeveless Levi jacket. And he did something he would not have thought possible. He guessed it was instinct. Maybe some sort of adrenaline pump—the kind you read about now and then in the supermarket checkout lines: Elderly woman lifts car, saves husband. In Dean's case, the headlines would stand in need of revision: Aging cunt strains back while hubby croaks. In short, Earl Dean swung on Dan Brown. He threw a left, and it hit something. He wasn't sure what, exactly. But he felt it in his hand, bone on bone. He kept his head down and threw again, a wild overhand right that missed everything, and then he was on his ass, his back against the fence. He knew at once that he had been hit. He could not immediately say where. At which point his head began to hurt. He put a hand to his face and found that his mouth was without feeling beneath it. He found as well that his nose was dripping blood. It covered his tie and shirt, the sleeve of his sport coat. He put a hand out behind him. He had in mind getting up, when the dog in the yard at last managed to break its rope. The article gave with a dull crack. The dog sailed through the air and attached itself to Dan Brown. Dean guessed it had him by the back of the leg, just below the ass.

The animal, a wiry-haired thing about the size of a German shepherd, seemed to have gotten a fairly good grip. Dean could see it swing around as Dan turned, hacking away with his right fist. The dog took several blows to the side of the neck and let go. It crouched, then sprang forward once more, this time getting him again on the forearm and for a moment the two of them stood there, man and dog. The dog with the man's arm in its mouth, the man hammering at the dog's head with his free fist, two, three, half a dozen times until suddenly the dog is lurching around in circles like a boxer with his legs gone. Dan Brown stayed right with it. He was putting the boot to it now, big black motorcycle boots pumping away like the jack end of an oil rig swinging in the moonlight until it was over, and the mongrel was laid out cold as the clay in the middle of a ragged yard. And for some reason Dean continued to sit there. He didn't quite seem to have it in him to get up.

A child had begun to scream, a young blond-haired girl. Dean saw her. She ran suddenly from the house. She was screaming at Dan Brown, something about what he had done to Buckie. It was hard to tell what was said because there was a lot of noise. All the other dogs were still barking and there were people yelling, trying to quiet the dogs, and other people trying to find out what was going on. At one point Dean was aware of the brunette from Dan Brown's looking at him over the fence. He could hear her shouting at someone, presumably the blonde. "It's Johnny Magic," he heard her say. "Looks like he tried to run away. I told you he was fucked up." She paused, then added something else: "No way," she shouted, "Danny's kickin' his ass."

Danny did in fact look like kicking Dean's ass would have given him great satisfaction. There were, however, distractions. The little girl took a swing at him with the stick. Dan Brown gave her the back of his hand and knocked her on her ass. The girl began to shriek and hold her nose. This brought two more people out of the house, what Dean took to be the girl's mother and an older brother. The brother was maybe twenty years old, a beefy blond with shoulder-length hair, and one could see right away that the kid was in something of a spot. The mother and girl were howling for vengeance. It was quite plain, however, that the kid knew Dan Brown and didn't want any part of him. "What's going on here?" he asked. He had to ask it a couple of times. You could see he was trying to sound like he might do something about whatever it was that was going on but was having a hard time convincing anyone of it. He was standing between his sister and the fallen dog, dressed in nothing but a pair of cut-off jeans and tennis shoes. The mother was back on the patio saying nasty things to her neighbor. At which point Dan Brown told her if she didn't shut the fuck up he was gonna kick her fucking cunt up around her fucking ears.

"What's going on?" the kid asked.

Dan Brown stepped over to where Dean sat propped against the fence. He reached down with one hand, pulled Dean more or less to his feet, and began to drag him out of the yard.

"You can't get away with this," the woman said. "Fucking low-life scum."

"Put a sock in it, bitch," Chuck said. He and Ardath were by now standing at the side of the house, at the edge of the back lawn.

"Look at Buckie," the woman said. "Look at what the low-life fucker did to Buckie. He's your fucking dog, Jodie."

"For Christ's sake, Mom, shut the fuck up, will you? What's going on here, anyway?"

Dan Brown dragged Dean past the kid and out into the front, retracing the route Dean had run.

As they passed in the night, it appeared to Dean as

if the kid intended to follow them. In the end, however, he seemed to think better of it and the last Dean saw of him he had gone back to his dog, where his mother was telling him to watch his fucking mouth. The last Dean saw of the little girl, she was still crying.

The brunette had run out to the front yard to meet them. She had the hose from Dean's Cyclone draped around her neck like a pet snake and Dean realized for the first time that he had forgotten his unit, that he would most likely not get it back, and that the lousy thing was probably going to wind up costing him damn near four hundred bucks.

Dan Brown still hadn't said anything to Dean. There was a nasty bite on his right forearm and he was favoring it. He used his left hand to push Dean up against the side of the carport and began to frisk him with it. Dean thought at first he was looking for a weapon. What he wound up with was Dean's wallet.

"Finish his ass off man." It was Ardath who spoke.

"Finish off Johnny Magic? You gotta be shittin' me, man. I got plans for Johnny Magic."

The tall man cracked his knuckles. "I got some plans for him too. I got some plans to beat his fucking face in."

"You're bleedin' all out the back of your fucking pants, man," Chuck said.

"Yeah, you are bleeding," the brunette added. She had an end of the hose in one hand and was swinging it around in circles. "He sure as hell beat the fuck out of that dog, though."

Dan Brown had Dean's wallet opened in his left hand and was shaking it out. There were only about three things in it, Dean's license, an old draft card, and a library card. The items fluttered like crippled moths in the shadows. Dan Brown gathered them to himself. "Travelin' kind of light, aren't you?" he asked.

Dean allowed the question to go unanswered. His nose was still bleeding. There was a bad taste in his mouth.

Dan Brown held up Dean's driver's license for Dean to see. "Now I know where you live, don't I?" He put the license in the pocket of his T-shirt. The rest of it he stuffed into Dean's jacket. "Can you dig the implications of such shit?"

Dean could in fact dig such implications. He even started to say something about it but the effort did something to his lip and the thing began to spurt blood, some of which traveled far enough to hit Dan Brown on the chest. Dan Brown looked at his chest and shook his head. "Look at yourself, Magic," he said. "You're one pitiful-looking motherfucker, you know that?"

"Bring him inside," the brunette said. "He can have some ice for his face. And you gotta have your leg looked at, Danny, the thing's bleedin' like a bastard."

"Jesus Christ," Ardath said, apparently to no one in particular. "Can you believe this shit?"

By the time Dean got his ice the big blond had gotten Dan Brown laid out on the dining room table and was working on his leg. Dan was lying on his stomach. His jeans were draped over the back of a chair. He was holding Dean's driver's license out in front of him and reading aloud all of the address changes written on it.

Dean stood at the edge of the kitchen. The brunette had given him a brown paper bag with ice cubes in it, which he now held to his nose and lip. A trail of cold water ran down his wrist and into the sleeve of his sport coat. The parts of his Cyclone were strewn across the living room floor. Dean took it that the brunette had been attempting to operate the unit.

"You've got to put water in it," Dean told her.

"Water?" the girl asked. "Who ever heard of putting water in a vacuum cleaner?" The girl had gone around through the hallway and come into the kitchen from the other side. She was standing at Dean's back. When he turned, he saw that she was now wearing one of the pink latex gloves that had come in the dollhouse. He noticed as well that the pizza had gone uncooked. It sat on a countertop near the bar, on a cookie sheet, in a modest puddle of water. The orange spatula lay at its side together with a jar of salad peppers. Apparently the girl had found Dean's Cyclone of more interest.

"That's what makes this thing different," Dean said. "Vacuum cleaners use bags and filters. As soon as the filter gets clogged, you lose air flow. Not only does the thing fail to pick up dirt, it blows dust from the bag back into the room. You ever notice how some vacuum cleaners smell when you run them?"

"Yeah," the brunette said. She extended her hand, examining the pink glove at arm's length. "As a matter of fact I did."

"Well the Cyclone uses water to filter the air, that's why they call it an air purifier instead of a vacuum cleaner. The air pulls the dirt in, leaves it all in the water. What comes back out is clean. You're not using the unit as a vacuum you can run it to get rid of odors. You can also use it as a humidifier."

The girl laughed. "It slices and it dices," she said. "You hear that, Danny? Johnny Magic knows what he's talking about. I want one."

Dan Brown was still studying Dean's license. "Looks to me like you don't stay long in one place, Magic. What the fuck's wrong with you anyway?" He turned

47

to the blonde. "Check this," he said, showing her the license. "Niggertown."

"Like this is the good part of town," the blond said. It looked to Dean like she was putting stitches in Dan Brown's leg. Dan appeared not to notice.

"Show me how the water goes," the brunette said.

Dean went with her to the sink. "You fill it to this line," he told her. The girl held the bottom of the unit as Dean turned the tap. He nodded toward the pink glove. "Looks like you found something you liked in that dollhouse after all," he said. He was still holding the bag of ice to his face. The girl watched as the water climbed to the mark. "Come on," she said. "Let's run the fucker."

Dean and the girl were running the unit when the blond finished with Dan's leg. Dean had thrown a little pine scent into the water so that Dan Brown's house had begun to smell something like the enchanted forest. The brunette was working furiously on the soiled carpet. Dean was standing in the middle of the room watching her. She was bending over in such a way that both her small breasts were plainly visible. It was impossible not to notice that her left nipple had been pierced with a small golden ring very much like the one in her nose. Dean stood with a beer in one hand, the makeshift ice bag in the other, and watched the girl. He was really rather shameless about it. She seemed, he thought, to be the thing that was keeping him going.

"Earl J. Dean," Dan Brown said. He was dressed again now, pulling on his belt. "I'd forgotten that was your real fucking name. We even had that math class together once."

"Mr. Davis. Pre-algebra."

The man seemed almost pleased that Dean remembered. "That's it," he said. "Pre fucking algebra. You pass?"

Dean nodded. It occurred to him that the semester of pre-algebra and Mr. Davis was also the semester in which Dan Brown had stabbed the guard in the throat, the semester of the knife. "I dropped the fuck out," Dan Brown said. For a moment he stood with Dean, watching the girl. Then he seemed to remember something else. "Well, don't just stand there watchin' them little titties all night," he said. "Do me a favor. Go see if those two morons have loaded the truck yet. I'll be out in a minute."

Dean, embarrassed that he had been found out, started toward the door. The girl appeared not to notice, or not to care. Nor did she appear to give much thought to Dean's passing. She continued to wail on the carpet. "Oh, and Magic," Dan said. "You try to run away again, you're dead meat. We understand each other?" Dean said that they did.

The truck was loaded. Ardath had taken to doing something to one of the scooters. He was on his back in the grass, a flashlight propped up by his head, staring up into the engine above him. Chuck was leaning against the back of the panel, smoking a joint. He looked up as Dean came out of the house.

"You're fuckin' lucky to be alive," he said.

"I remember," Dean said, "the night he killed that cop." He wasn't sure why he said this. He supposed it was a way of saying that he knew he was lucky.

"The cop was wrong," Chuck said.

A pickup truck passed in the street, its bed filled with tires. Chuck drew on his joint. The sweet scent of the dope mixed with that of the orange blossom. It was enough to make the odor of Clear Lake go away.

"The cop was a prick. He was throwin' his weight

around, shoving people, even stuck Brown's old lady in the chest with his stick. You know that?"

"No, I didn't."

Chuck nodded. "Big mistake," he said. "The man was in love with that bitch."

Dean said nothing. He was trying to imagine Dan Brown as a lovelorn swain. It was a hard one to get around.

"Papers didn't say shit about that, of course." Chuck said. "But that's why Danny didn't do that much time behind it. Fucking witnesses up the yin-yang. But shit." He paused to spit on the drive. "Try looking for a job when you got that shit on your record. Cop killer."

Dean made an effort at appearing sympathetic. He supposed the act had made the guy into something of a hero in a place like Clear Lake. The old outlaw fantasy. The opiate of losers. He wondered about what the security guard at the game had done, or the shop teacher, or the football player, and those were only a few of the ones he could think of, folks who'd managed to wind up on the wrong end of the Brown legend. A regular fucking Robin Hood, he thought of saying, but didn't of course and for some reason that started him thinking about what Dan Brown had said to him, look at yourself, Johnny. Fucking Johnny Magic, salesman of the month . . . You wanted to talk about the opiate of losers. Dean touched the tip of his nose with a finger. He looked into the smoked glass of the panel's rear door, at the red coffin, which appeared to float there above an invisible floor. "Guess somebody will be paying for this," he said.

Chuck looked at the back of the truck. It seemed to Dean as if the man had begun to smile, a wistful sort of thing, touched with a trace of sadness. It vanished quickly, however, even as it was forming, so that Dean was left to wonder if he had seen it at all. "Oh, yeah," the man said. He spoke softly. "You can go to the bank with that one."

Dean looked away. He looked into the dark street, the stench of Clear Lake. He thought of the girl, she of the long knife, Pomona Queen. He found himself wondering if she was anything like the girl in the house, the young speed freak who had appropriated his Cyclone, who, judging by the high-pitched hum still spilling from a kitchen window, was even now doing a number on Dan Brown's sorry carpet. He recalled the sight of her white face, somehow vaguely angelic, peering down on him as he lay bleeding in the cool grass, and he imagined another face as yet unseen, a face which, without more to go on, he could only imagine as the face from the label, dark, pensive. . . . He did his best to see it as Buddy Brown would have seen it before him, at the moment of his passing, flushed no doubt with the white radiance of eternity—God's eldest daughter—in the shadows of some dark place. At his side the bearded man drew on the joint, then offered it to Dean. Dean took it. There wasn't much left. Dean took his hit, then offered it to the man once more. Chuck just shook his head and Dean finished it himself.

"You have to wonder if this girl knows what she's in for," Dean said at length. Chuck studied the street in silence. Encouraged, Dean went on. "You have to wonder what she's like." The man started as a door slammed somewhere behind them, then turned to Dean as if hearing him for the first time. "You gotta be shittin' me," he said.

Dan Brown kicked Ardath in the boot to get him out from under the bike. After that they left. Dean rode in back, seated on the floor just behind the front seats. Chuck rode shotgun. Ardath rode at the back, alongside the coffin of Buddy Brown.

*   *   *

"So Magic," Dan Brown said. It was the first any of them had said since leaving Clear Lake. "Give us a song, dude. Let's see if you got anything left."

Ardath said, "Shit." Dean could see him shaking his head in the dark. The bearded man said nothing. Dean looked down the length of the freezer. He was pretending not to have heard.

"Magic," Dan Brown said. "You gonna sing at my brother's graveside, man, you'd better loosen up your fucking throat."

"For Christ's sake," Ardath said. "This suit can't sing. I can tell you that jus' by lookin' at him. This fucker can't do shit for shit."

Dean could see Dan Brown looking into the rearview mirror. "Guess you didn't hear me, dickhead. I used to party down to this cat. What was it, twenty years ago? I got me some good memories, Johnny." For a moment Dean found himself looking at Dan Brown via the mirror. "Bodine's," Dan was saying. "I remember one night in there. Shit, you probably don't even remember it. The band was finished. You were sitting at that piano with that little redhead I was asking you about. You were singing "One Night With You." Me and my old lady were sittin' in there at one of the back tables jus' waitin' around for someone to kick us out. Only they didn't. Charlie kept the place open that night. You sat up there at the piano and kept playing. A long fucking time. I remember that, man. Yeah." Dan Brown paused to shake his head. "The cat could sing," he said. "What can I tell you."

Chuck lit another joint. Ardath picked up something from the floor of the van and flipped it at Dean. It was a piece of gravel or a screw or something. Dean felt it hit him on the cheek. He felt the blood burning behind it. The desire to be gone was making him dizzy.

"Come on, man," Dan Brown said. "Show these fuckers how it's done, Magic. Make it plain."

Dean stared hard at the man who had struck him. The man's face was in shadow, outlined before the rear window of the van. It all ran together after that, the world beyond the glass. The colors overlapped, bleeding into one another like spilt paint, the reds and whites of passing cars, the colored neon of the bars and burger joints, the massage parlors and adult book stores, the harsh yellow glare of the spotlights strung above the gleaming metal roofs that filled the used-car lots, the big white marquee out in front of the Mission Drive-In with its blood red letters: CODE OF HONOR, A LICENSE TO KILL, the whole sorry mess of things with which they had replaced the groves and orchards his great-grandfather had come to plant. You had to wonder, Dean thought, what the old man would think of it, could he see it now, this valley of promise. At which point it occurred to him that at this very moment he was himself nearly as old as the man he generally referred to as the old man. The thought struck him as singularly unpleasant. William Tacompsy McCauly had been forty-one years old the night he died. Forty-one and already a successful businessman, a landowner, the father of two daughters, well on his way to becoming a wealthy and powerful man the night some nameless dipshit's stray bullet extinguished his light. A waste, they had said. If only, the McCaulys had said, and said again, a kind of whining litany to echo on down through the sad years and shit storms to come. If only . . . Earl Dean put his head back against the seat in front of him. He loosened his tie and, probably as much to his own amazement as anyone else's, did in fact begin to sing, the opening lines of Muddy Waters's "Hoochie Coochie Man," while Dan Brown, nodding, proceeded to beat time on his steering wheel with the butt of his hand.

He was not sure why he picked that particular song. Perhaps it was because he could remember very well the night to which Dan Brown had alluded, could still remember the keys of the old white upright beneath his fingers, the broken high C, the light swimming in a pitcher of beer, and the red-haired girl seated at his side. He had sung for her that night. Christ, he hadn't even known Dan Brown was there, lurking in the shadows with some love of his own. There was only one context in which Dean could place the evening. It was the night of Rayann's leaving and it had always seemed to him that he might have prevented it. The fact that he had not was a measure of his failure. He had failed in his own way as surely as the old man before him. Dean did not collect memorabilia idly, nor had he chosen at random when selecting those two pieces that now graced the otherwise bare walls of his room, the photograph of the red-haired girl and the old label. The two existed for him in some complex arrangement of interior harmonies, hieroglyphs in an existential code. They were fear and desire and they were meant for keeping him from the garden, and someday, perhaps, given the events now in progress, in the not too distant future, Dean would die and the garden would pass away for the simple reason that it had been there just for him.

"I'm a hoochie coochie man," sang Earl Dean, and his voice, stoked on fumes and Budweiser and sour memories, cast words like stones to clatter against the bare steel walls of Dan Brown's panel truck as it cut through the heart of the valley.

"You know something," Chuck said, "your buddy's not bad."

"You bet your ass he's not," Dan Brown said. "You bet your ass."

Ardath said nothing. Dean continued to sing, with memories as bitter as Dan Brown's were sweet, "Hey everybody, hey everybody knows I am . . ." And Dan continued to drive. North. Toward mountains lost in

the night, along hieroglyphic streets Earl Dean had of
late discovered he could read, like the pages of a book.
And in the eventual silence that followed the song, as
the red freezer groaned with the motion of the van,
sliding now and then on the slick residue of its own
spilled cargo, Dean stared from a window, and he read
his streets. As if there were a choice. Palomares.
Orange Grove. The Phillips Ranch Road. They came
fluttering out of the darkness, drawn by the lights of
Dan Brown's panel as surely as moths to a flame—in
Dean's mind, one of those blue electronic flames that
draw bugs only to electrocute them. If you listened,
you could hear them fry.

FOUR

*It was natural and fitting that two of the children of
Ygnacio Palomares should marry two of the children of Richardo Vejar. . . . Thus Tomas Palomares
married Madelena Vejar. . . . Don Tomas was a large
man, stout and hearty with a kind heart and a
cheery laugh. He wore a full beard and was a good-
looking man . . . he was honest but not shrewd. And
because he was not more aggressive he lost much
of the land which he had inherited.*

—F. P. Brackett

Perhaps, Dean thought, extending his meditation on
the electronic flame, the valley itself was such a light.
And the names on the street signs were the names
of those who had come, drawn from the long night of
eastern winters, of smoking cities, hard on the trail of
a thing they had heard of, a picture in the mind. Luise
Phillips had come from Prussia, at one point crossing
the Isthmus of Panama on foot, the entire stock of his
possessions strapped to his back. In Los Angeles he
met a certain Hyman Tischler, who was looking for a
man to take charge of his rancho. In fact, Tischler had
acquired his land through foreclosure from the Vejar
family. He had acquired the ill will of the Mexicans as
well, and when an attempt was made on his life, he
sold the land to Luise Phillips. He sold cheap, and
much of the purchase price was covered by a note that
Phillips redeemed by driving a band of horses to Salt
Lake City, where the prices were in his favor; he went
on to become the first man not of Spanish descent to
make his fortune in the valley. Others followed. There

was Slanker, the first constable, and Tonner, the first teacher. There were White and Geary and Mills. Eventually, there was Earl Dean's great-grandfather, William Tacompsy McCauly.

McCauly had come by train from New York City. The trip had taken him two weeks and left him in San Francisco, where he'd paid twenty-seven dollars for a mustang and ridden south. He'd recently sold a small farm near Ithaca and was looking for land in which to invest his money. Eventually he came to Los Angeles, and finally to the Pomona Valley, where he purchased twenty acres and set them out to navel oranges. He married Civility Fletcher and fathered two daughters. He later began a fumigation business that was to become the largest in the county. He held interests in a marmalade factory and a packinghouse. They might have named a street for him had he not, for no good reason that anyone could ever think of, saddled a horse, ostensibly to ride to Riverside for a meeting of growers, and rode instead a scant five miles in the opposite direction. It was a bad move. By morning the flies were buzzing above his eyes and the ashes of Chinatown had settled upon his remains.

The image had haunted Dean's youth. In fact, it haunted him still. He seldom spoke of it. This for a variety of reasons. For one thing there was seldom anyone around to listen. That he should have spoken of it on the evening in question, in the presence of Dan Brown would, a mere two hours before, have seemed quite inconceivable. And yet this is exactly what had happened. Who could say why? Perhaps some silence had grown unbearable, the weight of some memory too painful. Perhaps he had simply been too long alone. Perhaps he had whiffed too many fumes. The upshot was that at some point, in the aftermath of his song, Dean had spoken his mind. He had told Dan Brown that the name of this girl's band

and the name that had once appeared on his great-grandfather's packing label were the same. Like the old man's decision to attend the burning of Chinatown, it was a bad move. Dan Brown had swerved across two lanes of traffic, brought the van to a halt, hooked his arm over the back of his seat and demanded to know what the fuck Dean was trying to say.

Dean had seen at once the error of his way. In fact, he really had no clear idea of what he had intended to say. There was only this thing, this coincidence, or perhaps, depending upon one's take on things, this thing that was no coincidence at all. In fact, it had appeared to Dean, amid the wreckage he had so casually heaped upon himself, as if there were really two paths by which the material in question might be approached. Given the circumstances, he deemed the second a good deal thornier than the first. Still, he had waffled and said nothing and in the end Dan Brown had chosen for him. He had moved Chuck out of the front seat, shifted Dean to take his place and put to him such questions as could only be answered, at least in the beginning, with brief declarative sentences. Eventually, however, amid the fumes and half-light, Dean's answers had, like shadows at the end of day, begun to lengthen. A story had begun to form. At least Dean imagined that it was a story. He really had no idea what it sounded like. He imagined it all spasm and sweat, nothing but false starts and unfinished sentences, nothing at all like what flowed through the recesses of his heart. In those unseen caverns, the story ran clear as mountain water, every page a song.

Civility McCauly had, in her husband's long absence, done her best to carry on. Or at least she had done her best to go on living in the style to which she had become accustomed. William's daughters had gone to college. There were trips abroad. There was a summer house on the beach in Venice. Earl's great-grandmother had paid for things by selling things: the interest in the packinghouse, the marmalade factory, the groves. Unhappily the list was not endless, so that by the time Dean's grandmother came home from the East, divorced, with a child, in 1925, most of it was gone. A dozen acres of citrus were what saw them through the Depression, the *them* now consisting of the four women: Dean's great-grandmother, Civility; his grandmother, Melissa; his great-aunt, Winifred, who had never married, and never would, but had returned soon after college to live in the house she would eventually die in; and baby Alice, Earl Dean's mother.

Dean had often thought of them, out there in their fading Victorian the old man had once brought crafts-men from as far away as San Francisco to help build, ringed by their unkempt groves, their failing barns. It was, at least as Dean had come to imagine it, a setting worthy of the Irish moors. He supposed his mother's stories had helped, the way she had spoken of her fear of the big, dark house with its empty rooms, its shuttered, vine-covered windows. Her room had been on the second floor and often, at night, unable to sleep, she had slipped out of bed to sit at the top of the stairs, her attention riveted on that yellow slash of light that spread from the doorway at their foot, strain-ing to hear what was said as the three older women sat arguing long into the night, their voices mixing with the grotesque, high-pitched yapping of the coy-otes come down from the foothills to hunt jackrabbits among the groves. Nor was it uncommon for her to drift into sleep there, only to be awakened hours later by the screams of her grandmother echoing down a dark hallway—the old woman having, by that time in her life, fallen victim to terrible nightmares, debilitat-ing headaches, and spells of delusion. Not surprisingly, Dean's mother left as soon as she was able, at the age of fourteen, with a sailor she met one night in the lobby of the Fox Theater in downtown Pomona.

When the matriarch died, her daughters inherited the land. They fought continually over what should be done with it. In time, however, the last of the McCauly groves went the way of their neighbors. They were sold to developers, an acre at a time. It was, his grandmother told him, like selling pieces of herself; for already she had begun to cling to the notion that her holding of the land might pass as tribute to the father she had lost as a child. But the needs would not go away: the tract home for Dean's mother, a laughable series of business ventures on the part of Dean's aunt, everything from hat shops to show dogs, and finally, when it became clear his aunt was losing her mind, the live-in nurse who would care for her until the day she died, leaving what was left of the McCauly holdings to Dean's grandmother—a single acre, to which the old woman had taken hold with something like the death grip of a wounded pit bull. It was an heroic if somewhat pointless gesture. The age of citrus had come and gone. Tract homes were the cash crop then. They grew like weeds, naked pine stalks shining in the sunlight, with names like Cinderella, Clear Lake, Cedar Glen, Homes for Tomorrow. The home Earl Dean grew up in, bought and paid for with McCauly land, was within walking distance of the old house.

The desertion of her husband, Alice Dean had argued, made the purchase a necessity. It seems the sailor from the Fox Theater who had been Dean's father had gone out for cigarettes one night in Long Beach only to vanish "into thin air," as Alice liked to say. Alice was also fond of pointing out that Earl Dean had been seven months old on the evening in question, that it was the seventh month of the year, that there were seven colors in the rainbow, and seven archangels at the right hand of the Almighty. Such details were not lost on Alice Dean, though of course there was much that was. She fancied herself a Four Square Baptist. In fact, she was a daughter of Swedenborg and Blake. By the time her son was seven years old, she had taken up with a plumbing contractor by the name of Carl, and Earl had taken to spending a lot of time with his grandmother.

Dean called her Milly. By the age of ten he was as tall as she was. In his mind's eye he could see her still, just ahead of him there among those cool green corridors, hunting fruit amid the scant foliage, her white hair moving in and out of the dusty arms of light that sliced down through the trees. The grove had seemed a magical place to him then. He loved it as much as the old woman herself. He loved it as it was, full of disease. He loved her talk, her voice like the rustling of palm leaves in the dry summer air, telling him of how it had been, when the groves ran to the foothills, filling the valley with their scent, when William Tacompsy McCauly was king of the hill.

"King of the fucking hill," Dan Brown said. He had, in the course of Dean's narrative, taken to echoing certain phrases that caught his fancy. Dean would be forced to stop, to take his bearings, to start again. It was a distraction he could easily have lived without.

"Why do I find that hard to believe?" Dan asked. They were once again in motion. The dark shapes of the foothills that formed the northern end of the valley loomed before them. A bar by the name of Uncle Ned's sat some fifty yards off the road, its pink neon letters spreading a desperate glow among the bare limbs of half a dozen dying eucalyptus.

"Because he's related to this dick weed." It was Ardath who answered. Dean said nothing. He watched as the letters of the bar faded behind them, passing from sight. For him, the old man's status was an absolute. Something had begun there, with the gentleman rancher from the East. Dean harbored the conceit that it would end with him. For his own father he had little interest. The man had after all deserted him as an infant. Later they heard he had been killed, in a construction accident in Texas. The fact of the matter was, the man, like most men, had not left much to mark his passing: a broken home, a few unpaid bills, a pair of shoes in a hall closet. As far as Dean was concerned the man was of no interest, a shadow cast by a dream. William Tacompsy McCauly, on the other hand, dead now these eighty years, still loomed large in Dean's imagination, as large perhaps as the dreams that had driven him, as large and mysterious as the big, creaking house Dean had known as a boy with its hallways and staircases, its wild yards and dusty barns, its haunted groves. That was the man who interested Dean, the man who had posited a world of pastoral charm and wealth, spread the possibilities before the hopeful eyes of his kin with the ease of a street huckster flashing cards—each with a different position, boys—and then just as neatly folded his hand, saddled his horse, and rode off to die.

He had apparently been a man of action rather than words. He left no diaries or letters. He left the factory and the packinghouse. He left a fine Victorian, a wife, and two daughters. He left twenty acres of navel oranges, a yard full of fumigation equipment, and he left a barn. And in the barn, he had left the labels, freshly delivered, it would seem, as yet unused and with the event of his death never to be used, so that in handling them for the first time, in removing them from their trunk, in removing the waxed paper and the yellowed newsprint and gazing for the first time into the sad-eyed girl invention of some clearly mystic lithographer, Earl Dean had been willing to believe he was handling objects not handled since his great-grandfather had handled them himself, quite possibly on the very eve of his death.

On the surface, this label was a simple one—a dark-eyed girl before a coloring sky, the words "Pomona Queen" in gold above her head. For Dean, there was more to it. The girl was nothing at all like the happier images chosen by countless other growers. She was the sad-eyed lady and there was no way around it, and yet in the lines of her mouth there lay the faintest suggestion of a smile, just as if she really did know what two generations of McCaulys had worn themselves out trying to discover. She was the Mona Lisa of the Pomona Valley, a leg up on history, caught at just that moment in which some vision had been granted her of how it would all come down.

And now, it seemed, someone else had seen this label and chosen the name as the name for her band. It was not difficult to imagine how this might have happened. Dean's grandmother had donated one to the Pomona Public Library, where, year after year, untold numbers of schoolchildren had been made to march past it in the name of history. Anyone could have seen it. And yet it was not just anyone. It was someone. And this, for Dean, was not an idle concept. In a magical universe it was a symbol. For, in point of fact, Earl Dean was not exactly as he appeared. He was not, in his heart, a vacuum-cleaner salesman. In that black land he fancied himself a pilgrim, a seeker after hidden paths, a student of the theology of hope. Though generally speaking it was Dean's belief that theologians of hope were not immediately recognizable as such, that often they went about invisibly, in double knits and cheap polyester, at the wheels of aging mechanical wonders, in want and in tribulations, in motor courts and Holiday Inns . . . the desolate places of an unworthy world.

But then that was the stuff of the thorny path Dean had thus far managed to avoid and he saw no reason for pursuing it now, with Dan Brown. The man, after all, had his hands full with facts, forget what lay concealed beneath them—the hieroglyphic world, the script of angles. In fact, Dan Brown had, by the time they reached the end of Central Boulevard, managed to get his teeth into Dean's story much the way Melissa McCauly had once gotten hers into her acre of land and he was not about to let it go until he had gotten it straight, right down to the names of the four women. The man's attention to detail was somewhat breathtaking and Dean could not quite escape the observation that had he done as well for the faculty of Pomona High School, Dan Brown might have graduated with honors. Dean missed one name and the man was on it like a fly on shit, his big triangular head bobbing in the light of some passing car. "You just told me your grandmother's name was Melissa, fuck head," he would say, and Dean would have to backtrack, try to figure out who'd missed the last transition, himself or his host, and Dan Brown would jerk his bottle out of his jacket and take a few tokes. Crystal Meth? P.C.P? Dean had little experience with the post-sixties drug scene and could only guess at the nature of Dan Brown's habit. P.C.P., a cop had once told Dean, tended to induce erratic and violent behavior, enhancing physical strength, while, at the same time, rendering the user impervious to pain. The good news was that Dean, by this point, was fairly well fucked up himself—on fear, fumes, adrenaline, the beer he had consumed—for him an uncharacteristically large amount—on the very stuff of his own tale, perhaps. Because if these streets spoke to him of his great-grandfather, of the days of orange blossom and sage, they spoke as well of the red-haired girl whose memory Dan Brown had also managed to invoke. And so it was all tangled up there, in the corridors of the old mind—the girl, the old man, the valley, the theology of hope. In fact, it seemed to him that the last of these owed much to the first, that it was, by many counts, an edifice erected in her honor, of things she had given him. It even seemed to him that she had come to occupy a place in it. She was his judge of hearts. Should he hide at the bottom of the sea she would find him out. Should he sink to the bowels of Pomona and cover himself in smog she would command the psychopath, and the motherfucker would swallow him whole.

Dean first heard mention of a theology of hope amid the greenery and light of one of the canyons that creased the foothills north of town. He had gone there with Rayann. They'd heard of this place, of an older guy with money and good dope, a cool house, a radical tire swing. They'd heard right. The guy with money turned out to be a dropped-out, turned-on chemical engineer by the name of Bill. They had called him Engineer Bill after the television star who played with trains and showed cartoons. The Engineer Bill of the canyon showed cartoons as well. His, however, were chemically induced, and if you wanted on the engineer's train, you took his drugs and you rode his swing.

The object hung from an upper branch in a huge sycamore that jutted from the lip of the canyon. A hundred feet below, water trickled through a meager bed of stones. To start, one had first to climb the tree. Once situated on the appropriate branch, you hauled the tire in by means of a rope, put your legs through the hole, and launched.

You dropped a good fifteen feet before taking the slack out of the line and beginning to swing. The line itself was composed of equal parts rope and cable.

There was a spring of some kind near the seat that acted to absorb the shock of the initial drop so that the transition from falling to swinging was remarkably smooth, nothing like what the sight of the contraption would lead one to believe. In fact, it was this contrast, the discrepancy between what the swing looked like and how it behaved, that served to make of one's first jump an act of faith, or perhaps, for those to whom faith as defined by Paul in the tenth chapter of Acts was no longer a viable option, an act of hope. It was exactly the kind of rumination that still came to mind when Dean thought of the swing in the canyon. In all probability it was one of the ruminations that had issued from the tree itself, more or less verbatim, on the occasion of his first visit.

He and Rayann had been making their way along the dirt path that led to the engineer's house. In fact, they had just spotted the great man himself, in a Mexican pullover and faded jeans, at the foot of the sycamore. Dean's first assumption was that the guy was stoned, lost in some speech to the creatures of the canyon. Upon arriving at the tree's base, however, they saw that the man among the roots was quite silent, that the words were coming from the branches above, that there was a second man in the tree.

"I suppose," the voice said, "that this is what's known as the leap of faith."

The man on the ground looked at Dean and Rayann. He looked at Rayann a good deal longer than he looked at Dean, though out of politeness, Dean supposed, he addressed himself to both of them.

"Theology student," he said. "From the school down there on Foothill. New Testament theology, I believe." He yelled into the tree: "New Testament?"

"Faith as the eschatological moment." The words drifted down among the branches, like dying leaves.

"Pussy is afraid to jump," the engineer said. "He's

been up here half a dozen times now. Gets drunk, climbs the tree, pisses himself, then climbs back down. Jump, you pussy," Bill called into the tree.

"It does not belong to the man who is walking," the voice replied, "even to direct his own step . . ."

"If he's not going to jump," Rayann had said, "tell him to come back down, because we want to."

And Bill had looked once more at Rayann. He looked longer this time. He no doubt saw what they all did. She was five feet, ten inches tall. A hundred and twenty-five pounds. Skinny with curves. She had once admitted to being able to do more pull-ups than any other girl in her gym class. She had confided this to Dean as if it were a problem of some sort, as if her body pleased and embarrassed her at the same time, as if she really did not quite know what she had, or see what made her special, which of course served only to make her more special. Certainly she had never played the kind of games with that body that some would have. He had found her at once remarkable and the passage of time had served only to make her more so. She favored jeans and motorcycle boots then, though Dean liked to think of her in the flowered dresses she'd worn for the gigs. He liked to think of her barefoot under stage lights, and often when he saw her now, stalking the dark corridors of his heart, he saw her face with just that attitude of concentration she had affected when she played, anything you cared to name on an electric violin, fiddle tunes, country swing, all bearing the stamp of those ten years of classical training the old man had insisted upon. Eventually she would play in the canyon, a rendition of "The Devil's Dream" played in the branches of the sycamore that could still make the hair stand up on the back of Dean's neck, twenty years after the fact, twenty years after it had all been laid to waste. Of course the good engineer knew nothing of that on the morning in question. All he had to go on were the seventy inches of skinny curves, the waterfall of red curls. It had been enough.

"He's not getting down this time," Bill told them. "That's why I'm here. I'm going to see to it he jumps. It's for his own good. I suppose I was waiting for an audience." Upon which he pulled a wrist rocket from the leather satchel at his side, placed a marble in it, and fired it into the branches of the tree.

"For Christ's sake," the voice came down.

"Christ been a long time gone," Bill said.

"Flannery O'Conner," the voice said. "Christ among the trees."

"Jump, you pussy," the engineer said, launching another round, which must have hit something, as there was a sound—the plaintive cry of a wounded gull. Something moved among the branches, and then fell, and they could see that it was a rather pear-shaped man. The man wore black dress shoes and blue slacks, a white shirt, and red tie. He had his ass in a tire. He fell the requisite fifteen feet and came, as it were, to the end of his rope. The spring did its job quite nicely, however, so that one minute the man was falling, speeding past the branches in his descent, and the next, there he was, displayed for all to see, in breathtaking midflight, swinging farther than one would have thought possible, out over the distant streambed, the trees of the canyon, a brilliant red tie trailing heroically above one shoulder, a pair of black-rimmed glasses tumbling to the abyss below.

As it turned out, the man's name was Ross and they had soon taken to calling him Dr. Ross because of course he soon would be and because there was an old advertising jingle that went: "Dr. Ross dog food is doggone good," which someone had managed to remember and so he was stuck with it. Though to his credit, he never seemed to mind and Dean had always thought kindly of the guy. He was to become a regular among the people of the canyon. Always in his rumpled blue slacks, his white shirt, his cheap black dress shoes. It was only the tie that changed. Even the glasses remained the same. Someone had retrieved the pair that had fallen, patched them with duct tape, and Ross wore them for as long as Dean knew him, which, in actuality, was not long. Though it seemed to Dean now as if the duration of those days was difficult to measure, as if the canyon had affected time, bent it back upon itself in some way that had rendered conventional units of measurement obsolete. It seemed to him, for instance, that Ross had always been around, for days on end, so that there had been times when Dean doubted that the guy was a student anywhere. Once, however, he had shown up with a paper bearing his name, which had been published somewhere by someone and of which he had seemed quite proud. The paper was entitled "The Theology of Hope." At least this was how Dean remembered it. It seemed to him that, in its simplest form, it had espoused the notion that in a world where men could no longer count on proving anything as unlikely as the existence of a god interested in their affairs, one could at least hope for such a thing, that this hope might in fact inform one's life, that it might make a difference.

Perhaps this was a simple-minded way of stating the paper's thesis. Perhaps there had been more to it. Certainly there had been more to it. The paper had been pages long, for Christ's sake. It was lost was all, erased from the old memory banks, leaving only the phrase that, at some point in the wreckage that had followed those years, Dean had managed to recall. In fact, he had begun to dabble in the subject himself, in a strictly amateurish way, of course. The odd thing was, he believed he had a knack for it. It was akin to discovering one had a knack for selling vacuum cleaners. He had no desire to publish a paper or, for that matter, even to look up the now Dr. Ross. He supposed further that his hopes had little in common with the doctor's, though he would have been hard pressed to say exactly what those were. The man had on occasion spoken of the dynamic absence of the God Who Acts. Dean believed his own views to be even less specific, more arcane. In fact, it seemed to him that he had found their clearest expression in a single sentence, a footnote to a short story he had once read at Rayann's goading. The sentence, which Rayann had highlighted with a yellow marker, was just this: "The steps a man takes from the day of his birth until that of his death trace in time an inconceivable figure." Upon a first reading, the sentence had struck him as only interesting. Ultimately he had gone back to it with something more than a passing interest. Ultimately he had found that it pleased him to believe this was so. "Every man is on earth to symbolize something he is ignorant of," the author had elaborated, "and to realize a particle or a mountain of the invisible materials that will serve to build the City of God." Perhaps he was only his mother's son. One pursued such interests on the sly, of course. It was a little like sniffing girls' bicycle seats. Caught, one would deny everything. Alone, one might indulge oneself shamelessly. But then that was the beauty of the thing. In the soul's long sabbath, one was always alone. One could decipher to one's heart's content. One had only to keep one's mouth shut, one's eyes open.

And so it was that on the evening in question, in the dank heart of Clear Lake, in the home of Dan Brown, Dean had seen something, some fleeting glimpse, perhaps, of that angelic cryptography it pleased him to postulate, hidden, in each moment. The bearded man had said Pomona Queen. A current had arced somewhere in the night. Or at least one might hope that a current arced somewhere in the night. One might hope as well that the arc held, and curved away, into the past, connecting, for the sensitive hip to such events, a series of points, as in some cosmic paint-by-the-numbers kit, and Dean had seen once more in his mind's eye the old label with its sad-eyed girl, its golden letters, its crimson sky, which, when you thought about it, must have been very much like the sky a mother and her daughters once saw from the third floor of a fine Victorian the night the citizens of Pomona put the torch to Chinatown, never guessing that at that moment, as the pitiful shacks of the Chinamen went up in smoke, their own hopes and dreams were going up, too, that the guy they were counting on to make it all happen had already bought his, that they were like the straight man in an old joke, the one in which a man is away in the army when his mother dies, and it falls to his sergeant to give him the bad news. Only the sergeant is not sure how to go about it. So what he does is, he assembles his men, and he says: "Okay, men, everyone with a mother, step forward." And our man starts forward. And the sergeant barks: "Not so fast, Wilson." They were like that, Dean thought, his women. And he could almost see them there, slender in their long housecoats, huddled in the darkness before some south-facing window, and somehow, in this particular vision, it had fallen to Dean himself to bring them the news. "Every family with a husband and father," he could hear himself say. . . . And there they would come, turning to him across time, all wide-eyed and innocent, waiting on the gifts wise men bring and it would be for him to set them straight. "Yo, McCaulys," he would say. "Not so fast there. Yours is down in Chinatown, dead in the street."

*   *   *

"Shit," Dan Brown said. "I didn't even know there was a fucking Chinatown."

Dean was stopped short. He scarcely knew anymore what he was saying. It would appear he was able to talk one story while thinking another—a marketable talent, no doubt. Dan Brown's words, however, jerked him back into the present like a choke chain. He saw they had gotten as far north as Foothill Boulevard, and were in fact now traversing a stretch of road that had once served as part of the first transcontinental highway and managed to have at least one song and one television show named after it. It was, Dean suspected, in all probability the route by which the first Brown had made his way into the Valley of Promise, in a model-A Ford, untold years worth of useless belongings tied to the roof. "It was where Buffums is," Dean said at last. "There were only a couple of blocks of it."

Dan Brown nodded, as if giving the matter some thought. "And they burnt the fuckers out."

"Actually, most of them were gone before they burnt it." He could see that Dan was somewhat disappointed. He felt obliged to explain. "The citizens had formed something called the Non-Partisan Anti-Chinese League." The name had a way of rolling off the tongue, as it had done fifteen years earlier at the time of Dean's first reading of F. P. Brackett's gargantuan history. "They boycotted the Chinese-owned businesses," Dean continued. "Forced most of them into Los Angeles, then went down and burned what they had built. My great-grandfather was the only casualty, or so they say."

Dan Brown laughed out loud. "Sounds like one of your kin, Magic. Wrong spot at the wrong time." Brown laughed once more. "Fucker was probably down there trying to sell some poor slant-eyed bastard a vacuum cleaner."

"No one knew what he was doing down there,"
Dean said. "That was the thing." By which he meant
it was the thing that had put the bug up the asses
of two generations of McCaulys. "Like I said," Dean
continued, "my grandfather was a grower." He was
telling it now the way it had been told for eighty years.
He could have gone back to thinking about Rayann
but he clung to the moment, lest some interior digres-
sion get entirely out of hand and carry him down the
thorny path after all. "The growers were getting
screwed by the packers and shippers and they were
trying to figure out what to do about it. People like
my great-grandfather could grow the fruit, but when
it came time to get it to market they had to go through
a commercial shipper. These guys had the whole area
divided into territories and they refused to compete
with one another. They could offer very low prices to
growers. Sometimes they didn't even buy at all. They
handled the goods on consignment, and forced the
growers to guarantee them against loss. It was a bad
scene. At any rate, what happened was, the growers
began to pack and market their own goods. They
called it cooperative marketing. They formed their own
associations. They established their own local brands.
They labeled them, and they got them to market. My
great-grandfather was the first president of the
Pomona Fruit Exchange. The night he died, he was
supposed to have been on his way to a meeting of
growers in Riverside. No one could believe it when he
didn't show. No one could believe it when they found
him dead. His friends thought all kinds of things, like
maybe somebody in the packing industry'd had him
shot. But nothing ever added up. And they could
pretty much track his horse. I mean it has always
looked as if that was just where he went, like maybe
he was just curious or something, went down there to

have a look. It was dark. These assholes start firing off a few rounds, raising a little hell . . ."

Dan Brown finished it for him. "The old man eats a bullet."

Dean nodded. "Through the lung. They always figured they might have been able to do something for him had anyone found him in time. He tried to make it by himself. He fell someplace north of town, about a mile from home. Bled to death in a neighbor's grove."

"Well, then, how the fuck did—"

"They know he was in Chinatown?"

Dan Brown just looked at him.

It is an old question. "They found his leg," Dean said.

This gave Dan Brown pause. "No shit!" he said. The idea seemed to lighten his mood. "You mean somebody cut the fucker off?"

Dean was forced to admit the limb in question was an artificial one.

Dan Brown looked disappointed once more. "Shit," he said. "How old was this fucker anyway?"

"Forty."

"Wha'd he do, lose it in a war?"

Clearly Dan Brown was still clinging to hopes that some further act of violence would yet be revealed and Dean was forced to disappoint him one more time. "A horse fell on it," he said. "They couldn't get it to heal right." Dean was not sure about how much more to add. "He eventually developed a tumor behind his knee," he said. He was thinking about how little of this man there was to know. Milly, Dean's only real source of information, had been a small child when her father died. Her memories were somewhat vague and scattered and yet she had clung to the more vivid as if they were precious stones kept hidden away in the dark folds of her heart. She could, for instance, remember quite clearly the morning the doctor had come to give her father the news concerning his leg. She had in fact, on more occasions than one, shown Dean the exact spot where she had stood, had positioned him before the open doorway where the sunlight had once streaked the papered walls before which her father had lain, his eyes on the ceiling. She had described the broad back of the doctor, and the way the men had spoken, in hushed tones. She had told it in such a way that eventually Dean had appropriated the memory for himself, just as if he had been the one waiting there, in the hallway with the half-heard words and the still-dark house and the morning light. In Dean's version, however, there was a twist. In Dean's version, he was not only in the hallway, he was in the bed as well, and the pale, stiff profile of the man beneath the sheets was his own.

"And you know all of this shit," Dan Brown said at length.

Dean found that he had lapsed into silence once more, that once more he had been caught drifting. He was a moment in replying. He found Dan's voice difficult to read. Somehow he felt the man to be genuinely impressed. What he wanted to say was that all things considered, it was really not very much shit to know. What he said instead was, "It's my family." He looked at Dan Brown when he said it. "It's what remains," he added. Dan Brown turned to him and smiled and it was, Dean thought, a smile not tainted by contempt or malice. It was the genuine article. He extended his palm for Dean to slap. When Dean did so, he slid his palm away, hooking Dean's fingers with his own in some variation of a gangland handshake and Dean was given to understand that his afterthought had been pure inspiration, that he and Dan Brown were, for perhaps the first time that night, on the same wave length after all. Dean took it as cause for hope, as if his story had not been told in vain, as if the immeasurable gulf that separated him from the man behind the wheel might in fact be bridged. As if, in the end, they were brothers after all, fellow participants in the species' slow ascension toward the lights.

They had by now come to a point midway between the towns of Claremont and Upland, a peculiar stretch of no-man's-land where everything had been imaginatively named the midway something: The Midway Tractor Rental Company, The Midway Bar, The Midway Motel. Dean used the opportunity to ask for a beer, to collect what were left of his thoughts, to comfort himself in the belief that soon this bartender they called The Stench could take his place, if not in the panel, at least in the heat of Dan Brown's relentless cross-examinations. He went so far as to believe that perhaps the man's story would work in some way to alter Dan Brown's plans. Flushed with the thrill of his small victory, there seemed in fact no end to what one might hope for and he turned his attention to the lights of the valley made visible by the elevation of things up where old Route 66 leaves the town of Upland and enters the town of Claremont.

FIVE

*It came about that Cyrus Burdick, the pioneer Amer-
ican in Pomona, chose for his home the identical
spot which had proved so attractive to the original
grantees. . . . The first planting was about five hundred seedling orange trees bought of a French nurs-
eryman in Los Angeles. It was then supposed that
orange trees would not do well if planted by day-
light, so the holes were dug, and the trees brought
out under cover, and Mrs. Burdick held a lantern
while Mr. Burdick and his helpers set them out by
night.*

—F. P. Brackett

The Stench lived with a potbellied brunette in a run-
down California bungalow. The house, stashed at the
back of a long, narrow lot and sandwiched between a
Taco Bell and the Midway Tractor Company, was Dan
Brown's first stop upon reaching the northern end of
the valley. Dean had gone with the others to the door.
He had seen the brunette.

Unhappily, the Stench himself had not been home.
He had, according to the brunette, gone to a liquor
store down the street to use the phone. The girl,
clearly skittish, had invited them to wait. Dan Brown
had declined.

"We'll wait over here," he told them as they walked
away, down the dark drive, circling back into the lot
of the Taco Bell, where the panel sat before a plain
block wall. "I want to give this asshole a little surprise,
make sure he's telling us everything he knows. Besides
that," he said, waving toward the Taco Bell, "I could
use some fuel."

So they had gone to the take-out windows and

returned to the panel armed with burgers and burritos. Ardath had pulled a few fresh beers from Buddy Brown's coffin to wash them down, and Earl Dean, much to his dismay, had been returned to the front seat to continue the tale he had been rash enough to begin on the ride up. And he was there just now, an as yet untouched burrito warming his thigh, trying as best he could to bring his sorry tale to some satisfactory conclusion, rambling on, as others of his tribe had done before him, about how everything had pretty much gone to shit after the old man died, about how the land had been lost, the business ventures sold, about how, finally, it had all come down to a single paltry acre to which Dean himself was now the heir, at which point Dan Brown had stopped him.

"No shit," the man had said, impressed once again. "You mean you're going to sit there and tell me you're a fucking landowner."

And Dean had been forced to tell him the rest of it, about how he'd been up north when he'd gotten the news, about how he'd come home only to find the house already occupied by Carl and his mother. He had described the manner in which Carl had sat him down at the big oak table in the dining room and given him the financial report, told him all about mortgage payments and taxes, broken pipes, old wires, the city's demand to do something about the barns and fumigation equipment, and so on and so forth, all the reasons in other words why his stepson, given his station in life, would never in a million years be able to do anything with the property besides sell it immediately for a poor price. The man had gone on to point out that he on the other hand, having deeper pockets, would actually be able to do a little something with the place, fix what needed fixing, meet expenses. . . . At the very least, Carl had explained, he could manage the place long enough to get a decent price, at which time he had made his offer. He would be willing to take the property off Dean's hands. There had been papers on the table. All Dean need do was sign.

Dean had sat for some time that day, listening to his parents. Beyond the dusty beveled glass of the downstairs windows he had been able to see the tops of the dead trees and the smudged orange light of late afternoon as it snaked along the roof line of Carl's new Winnebago. The man had wanted him to sign a quitclaim deed. In return he was prepared to give Dean a check for twenty thousand dollars. "You can look at it this way," Carl had informed him. "You can't afford to stay here. I can. I could stay here myself. I could even hire someone to stay here for me, make a few improvements. . . . Shit, I'm here five years, pay the taxes, I could claim the place." Carl had paused, allowing this last piece of information to sink in. Dean had imagined that he was being invited to ask what Carl was talking about. He had elected to deny his stepfather this pleasure. The man of course had told him anyway. He had produced his dog-eared copy of *The Real Estate Handbook* and read from it, aloud. He had done so with all the zeal of a fundamentalist preacher citing scripture. In fact, Dean thought, the man had appeared slightly deranged, his forehead glowing cherry red, his eyes alight with the gift of the spirit. Adverse Possession was the ticket. If Dean didn't act soon, Carl would simply withdraw his offer, then sit on the place long enough to claim it himself.

Dean had told him he would have to think about it. "Think about what?" Carl had asked him, the light fading in his eyes. He had looked at Dean's mother, as if making some appeal to the seat of reason. "What's to think about? Take it or leave it, pardner. That's my offer."

Dean had left it. He had taken up residence in a tiny one-room apartment just north of downtown Pomona. He had taken stock of his options. Dean had, for the past two or three years, been living basically out of a 1971 converted Dodge maxivan now parked at a friend's place in the Owens Valley. It was not a bad place to be. Half an hour's drive could put you in the Sierras. In the summer the air was hot and dry and the nights smelled of greasewood and sage. He had begun to paint again there, something he had not done in years, desert landscape jobs, complete with cactus and cow skulls, the dry riverbed, the sun-bleached stone. In fact he had found that there was a market for such items at assorted local craft fairs and roadside galleries. He managed a class now and then at the community college near Reno. He occasionally filled in on guitar with the local bluegrass band. He worked part-time for a local landscape architect, digging trenches for sprinkler systems, clearing rock. In short he had done what there was to do, to get by, still managing, at those rare times when called upon to explain himself, to dress it up as some kind of alternative lifestyle. But then one was not really called upon to explain oneself all that often and he had assumed that he was not so different from everyone else. In the end, one had one's road and one had one's burden. One soldiered on. It even pleased him to think from time to time that his grandmother would have approved of the painting. For she had once been quite proud of what she considered his talent and there was still a watercolor he'd painted for her in 1958 hanging on a wall of the old house, a tugboat parked before a barn, which she'd had framed at a shop in downtown Claremont at considerable expense. The problem now, however, was that while this jack-of-all-trades routine might pay the rent in the Owens Valley, it was not going to buy him jackshit in the valley of ashes. He had consulted with a couple of realtors, and found to his great disappointment that Carl had been about right. The land was not exactly in the most desirable part of town and the profits he would realize from some sort of distress sale, when everything was paid off, were not going to be much different from what Carl was offering him. Nor was Carl far off the mark about winding up with the property himself, should he occupy the house, make improvements, and pay the taxes, for a period of five years. There really was a provision called Adverse Possession. And yet he could not quite bring himself to sign the papers.

It had to do with more than money. There was a big piece of Dean's life tied up in that chunk of ground and when he had come down to stand in the rutted drive for the first time in nearly a decade, he had been struck by two things. He had been struck by an emotional response to the place he would not, after all this time, have thought possible, and he had been struck by the enormity of his betrayal. The condition of the house was shocking. The white paint was all but gone, buried beneath years of dirt and mildew, dust and dying vines. The barns had been condemned. The rose gardens Milly had once tended with pride had gone to weeds and naked thorns. Carl and his mother were there of course, sitting on the place like a pair of aging vultures, but clearly no one had been there to do any work for a long time. Dean had, on occasion, called his grandmother in the course of his travels. Never had she asked for anything. She had died suddenly of a stroke. And yet he saw at once, standing before the house, how it must have been for her, how the enormity of it must have broken her heart. What he wanted to believe was that there was something still that might be done. If the steps a man took from the day of his birth till that of his death were to trace in time some secret symbol, if every man had come into this world to symbolize something of which he was ignorant, perhaps it was for Earl Dean to claim the land as his great-grandfather had claimed it before him, to seek a closure. It was exactly, of course, the kind of thing to which a man of his persuasion might cling. And yet it seemed to Dean that more often than not, that was what soldiering on came down to, some mental sleight of hand. Everyone did it. You had your causes. You had your flags. Alice Dean had her four angels holding back the winds of the apocalypse. She had blood and water and her baby Jesus. Dean had alternate lifestyles and secret paths. In short he had elected to make a run at it.

He had come upon an ad in the local paper. He had made a phone call, was given an address. That night he had driven to a small shopping center on Central Avenue. He'd sat in a room with two dozen other desperate men. He'd watched as Bill Frank did his thing with the blackboard and the numbers. With each consecutive meeting the number of desperate men had shrunk until finally he was part of a graduating class of an even half dozen, a small, poorly trained but highly motivated group of misfits ready to sell the Cyclone Air Purifier to the world. The remarkable part was that after two weeks on the job, Dean was up nearly two thousand dollars.

He had also taken a day job with a maintenance outfit where he was being instructed in the fine art of shampooing carpets. Now if a man could build up a little route. Shampoo carpets by day, sell vacuum cleaners by night . . . There was, perhaps, light at the end of the tunnel. Granted the tunnel was one long piece of shit for an aging hipster with a degree in studio arts. But there you were. You picked your place, you made your stand. And so it had been with Dean, into the night, upon these hieroglyphic streets in a valley rife with ghosts, armed with Cyclone Air Purifiers and dollhouses . . . right up until the night in question, the night upon which Dean's plans for karmic closures and Betty's words about a hot one had cross-circuited with some valley bimbo's lust for free gifts and Dean's own footsteps in time had doubled back upon themselves in a highly undesirable fashion and landed him here, in the company of a walking nightmare from his past, a dusted psycho with an interest in valley history and a vision of justice that called for Earl Dean to sing over the grave of his murdered brother. In short, Earl Dean's movie had run afoul of Dan Brown's. The theologian and the outlaw, in the valley of the Quick Decline.

And yet Dan Brown was not without sympathy for what Dean was trying to do. He liked the part about someone trying to steal Dean's land almost as much as he liked the part about the old man's violent death on the streets of Chinatown.

"You want this fucker off the land," Dan Brown said. "Say the word, dude, we'll go down there tonight."

"It wouldn't do any good. . . ." Dean began. He was trying to say it wouldn't do any good to move the guy off if Dean didn't have the money to move on. And of course he wouldn't have the money if he didn't have a job. And if he didn't get back to work soon . . . The remote prospect of perhaps salvaging the night danced before him in a tantalizing fashion.

Dan Brown, however, was already off on a new flight of his own. "That's where we bury my brother," he said. He punched his steering wheel with his fist. Dean was effectively halted in his latest reverie. He endeavored to formulate a response. "What?" he asked. "Jesus," Dan Brown said. "Clean your fucking ears, man. I said, that's where we bury my brother.

We throw this motherfucker that's in there off, put the fear of God into him while we're at it. And we bury my brother. And you sing at his grave." Dan Brown paused. "It's what remains, magic man, you said so yourself."

Dean sat in silence as the recent moment of inspiration he had been so proud of turned around to bugger him in the ass. There really was nothing left to say. The man at his side had his own agenda. He held his own counsel. In his mind he and Dean did in fact go back. They were bound, if not by blood, then by the land itself, by the valley that had spawned them both. Forget that the old order had been stood on its head, that the Oakies had once worked in the groves with the Mexicans, that perhaps some relative of Dan Brown's had even worked for, if not the old man, at least for his wife, or his partner in the fumigation business, had stalked those green corridors as had Dean himself. A fine irony, no doubt, were it so. Dean did not imagine that anyone would ever know. He had no intentions of taking it up with Dan Brown. He'd spoken his mind once tonight. One could see where it had gotten him.

As Dan Brown talked, he had, Dean noticed, begun to punctuate his words with the butt end of the beef and bean burrito he held in his right hand. It was a gesture which, aside from highlighting a word here and there, was also covering the dashboard of his truck with tiny beads of grease. Dean had thought of saying something but then, like his idea about the groves and the men who might have worked them, it seemed to him the kind of observation one might do well to consider from several angles before committing to. And so he had held his tongue once more, and watched, as the orange dots multiplied, as his most recent plan for saving himself went the way of those that had preceded it, withering in the heat of Dan Brown's rhetoric. The man was as full of outlaw fantasies as was Dean with his theology of hope and when he had it rolling he could keep it going at great length. What stopped him just now, in his dictation of the details of his brother's burial, was, at long last, the sight of the grease on his dashboard. By a peculiar twist of logic, however, Dan Brown was able at once to blame Earl Dean. "Jesus Christ," Dan Brown said. "Watch the fuck out, man. You're getting grease all over the fucking paint job." At which point he handed Dean a napkin. "Wipe that shit up, man. And I mean now." He made another stabbing motion with the burrito, which in turn deposited more grease on the dash. Dan didn't see it of course. He was looking at Dean, and there was, Dean thought, a kind of terrible beauty in the way the man's mind worked. He kept you guessing. He was twisted, to be sure, but he had his qualities. He was like the rat, adaptable, clever, impossible to eradicate. And he would always be there. It was the thought which came to Dean as he wiped away what he could of the grease. The brave ascension to the lights would stand in need of revision. Dan Brown was what they would get, when the rest of it had gone to shit, when the last theologian of hope had been boned and gutted. Dean could see it quite clearly now. His recent sense of camaraderie had led to a rash optimism. Dan Brown would be their reward after all, cold rat eyes flushed with victory, burning in the darkness. "I want every bit of that shit off there," Dan Brown told him, and Dean continued his labors as Dan Brown watched, while Ardath groaned and shifted his weight and said, "I don't even believe this shit." At which point Chuck moved his head up into the front and said, "There he is."

Dean looked toward the highway in time to see a heavyset man with bright red hair sticking out from the sides of a tractor cap come humping along the shoulder of the highway, passing beneath the light of the Taco Bell. Dan Brown put a hand on Dean's arm and smiled, showing his silver tooth. "Let's go," he said. "I want to give this fucker a surprise."

This time they went to the back of the lot and hopped the wall, effectively putting themselves in position to meet the Stench as he approached from the opposite direction. It was, Dean assumed, to be part of the surprise. He tried briefly to put himself in the bartender's shoes, to imagine what kind of picture he and the others must make, three bikers in soiled denim and Harley-Davidson T-shirts, one neutral observer in a blood-spattered sport coat.

Once over the wall, Dan Brown paused for a couple of tokes off the cigarette from the bottle. When he was finished he had something to say to Dean.

"That old man of yours," Dan said. "All those years and no one ever knew what the motherfucker was up to."

Dean admitted that this was so.

Dan Brown laughed. "Shit," he said. "I been thinkin' about it for about five minutes and I can tell you what the bastard was up to."

They were headed across the dirt lot now, toward the cover of the trees, and Dean could just make out the unfortunate bartender as he passed by the far end of the wall, silhouetted for a moment in the lights of the highway.

"Goose is goose, ginny is ginny," Dan Brown whispered, "slant-eyed pussy just as good as any."

They caught the Stench about five feet from his rear door. He was carrying a sack of beer and when he saw Dan Brown coming at him out of the shadows, he dropped it. The act was accompanied by the tinkling of breaking glass.

Dan Brown ignored the bartender and went directly to the fallen bag. "Teach you to buy bottles, fuckhead," Dan admonished him. He had begun a search of the bag's contents, looking for survivors. The bag had apparently contained a pair of six-packs. Dan Brown pulled a bottle from the wreckage and twisted the cap. Beer foamed out white in the moonlight and spilled across his tattooed knuckles. He pointed at what was left in the bag and invited the Stench to help himself.

The Stench, in apparent confusion, thanked him. When he bent to find one for himself, however, Dan Brown took the opportunity to boot him squarely in the ass. Everyone else could of course see it coming. Ardath hooted. The Stench pitched forward, landed on top of the bag, and skidded across the muddied ground on his stomach. Dean could hear the sound of more glass breaking beneath him. When the Stench had stopped sliding he rolled over and sat on his butt in the dirt.

"I had nothin' to do with it, man. I swear it," the Stench said.

"You should have called me, dickhead."

"I didn't know your number, Dan. I told Charlie."

Dan Brown walked to where the fallen man now sat. He squatted on his haunches, a position which brought his face within inches of the bartender's. "So okay," he said. "So tell me now."

It seems that these girls had shown up, four or five of them, along about four in the afternoon, all of them fucked up. Buddy had been there at the time, seated alone at a corner table near the jukebox, which was where it started.

The Stench was unable to tell them precisely what had started or why. It was like one minute Buddy was sitting there swapping insults with these cunts and the next minute there was a big fight in progress. Or rather, there was a big shouting match. Buddy had squared off with this wild-looking bitch with blond dreadlocks, nose rings, tattoos, leather jacket, the whole nine yards. At which point someone, it was difficult now to say who, had begun throwing empties through one of the windows, an act that had precipitated the Stench's own involvement.

Now Dean had, at one point in his life, spent a fair amount of time around the bar in question and in his mind's eye could just about see the scene. He could see some guy like the Stench waddling out from behind the bar and into the sunlight, which, at just that time of day, would be streaming in through an open front door. He could see how the light would be streaked with dust and filled with the noise of the traffic coming in off old Route 66, where the faithful would be lining up in traffic after a day's work. And he could see how the Stench would have this weary look about him and how he would set about tossing the girls into the lot with all the enthusiasm of a guy sitting down to unlace his shoes after a long day at the office.

The Stench had, by his own admission, given Buddy Brown a shove toward the lot as well. The deal was, though, he was quick to point out, Buddy seemed to be having a pretty good time. "I mean like the dude was laughing his ass off," the Stench told them. "What can I say? I mean here are all these cunts, and here's your fucking brother, laughing, pinching titties, everybody yelling their fucking heads off. The guy was in hog heaven. The thing is, I can't have people busting glass like that, man. Happens on my shift, Charlie's

gonna take it outta my fucking pay." The Stench
paused to wipe his mouth with the back of his hand.
"I didn't think it was any big deal," he said. "I figure,
they all roll around out there for awhile, work up a
good thirst, it's all over. You know what I mean?" The
man looked rather imploringly toward the four faces
peering down at him from the night sky. He might as
well have looked to the Four Horsemen of the Apocalypse. At last he wiped his mouth once more and went
on.

"I went back to the bar," he said. "About three
minutes later, I hear somebody scream. Next thing I
hear is Buddy's voice. He's not out in front any more.
He's in back, by the steps. And there's something
weird about the guy's voice. I go back there, and there
he is. I mean the guy is bleeding like a fucking stuck
pig." The Stench paused to indicate the area of the
wound. "He sort of comes through the door, leans
against the wall, then spins around and starts off outside. By this time, I'm right behind him. I got a bar
towel with me. I figure, get him to sit the fuck down
or something, get some pressure on it, I can get back
to the phone. So anyway, I run out and that's when I
see these cunts again. They're driving this piece-of-shit
van. And I see the blonde too. Only she's not in the
van. She's outside the fucker. The van is trying to pull
away and she's on foot. Got her jacket in her hand
and she's running after the van, screaming her head
off for the thing to stop. Which it does, and she's
gone. I mean it had to be her, man. Bitch is a fucking
amazon. So by now, Buddy is way the fuck around in
front of the bar trying to get on his fucking bike. I get
to him. I get him the towel. I'm trying to make him
sit down. He does, for about fifteen seconds, just long
enough for me to get back into the bar. I got the phone
in my hand. I hear an engine. I turn around, and there
goes Buddy. Fucker is blasting off down the side of

the road, man, gravel flying all over the cars lined up at the light. I see him hang a right on Central, and the fucker is gone, man. What the fuck am I supposed to do? Buddy's gone. The cunts are gone. As far as I know, Buddy's gonna get himself to the fucking hospital. I mean he was headed in the right direction. . . ." The Stench's voice trailed away from him, finally petering out altogether. "The cunt got this band," he said finally.

"Yeah, yeah, we know all about the fucking band," Dan Brown said, cutting him off. "That's it? You were right there and that's all you got?"

The Stench nodded. He looked like a man who would have been only too happy to give more but who had been cheated in some terrible karmic way. With nothing more to say, he sat in the dirt and considered the toes of his boots.

Dan Brown stood above him, hands on his hips. He looked at the man seated before him. He turned his face to the dark branches above his head. The moonlight slipped down through the limbs and Dean could see the silver in Dan Brown's pony tail where it lay across the soiled denim of his jacket.

"There was one thing," the Stench said. Dan Brown looked at him. "I think these chicks had some fliers."

Dan Brown dropped his hands to his sides, as if maybe he was thinking about using them for something. "What the fuck are you talking about?" he asked.

"Fliers," The Stench said again. "I mean I didn't actually see one, but I think that's what they came in for, 'cause I saw one of them with a stack of paper. . . . And these bands do that sort of shit. So I don't know, man. . . . I mean you find one of those fliers, might at least tell you where the next gig is."

Dan Brown stood over the Stench for some time. He looked like he was trying to decide if this last piece of information called for any kind of violent reaction. The Stench looked like he was probably trying to decide the same thing. He stayed where he was, on his ass, in the dirt.

"Fliers," Dan Brown said at last. "These cunts have fliers and this is the first anybody tells me about it." The statement was greeted with silence. "I want you to know something," Dan Brown said. "This motherfucker is starting to piss me off."

It was not immediately clear to Dean who it was that Brown was addressing, or if the said motherfucker was the man at his feet or the situation in general. Dan Brown stared into the ravaged trees, then turned abruptly and started off in the direction from which he had come. He did this so suddenly that the others, Dean included, were taken by surprise, and there was a beat in which they found themselves standing there without him, staring down on the Stench, who was suddenly beginning to look very much like a man with a new lease on life. In the end there was nothing for them to do but to turn around and trail after Dan Brown, who by now was halfway back to the block wall.

Dean walked in the middle. He had the bearded man in front and Ardath at his back and he found himself thinking once more about this girl, Pomona Queen. He had the bartender's description to go on now, with which to build upon whatever it was he had begun in Dan Brown's house. She was his sword maiden, he thought suddenly. He liked the ring of it . . . anointed in blood. . . . And it seemed to him that she waited for him out there somewhere, in leather and lace, blond dreadlocks shining in the light of an immense neon Taco Bell, a knife in her hand, alone before an approaching darkness.

* * *

The darkness was noticeably dragging a leg by the time they reached the lot. Dean supposed the thing was starting to stiffen up on him where the blonde had stitched it. Perhaps if it stiffened up and fell off, Dean's sword maiden would stand half a chance. It was the thought that sustained him as he climbed once more into the back of the panel.

"So where to?" Ardath wanted to know.

Dan Brown started the truck. "The Mid-Dump," he said. "Fliers my ass. You two dumb shits couldn't get a line on one of these fliers?"

"Hey, man . . ." It was Ardath who spoke. "No one said anything to us about fliers."

There was a suicide knob on Dan Brown's steering wheel. The thing was shaped like a small silver skull with ruby red eyes. Dan Brown used it to steer with, whipping them around in the lot, then out to the street, where the traffic crawled slowly along Foothill Boulevard.

They rode for several minutes in silence. As they slowed, approaching a red light, Dean noticed a Mexican kid of perhaps fourteen. The kid was running up and down a concrete island in the middle of the street, peddling his wares to passing motorists. In this case the wares were flowers, gaily colored bouquets wrapped in brightly colored foil. As Dan Brown stopped for the light the kid waved a bouquet in the open window of the panel truck. Dan Brown swatted it away as one would a gnat. "Why do I get the feeling that some motherfucker is trying to put me together?" Dan Brown asked.

Dean thought of saying something clever on the general condition of man, then thought better of it. The kid with the flowers thought Dan Brown was talking to him. He rattled something off in Spanish, too quickly for Dean to catch. "Go fuck yourself, pancho,"

Dan Brown said. The kid stared. "Better yet," Dan Brown told him. "Go get me your sister." Dan Brown laughed. "Least in T.J. the little fuckers are trying to sell you some poontang." Dan turned once more to the kid. "Dónde está su . . ." Dan Brown paused. "What's the fucking word for sister?" he asked. No one said anything. Ahead of them the light turned green. "Seester," Dan Brown said, affecting a Mexican accent. "We fuck your seester. Five dollars . . ." The kid suddenly looked more scared than pissed. Dean could see him scurrying off toward another car as Dan Brown pulled away. At the next intersection there was a guy selling oranges but they made the light and up ahead Dean could see what he knew to be the faint glow cast by the lights of the Midway Bar. At least in terms of exterior lighting the glow was faint.

For Dean it was a regular aurora borealis. For if the specter of the old man still stalked the groves, the Midway Bar belonged to the red-haired girl. Everything, it seemed, belonged to someone. The entire valley had been carved into pieces and he was granted a kind of vision of what lay beyond the smoked glass of Dan Brown's windows—the pale grid of the dead. It was what hovered above the more concrete grid of shingle roofs and paved streets, the ordered swirl of their lights. He saw too what went down there, how there was really not one square foot to which some sad ghost had not staked a claim. The situation was, as one might imagine, not without its unseemly side, the dead being scarcely more magnanimous than the living. "I lost my virginity here, you useless fuck." And some other ghost says, "Up yours, dickhead. My piles fell here in eighty-two." And suddenly you have a terrible fight on your hands. Ghosts groping for half-remembered testicles, gouging at sightless eyes . . .

"If I ever thought," Dan Brown said suddenly, apparently taking up where he had left off before the kid had interrupted him, "that someone was trying to put me together, I would pity that motherfucker's sorry ass." Dean heard the pronouncement but he was thinking about his ghosts and it took him a full fifteen seconds to appreciate the fact that, via his rearview mirror, the man was looking directly at him.

SIX

Other sports of San Juan Day were horse racing and cock fights. . . . On these occasions the Burdicks and other American families were always invited, for the generosity of the Mexicans was unlimited. . . . Even when the smallpox raged and whole families were wiped out, they did not desert each other. . . . It was doubtless this lack of precaution which accounted for the terrible toll which the disease levied upon the Mexicans. And it was even worse among the Indians, as will be noted later.

—F. P. Brackett

If there was an oasis in the Pomona Valley, it was the town of Claremont. Its founders, the Pacific Land Improvement Company, strapped in 1887 with a full-blown ghost town, after an initially promising boom, had cut a deal with the fledgling Pomona College. They'd offered the institution the use of an otherwise empty hotel, together with two or three hundred jackrabbit-infested lots, if the college would move to Claremont. It did. Others followed, and by the time Dean was a kid there were something like five small private colleges in and around the town, which was ringed with older neighborhoods, with tree-lined streets, with wooden two- and three-story homes. The colleges owned much of the town and they had worked at creating a certain college-town ambience. The extent to which they had succeeded was, to Dean, growing up, a kind of minor miracle. It was also a major thorn in his side.

The fact of the matter was, it should have been his, these tree-lined streets, these ivied halls with their reek of privilege and money. It was the world to which he should have been born, had the old man only held up his end of things, gotten old and rich instead of dead young. The town was a symbol and so was Rayann. He came from Pomona. She lived in Claremont. It was no small deal. He didn't just come from Pomona. He was her native son, born and raised in a tract home, a front yard filled with Carl's plumbing trucks, the backyard with his collection of Hudsons, so that when he won that painting contest during his freshman year in high school and got as his prize a series of art classes that met on Saturday mornings at Scripps College it was no small deal either. If there was a good life left in the valley it started somewhere north of the old Santa Fe rail line and the classes were his letter of introduction.

It became his custom to drive to town in the white Hornet he had gotten from Carl, then walk the rest of the way, his sketch pads beneath his arm, shuffling through the fallen leaves, the autumnal light, just like he was on the trail of some bright future. And then one morning in late November, at the corner of Yale and Eleventh, he was stopped by the sound of someone playing the violin. He supposed it had something to do with the light and the leaves and the time of day and the tree-lined street and the old wooden houses. The music came wafting along a narrow dirt drive at the side of a white colonial with green trim. There was a Peugeot station wagon in the drive and a Volkswagen bus with a MAKE LOVE NOT WAR bumper sticker on the rear glass. There was an alley in back of the house and working his way around to it, peering over a vine-covered fence, he discovered the musician was a girl. She wore a T-shirt and jeans. It is not likely he would forget. She was tall. She had a thin, somewhat boyish build. Dark red hair spilled over her shoulders. The arms that made the music were white as starlight and he may as well have been Saul of Tarsus, struck blind on the road to Damascus. This girl had it in her power to make him whole. It was that simple. She was everything he had been denied. Everything to which he would aspire. It all helped of course, the trees, the light, the music, even that Volkswagen bus in the drive. Make love not war. Indeed.

For six weeks, the length of his lessons, he imagined himself walking down that drive, knocking on her door. He never did. He got as far as the alley. He listened to her play, "Dark Eyes," "The Arkansas Traveler," "Sweet Georgia Brown." He purchased a secondhand guitar from a pawnshop in Pomona. It became his secret ambition to sit with her on that wooden porch, lay down some bass lines and chords, lay her down as well, as far as that went, in that chaise longue, say, the one that sat beneath the tree at the edge of the grass. And then one day he went and she was gone. A month passed. He had begun to despair, to consider something rash, when suddenly she came back into his life. It happened along about two o'clock in the morning at the side of the Midway Bar, effectively putting a charge on the place no amount of time was going to erase.

For years, in the years before time, and long before the building of the San Antonio Dam, the waters that flowed from the mouth of the San Antonio Canyon brought with them the debris of the mountains. Eventually, this debris, the rock and the gravel, came to form a great alluvial fan. It was upon this fan that the towns of Claremont and Upland, as well as a good part of Pomona, were built. Chino, farther to the south, got the topsoil. Claremont, Upland, and Pomona got the rock. In order to do any planting, as was required by the citrus industry, it was necessary first to remove the rock. As a consequence there was a lot of it around.

Some had been used as building material. The Midway Bar was of the rock-building era. From the outside, the structure was squat, gray, and colorless. Inside, many of the stones in the walls had been dusted in festive shades of hippie Day-Glo and surrounded a badly scarred black-and-white linoleum floor, which ran through two rooms of unequal size. In the back room a redwood picnic table languished beneath a single dim light. The front room was jammed with a bar, a quarter pool table, a handful of card tables, and metal folding chairs. There was a jukebox on one side of the front door and a cigarette machine on the other. It had been that way for as long as Dean could remember. The building occupied high ground and on a clear night, the lights of the Pomona Valley could be seen in all their mediocre splendor, cast among the dark folds of the surrounding hills.

Dean knew about those lights. Their meager swirl still burned in his memory, stamped there like some circuit, rife with concealed meaning. He knew of the silence that would descend when the traffic had gone and the bar had closed and he knew what the sun would look like as it peaked the distant mass of San Gorgonio. Rayann had pointed it out to him. Just like she'd taught him the opening arpeggios of "Minor Swing," or pointed out that passage about the steps a man takes in time. Of course he liked to think that he'd pointed out a few things to her as well. He'd introduced her to Milly, to the ghost of William McCauly. He'd shown her the old opera house in downtown Pomona, buried in its sad layers of faded stucco. He had gone down on her in his great-grandfather's barn with the sunlight slicing down through the cracks in the roof like so many projectors drawing lines in the dark and she had said it was the first time and

he'd always figured he had the Midway
bartender whose name he'd long forgotte

He had been going there off and on for
more. He wasn't old enough, but then the
little slack on details at the Mid-Dump, so long
played it smart, went with older friends, hung
the back room. They were especially easy on girls, so
long as they looked good and kept a low profile. Rayann had the looks down, it was just that keeping a
low profile had never been a part of her act. And there
was something else about her as well, the boyish lines,
the perfect complexion. Bartenders were carding her a
decade later, even after the lines had begun to blur
and the light had died in those green eyes. A bartender had carded her on the evening in question,
leaving her to strum an old Sears Silvertone in the
parking lot while a pair of friends stayed inside to finish off a pitcher.

Dean could not quite believe it at the time. He had
gone with a pair of friends himself, a couple of hicks
from P town, the Craven brothers. One had a job at a
gas station. The other was chronically unemployed.
Neither had a car but both were old enough for bars
and Dean went there with them from time to time,
driving them in the white Hornet, which they were
desperate to get their hands on, chop and channel it,
you understand. Bill favored mint green, Ned candy-
apple red, and when Dean climbed out from behind
the wheel and saw this girl on the back porch he was
struck dumb, both with wonder and shame. In fact he
believed he had faked a coughing spasm and sent the
brothers Craven in ahead of him so as not to be seen
with them.

It should be pointed out that seeing someone like
Rayann at the Midway was not then as unusual as it
might seem now. For there had been a time when the
place had enjoyed a brief stint of hip respectability, a

, where Claremont College professors could rub shoulders with bikers from Pomona. In fact Dean had first heard of the bar from the man who taught the painting class and he made a point in those days of getting there as often as he could, even if it meant hanging out with guys still into pompadours and pointed shoes. It should also be pointed out that this era of hipness was fairly short lived and by the time Dean left the valley, enough serious violence had gone down at the place to scare away the intellectuals. The outlaws had reclaimed their turf. By the mid-seventies the Midway had become the Mid-Dump, stone Dan Brown territory, and had been ever since. Still, for Dean, the place would always be haunted by some vestige of that old magic, the place he had been too young for, the place where college professors had lined the bar in their blue jeans and cotton workshirts, passed their joints and laughed their knowing laughs, the place he had spoken to Rayann for the first time— some witty remark no doubt, though in point of fact he no longer had any idea of what had been said and could only hope that it had been a remark of some wit. But then one hoped for a lot of things, pillaging the shadows of one's past. The upshot was that Dean had, on the evening in question, been in possession of a case—the hand of God it had seemed to him at the time. The thing had rested in the trunk of the Hornet, Budweiser in the bottle, and before the night was over he and the redhead had found the bottoms of most of them. They'd sat on the hood, their backs against the windshield, swapped songs and one-liners at the expense of the valley, and they'd seen the first pale light as it spread from the east. Earl Dean had been nineteen years old at the time. He had unearthed a heart much like his own at the side of the Midway Bar, halfway between the towns of Claremont and

Ontario. In fact, he had fallen in love there, the lights of Pomona strung like jewels at his feet.

It was of course a long, long time between that night and this and yet he was amazed, pulling into the lot, to see how little the place had changed. There were not many places in the southern half of the state one could say that about, and what Dean felt at seeing the bar was not unlike what he had felt upon walking out of Dan Brown's house, inhaling the scent of orange blossom, catching his first glimpse of the old panel parked in the drive.

Chuck wanted to piss before he went inside and the others waited. Dean listened to the voice of Charlie Daniels spilling from the bar, the soft spatter of urine on hard-packed dirt. The night air burned his lip and the lights of the Pomona Valley rolled away before him as they'd once done for a nineteen-year-old kid with a hard-on and a case of beer. It was enough, he imagined, to make a grown man puke.

As Chuck pissed, Ardath began an inspection of the concrete steps leading toward the back door of the bar. Dean could see him there, bent at the waist in the shadows. He appeared to be touching something with his finger. At last he straightened and turned toward the van, where Chuck was now buttoning his jeans. "Danny," Ardath said. "Check it out, man."

They checked it out together. The steps were spattered with blood, though perhaps spattered was too gentle a word. It streaked the corroded handrail and the concrete. It spotted the stones that framed the doorway. In fact, it was everywhere. The more one looked the more one saw. When Dan Brown had seen enough to satisfy himself he went up the steps and into the bar, the others with him.

*　　*　　*

In the year or two following Dean's graduation from high school a girl everyone called Fall Down Debbie occasionally tended bar at the Midway. She was not unattractive in a plump, cowlike way. Her parents had money and were understandably horrified by her choice of company, her drunkenness, her sliding reputation. It was said the old man once showed up at the Midway and tried to drag her out of the place, physically, by her hair. Debbie had managed a death grip on the bar, however, and after extracting two or three handfuls from his daughter's scalp, the old man had given up, disowned her on the spot, much to the delight of the Midway regulars, and lurched back out to his waiting Mercedes, only to find that someone with a sense of humor had flattened all four tires.

That of course was by now ancient history. For Dean it was of another life, so that he was at once both horror stricken and delighted to see none other than Fall Down Debbie, twenty years older, to be sure, but clearly recognizable, standing behind the bar and running a filthy bar towel around the lip of a glass pitcher.

There was a Confederate flag nailed to the wall above Debbie's head. Before her lay the cool green felt of a quarter pool table, as soft, as shimmering as any delicately manicured lawn touched by morning light. There were certain places, a leggy brunette had recently explained to Dean at a crafts fair in Big Sur, which could serve as doors to other physical planes. The purpose of the crystal she had pressed into Dean's hand was to see through the time block. Once through the block, one should, theoretically, of course, be able to maneuver by way of the various poles. "We are looking," the woman told him, "for a small group of people who can work in the realm of the incomprehensible." The woman had eyes like the sky in that hour before the dawn. She also, as it turned out, had a traveling companion, a bearded Goliath in an aging pickup with whom she was making the circuit, and Dean had gotten nothing more out of the deal than the useless piece of rock. And yet now, standing there in the smoky light of the Mid-Dump, Fall Down Debbie back of the bar, a six-pack beneath his belt, his head still ringing from Dan Brown's punches, he was possessed of a sudden illumination. Dan Brown's house. The panel truck. The bar. The name of the band—magnetic poles in a field of time. It occurred to him as well that he had, after all, been working in the realm of the incomprehensible most of his life.

There were perhaps a dozen people in the bar, men and women. Most wore denim and leather. The men favored facial hair and tattoos. The air was dirty with their smoke. Dean was aware of their glances, of the uneasy silence that had fallen upon the room. His immediate impulse, however, was to laugh. The scene appeared to him as something out of a B western, what with Dan Brown looming up there before him, his back black with shadow, his boots spread shoulder width. The impulse was cut short by something else, something one felt along the hairs at the back of one's neck. It was the energy. There was really no other way to say it. The room was alive with it. There was no one in the place who did not know what had gone down, not at this point. They knew about Buddy Brown, and they knew Dan Brown had come to handle it. The pale horse was parked outside and Death had come to pay a visit. You could reflect, as Dean had earlier, on outlaw fantasies and the opiate of losers. The fact was, Mr. Brown had a way of creating his own reality. There may have been some folks in the room unhappy with Dan Brown's movie but it was highly unlikely any of them would get it together to walk off the set.

"Danny," Fall Down Debbie said at length, and

there was, Dean thought, a slight tremor in her voice. "I'm sorry."

Dan Brown approached the bar. "Coupla pitchers," he said.

Debbie filled two pitchers and set them on the bar. The second thing she said was, "On the house, Danny." The third thing she said, after a long pause, was, "Am I seeing things, or is that Johnny Magic?"

"The very motherfucking one," Dan Brown said. "He just showed up at my crib. He was trying to sell the old lady a vacuum cleaner."

Fall Down Debbie laughed out loud. She had a deep, throaty laugh, which, it seemed to Dean, had not changed much in twenty years. Her face, which time had stretched wider and turned harder, spread before him a smile so wide it seemed to him something a man might fall into and be lost.

"So much for the sport coat," Debbie said. "What happened to his face?"

"Johnny's having himself quite an evening," Dan Brown said. "He's already stepped in dog shit, broken his vacuum cleaner, and tried to jump bad on his old friend Dan Brown. And dig this, Debbie, the evening is still young."

Debbie filled a glass and pushed it in front of Dean. "What's it been?" she asked him. She was still grinning. "Twenty years?"

Dean shook his head. "I guess. How are you, Debbie?"

"Fat and fucked up. Last thing anybody told me about you all, you'd gone to New Mexico or some place with Rayann. That right?"

"Rayann died, Debbie."

Debbie stopped smiling and began to wipe absently at the bar with her dirty towel. "Lots of people died," she said, and then began to name names. "You remember Racetrack Bill? Doctor told him his liver was fucked up. They gave him about a year. Drove his bike off San Dimas Canyon Road." She continued on down the list: Frank, Stacy, Jim Hoyt. Some of the names Dean could put faces to, others he could not. It was clear, however, that Debbie had given the subject a good deal of thought. She was still going when Dan Brown silenced her with a wave of his hand.

"I got my brother out there in the truck," Dan said. "Johnny here is going to sing over his grave. You're fucking officially invited to attend."

"Attend where?"

Dan Brown looked at Dean. "We're still tryin' to work that out. Right now I want to know if you can tell me anything about this band, Pomona Queen."

"It's a girl's band."

"I know it's a fucking cunt band," Dan Brown said. "The Stench tells me they were in here handing out fliers. You got any left?"

Debbie shrugged. "I wouldn't know," she said. Dan turned suddenly on the patrons at his back. Most were already looking in his direction, waiting, it appeared, to see what would happen next. "What about it?" Dan Brown asked. "I want to know if there are any of these fucking fliers left around here or not."

The request was met with an immediate silence. Eventually, however, a thin, bearded man with bad teeth rose from a metal folding chair and walked into the back room. When he returned there were two sheets of paper in his hand. The man was dressed in a pair of grease-stained coveralls into which the name Frank had been stitched with red thread upon a white oval above his heart. He placed the papers on the bar between Dean and Dan and returned to his seat without saying a word.

Dan Brown picked them up almost at once so that Dean was afforded only a brief glimpse. What Dean saw was the black-and-white Xeroxed photograph of a girl with a guitar. He saw the words Pomona Queen in baroque script. The girl's photograph was surrounded by smaller chunks of writing, what looked to be club dates, but nothing Dean could read. Dan Brown waited until Frank had returned to his seat, then looked quickly at the fliers, folded them in half, and stuffed them into the vest pocket of his jacket. The entire transaction had been carried out in silence. Dean could hear Debbie in back of the bar, squeezing the water from a dishrag.

At last Dan Brown smiled. He swiveled back around on his stool. "We're in business," he said. The words had a kind of finality about them that Dean found chilling. Dan Brown glanced once in his direction, a portrait of grim satisfaction. With eyelids at half-mast there was something almost reptilian about the man's face, the wide, flat brow, the narrowed eyes, powerful neck. The boa constrictor with an eye on the lamb.

"Who are these cunts, anyway?" It was the bearded man who spoke. He seemed to be addressing himself to Debbie.

"Who gives a shit who they are?" Dan Brown asked. "We know where now. You two assholes woulda been lookin' for 'em all night long."

"College girls," Debbie said.

"College girls?" Dean asked. He asked almost as a reflex action and was then aware of Dan Brown staring at him.

"That's what they tell me," Debbie said. "Pitzer, Scripps, one of those places." The places she was naming were private colleges in the town of Claremont.

"Rich pussies," someone ventured from the room behind them. Dan Brown didn't bother to turn around. He continued to address himself to Debbie. "So what are they doin' in here?"

Debbie drew another pitcher. "I believe it's called slumming," she said.

"Yeah," Dan Brown said. "Let me tell you this. One of them has just about slummed herself into an early grave."

Debbie just looked at him. Another voice issued from the room. It said something Dean could not quite catch. He believed it said, "Right on."

"The Stench says it was one of these cunts from the band knifed my brother."

Fall Down Debbie shook her head. She took up her bar towel once more and drew it along one side of the scarred wood. "I don't know, Danny. I heard something about it. Stench says there was this blonde running down the road or something. . . ." Debbie's voice trailed away. A metal chair grated on the linoleum.

"And the blonde was arguing with Buddy, and the blonde was with the band." There was something in Dan Brown's voice that asked to be challenged.

Fall Down Debbie declined the gambit. She shook her head. "I don't know, Danny. I really don't." She looked him in the eye just long enough to be convincing, then turned to Earl Dean. She hooked a lock of dark hair behind one ear. "You know your nose is bleeding?" she asked.

The Mid-Dump was possessed of a single bathroom. A dingy little place you could always count on to reek of human waste, just like you could count on the graffiti, the stopped toilet, the quarter-inch of water sure to cover the floor. Some lunatic had ripped the door off back around 1969 and no one had ever gotten it together to put on a new one, making it necessary to do whatever business you'd come to do in plain view of most of the patrons. Dean had come to do something about his nose.

The thing had bowed out some on one side but

didn't seem to hurt badly enough to be broken. Dean bathed it in rusty tap water. He washed off the dried blood and rinsed out his mouth. He ran his wet hands back over his head to slick back his hair, then took a moment to stare at his misshapen reflection in the small, battered mirror that hung above the sink. There was a survivor for you, Dean thought, considering, not himself, but this fragile piece of glass, the same that had hung there for perhaps twenty years or more, having survived uncounted brawls, dusted vandals, sexual encounters best not imagined at length. If this mirror, like Beale Street, could talk, who then would have to walk? Well, there was just no telling, thought Dean, and he found himself thinking once more of the girl. She seemed, in his mind's eye, to have made the rather abrupt transition from street-tough white trash to . . . here he hesitated. An English major with a flair for knife fighting? An art student with a taste for funk, in suddenly over her head? Perhaps the tattoos had been paste-ons, the dreadlocks a wig. Perhaps even as Dean stared into this milky glass, she was showered, chastened, and afraid, huddled in the office of some college adviser. Perhaps the long-distance call had already been made, a ticket placed in the mail, a lawyer retained. . . . It was probably, Dean thought, the best that one could hope for.

Dean's dress shirt and tie were history. The tie went directly into the large, alley-sized trash can that rested against one wall of the bathroom. The shirt did service as a towel, the Mid-Dump being, predictably, fresh out. When he was done with the shirt it followed the tie and had it not been for the fact that the trash can was already filled to overflowing, he probably would not have noticed the flowers. As it was, he gave the shirt a bit of a push, just to get it down into the container, and was surprised to see a red, long-stemmed rose emerge from beneath a sheet of newsprint. One simply did not expect to find long-stemmed roses in the bathroom of the Mid-Dump. Lifting a corner of the newsprint, he saw that there were others, at least two dozen, their stems still wrapped tightly in handsome violet foil. The flowers had been mashed down with the rest of the trash and then, or so it appeared to Dean, very deliberately covered with several pages of newsprint.

He noticed something else as well. First he noticed the dirt, and then the blood. The flowers were streaked with both and it occurred to him that the roses had been on the ground, that they must have been there when Buddy Brown was stabbed and that someone had deliberately gathered them up and put them where they would not be seen.

Dean stood for some time in the poor light, examining the flowers. At last he reached down and covered them with the newsprint once more. He put his sport coat back on, over his T-shirt, pissed in the sink, and went back out into the bar.

The bathroom was located just off the Mid-Dump's smaller, back room and coming out of it, Dean found himself staring toward the side door by which he and the others had entered. By necessity he turned toward it and for a moment it seemed to him that the doorway was quite empty. The door itself stood propped open upon the blood-stained concrete. At which point something moved at the edge of the night. The Budweiser sign flickered and he saw Ardath. The man moved out from a shadow and leaned against the doorjamb, his face distorted by an unpleasant smile. Dean turned away. He was moving into the main room when the man called to him.

"Yo, dickhead," Ardath said.

Dean noticed that the room was empty.

"It ain't in there, man. It's out here."

Dean looked at Ardath. The man's hair was lit up like snow in a sudden flash of light. He was gesturing toward the darkness. Dean hesitated briefly, then crossed the room and walked out onto the concrete porch. He saw at once where the others had gone, the patrons of the Mid-Dump. They had gone to view the body.

Dan Brown and the bearded one, solemn as a pair of backwoods preachers, stood at the rear of Dan Brown's truck. The back door was open, the freezer lid raised. The others filed past it in an orderly fashion. Fall Down Debbie stood at the rear of the line. Dean was considering this procession when he felt a hand in the small of his back. Ardath gave him a shove and he went down the steps in a hurry, fairly stumbling onto the dirt lot. Dan Brown raised his eyes at Dean's approach.

"Dude was lookin', man." It was Ardath who spoke, walking onto the dirt behind Dean. "Dude was fucking lookin', man."

Several of the men in the lot looked at Dean. The silence, save for the occasional rush of a passing car on Foothill Boulevard, was absolute.

"Looking for what?" Dan Brown asked.

"Lookin' to run, man. I saw him come out of the head. Suit was checkin' out the door, man."

"I was comin' out of the bathroom," Dean said. "Hard to come out of the bathroom without looking at the door. It's right in front of you."

Dean heard the man behind him curse softly beneath his breath. Dan Brown appeared to be giving the matter some thought when a pair of headlights swung suddenly off the highway and came bouncing across the rutted dirt of the lot. The lights were attached to a battered Volkswagen Bug, which lurched to a stop about six feet from the back of Dan Brown's panel.

Dan Brown looked at Dean a moment longer, then turned to face the car. The headlights died. A door creaked open. What emerged was the skinny brunette with the scar on her shoulder.

"Some fucker stole my Cyclone," is what she said.

Dan Brown just stared at her. "What do you mean, some fucker stole your Cyclone?"

"I mean some dumb Mexican showed up asking about Earl Dean. When he saw the Cyclone he asked for a receipt. When I didn't have one he took it. . . ."

"You let him."

"Let him shit . . . Look at this." The girl extended her lower lip. Dean was too far away to see anything himself. Dan Brown took a step toward the girl.

"You mean he hit you?"

"He pushed me down. I hit my chin on the table and bit my fucking lip. Then the bastard went out and broke in to Magic's car and took all of his Cyclones."

The girl looked at Earl Dean.

Dan Brown just stood there, his hands on his hips. "For Christ's sake. You drove all the way up here to tell me this shit?"

"I came to tell Johnny Magic," she said.

"So how did you know he was going to be here?"

"Hey, you said you were going to find the Stench."

The girl said this in a somewhat defensive manner, after which she and Dan Brown traded stares in the murky light. Dean, watching from the far side of the truck, was struck by a pair of items. On the one hand, he had the distinct feeling that Dan Brown thought there was something wrong with the girl's story. On the other hand, it became apparent to him for the first time that the girl was Dan Brown's.

The resemblance, seeing them standing there facing one another, was so obvious he did not know why he had not seen it at once. Nor could he say immediately why the idea should strike him as odd. The fact of the matter was, he had assumed from the first that the girl belonged to the blonde who had answered the door in Clear Lake. Upon reflection, however, an answer to these questions presented itself. He had simply found it incongruous to imagine Dan Brown as human enough to father another living soul. It was an absurd notion of course, living souls being fathered by the likes of Dan Brown and worse on what was no doubt an hourly basis. Still, one was entitled to one's feelings and he could not help thinking the girl's misfortune ran even deeper than he had first imagined.

"Listen," the girl said. "That fucker stole my Cyclone. I want it back. . . ."

Dan Brown turned his back on her and walked toward the truck. The girl fell in behind him. "That was mine. . . ."

Dan opened the door of his truck. "You got a receipt?"

The girl put her hands on her hips.

Dean had listened thus far in silence. He was about to ask the girl something about the Mexican when he felt Ardath shove him once more from behind. He shoved him in the direction of the panel. "I'm tellin' you, Danny," the man said. "This suit was looking to run."

Dan looked at them across the roof of his truck. "Get in," he said. "We're outta here."

Chuck shut the lid of the freezer, closed the back door, and opened another. He pulled a seat back forward, inviting Dean into the darkness. "Let's go," he said. Dean was once more aware of Ardath on his tail, cursing beneath his breath as they both crawled into the reeking interior of the truck.

Dan Brown was in himself now as well, saddled up, his offspring having positioned herself at his window.

"That fucker stole my Cyclone, Danny. I want it back."

Dan Brown shook his head. "Johnny Magic will get you another one," he told her.

"I don't think Johnny Magic works there anymore," the girl said.

"Yeah? I thought he was the one you came looking for."

The girl said nothing, and it seemed to Dean as if, in the look which passed between father and daughter, some obscure point had been scored by the former.

"Get home," Dan Brown said at last. "That's Kim's car and she needs the fucking thing for work, you understand me? Get it home and stay there."

As Dan Brown started his truck and backed it around in the lot Dean was afforded a last look at the girl. She was standing at the side of the battered Bug. Her arms were folded at her chest. Her eyes had the appearance of holes that had been punched in her face, allowing the night to show through. The effect was, Dean thought, rather startling. The car at her side was sitting at an odd angle in the uneven lot, with one door hanging open, as if with fatigue. The interior was quite black, with the exception of one brilliant pink latex glove which lay across the passenger side seat and hung out of the darkness like the pink tongue of a spent beast and Dean found himself thinking rather suddenly of another girl and another time, of a girl with haunted green eyes and rosin dust in her hair, a girl long since gone to the long home. One more creature of the night—his special weakness.

He thought of the barn owl his grandmother had once kept in an upstairs room of the old house, she of the broken wing. And then he thought of something else too. He thought of the roses he'd found covered with newsprint in the bathroom. It would not do, he thought, to forget the roses.

*   *   *

From the bar, Dan Brown drove south on Central Avenue for a mile, then turned west. Dean assumed they were going to intercept the girl, that Dan Brown now knew where she was. Still, without a better look at the flier, he had no idea of where they were headed. They had driven for perhaps two minutes in silence before the voice of Ardath was heard once more.

"I'm tellin' ya, Danny," the man said, his voice having assumed something like the whine of a petulant child. "This asshole came outta that head lookin' for the door, man." Dean had been aware of the guy staring at him in the darkness, almost without letup, since leaving the Mid-Dump; now he felt the guy kick him in the sole of the shoe with his boot.

"The pussy was gonna run, man. I could feel it."

Dan Brown shook his head, much as he had done while listening to his daughter bemoan the loss of her Cyclone. " 'Cept you scared his ass out of it. That right?"

"Hey, man. Damn straight." He kicked Dean in the shoe once more.

Dan Brown adjusted his rearview mirror. "That right, Magic?"

"No," Dean said.

"Johnny Magic says no," Dan Brown said.

"He was looking straight at the fucking door."

"I told you, man." Dean said. "You got to look at the door when you come out of that head. It's right in front of you."

"You callin' me a liar?" Ardath asked.

"Not necessarily," Dean said.

"Not necessarily," Ardath mimicked. "He's cute, Danny."

"Maybe you've just got dog shit for brains." Dean added.

He wasn't exactly sure what had made him say it. It was different than swinging on Dan Brown. That had been a kind of instinct, involuntary. This was something else. Dean had never tried to pass for a hard guy, but then he could not exactly remember having had to sit still for so much shit in a long time either. The guy at the back of the van was not Dan Brown and a dull, throbbing anger had at last begun to override the stone fear with which all of this had started. The alcohol probably helped.

The words, however, were scarcely out of Dean's mouth before Ardath was on him, with a fury for which he was not prepared. And it occurred to him, even as his head began bouncing off the back of Dan Brown's seat, that the alcohol had done him one final disservice, that perhaps he could have sat still for just a little more shit after all—not exactly the blind and righteous fury with which he had imagined his own attack unfolding. The guy had him by the throat with one hand and was bouncing punches off his head with the other. The punches fell like rocks, three or four of them while Dean was still trying to get a handle on what exactly was coming down. When he did he began to struggle. His wingtips drew sparks from the van's metal walls. He drove a thumb into Ardath's eye and heard him yell. A punch fell squarely above his own eye, closing it almost at once. Things became difficult to keep track of.

At some point he became aware of the panel lurching wildly through a series of turns. He felt the ice chest against his shoulder. He felt Ardath, thrown slightly off balance, loosen his grip. He fought for air. He felt himself sliding on his back toward the front of the panel. Ardath and the freezer slid as well, as the van came to an abrupt stop. And all at once he was aware of the light, of the rear door standing open to the night, of the blond-haired maniac with the viselike grip being pulled away from him, and after that the action was all outside.

Dean could hear it from where he lay, wedged between the red freezer and a bare metal wall, having assumed the full survival position of an injured stinkbug. He could hear the voice of Dan Brown cursing in the darkness. He could hear the wicked sounds of bare fists landing. He pulled himself painfully on to his ass and looked around. Chuck had gotten out of the truck. Dean was alone. They were somewhere on the north side of town. Big old houses down here, Victorians, three stories high, and old chestnut trees weaving dark patterns before the streetlights and tearing slabs of concrete from the ancient sidewalks. The houses had long, sloping yards and windows lit by yellow lights and for the second time that evening, Dean ran.

It occurred to him later, he should have at least looked at the ignition, as it seemed quite likely Dan Brown would not have pulled the keys. As it was, he did not look at anything, save the branches of the chestnut trees and the yellow lights of the houses. All he really wanted was out. He pulled himself over the front seat, went feet first out the right front door, where he stepped squarely into the path of an oncoming car.

It was a small car, a sports car of some kind. The thing was driven by a woman. Fortunately, she was nearing her driveway and already on the breaks. Dean was probably going as fast as she was. Still, the car took him low on his right leg and flipped him across the hood and onto his shoulder. He rolled to his hands and knees and made it to the curb. He heard the woman scream. Lights blossomed among the shadows. Soon a man's voice could be heard, issuing from one of the yards. Dean crawled up onto the damp dirt beneath one of the trees and was just about to the sidewalk when Dan Brown took hold of him by the

collar of his sport coat. He pulled Dean to his feet and
turned him around, and Dean could see, for the first
time, the woman who had run over him. She was
standing in the street, next to her car, her hand over
her mouth.

"Not a mark on him," Dan Brown said.

The woman said nothing. A man's voice called her
name. The woman looked toward a house. There was
a man there now, a big man in a white T-shirt moving
down across the yard. There were other people in
other yards as well—pale shadows among the trees.

Dan Brown dragged Dean around to the back of the
truck and pushed him in. "No harm no foul," he said
to the woman.

The man in the white T-shirt said, "Hey there . . ."

Chuck said, "These fuckers will have the pigs down
here in about two seconds." He said this beneath his
breath as Dan was shoving Dean into the back of the
truck.

"No shit," Dan said. He pushed the door shut after
Dean and ran around to the driver's side. The last
Dean saw of the woman who had hit him, she was
still standing in the street, surrounded by a small collection of neighbors. The man in the T-shirt had his
arm around her shoulders. There were perhaps a
dozen people present. Dean could see their faces
receding in the shadows of the trees as Dan Brown
pulled away.

Dean had to crawl over Ardath's legs to resume his
position near the front of the truck. He did this without looking at the man's face. His body seemed to
have gone mercifully numb. Perhaps he was in shock.
There was nothing more than a faint tingling sensation
in the leg and shoulder which had taken the blow. The
pain would come. He was sure of that. It was just a
question of time. When he looked down along his leg,

he saw that his slacks had been ripped, his leg skinned. His sock was crusted with dry blood. It was hard to see more. Dan Brown had his hand on the suicide knob, swinging the car this way and that among the dark streets, then out onto Town Boulevard, headed toward a freeway on ramp. He kept checking the rearview mirror. As they approached the intersection that marked the on ramp, Dean saw the traffic light turn yellow. Dan downshifted, getting scratch as he swerved to miss the car slowing before him, sailing past it on the right, then turning hard, just as the light turned red, up and onto the on ramp. The turn was hard enough to throw the freezer against Dean and for a moment he found himself pinned to the wall by the enormous weight of the thing. Then they were on the ramp, gaining altitude fast, and the freezer was sliding away from him, banging over the metal floor, headed for the rear of the truck. Dean heard the blond man grunt. He waited for the sound the freezer would make as it crashed against the rear door.

The sound never came, as least not with the ferocity which Dean had expected. What came in its place was nothing more than a dull thud, followed by a rush of cold air, an explosion of light, as the door, apparently never satisfactorily latched, swung back on its hinges. The event was accompanied by the din of screeching brakes as the cars behind took measures to avoid the freezer suddenly bouncing toward them.

At some point in its descent, the freezer's lid sprang open. Shards of ice flew like sparks before the headlights of an approaching car. Tires skidded. There came at last the inevitable dull crunch of metal finding metal, of breaking glass. It was impossible, from Dean's angle, to see exactly who hit whom, or how many cars were involved. What he did see, however, and he saw this quite clearly, was the body of Buddy

Brown. Somehow it had been thrown clear of the freezer and for one magical moment appeared simply to hang there, amid the glare of lights, the shards of flying ice and glass, as if poised for flight. The spectacle was unlike any Dean had yet seen and his first impulse was to dismiss it as some kind of elaborate fakery, a Caesar's Palace variation on the Day of Reckoning. His second impulse was toward the numinous. It was Buddy Brown he had seen, cleansed in the blood of the lamb, naked and in snowy splendor, reaching out for a seat at the right hand of his Lord. Unhappily it was not to be, for Dean was witness as well to his fall, and it was, he thought, a moment of profound sadness. The man had taken his best shot and he had been denied. The darkness would have him.

They went on of course. Dan Brown hit the brakes once, hard enough to close the rear door, and then they were gone, one more car among many, the lights of the San Bernardino freeway strung before them, a delicate silvery web spiraling into the dark folds of the old Phillips ranch where Earl Dean's great-grandfather had, on a day more promising than the present, once gone to secure his water rights for the freshly plowed ten acres he intended to turn to navel oranges. The interior of the van was as dark, and as silent, as the tomb. "As I live and breathe," Dan Brown said at last, his voice barely above a whisper. "As I live and breathe." He said it one more time. "Magic. You are dead meat."

SEVEN

Doubtless a little search would bring to light old fences or buildings anywhere in the Valley, or stones upon the mountains, still bearing the inscription, "We Sell the Earth." No one who lived within forty miles of Pomona in the late eighties . . . will forget R. S. Basett and his cheerful, indefatigable, hustling ways, as he burst into town and began to sell pianos and other musical instruments, sewing machines and everything else, but especially real estate.

—F. P. Brackett

Dan Brown exited the freeway at White Avenue. They were headed in a southerly direction when Ardath began to bang his head against the side of the van. Dan Brown ignored him for half a mile before adjusting his rearview mirror the better to see him with and saying, "What the fuck." Ardath responded by banging his head once more against the metal wall. Dean looked at him for the first time since climbing over his legs. The man was cradling an arm, rhythmically bouncing his head off the interior wall. "It's my fucking arm," Ardath said at last. "Fucking Buddy got me on his way out. I think the bastard is broken."

Dan Brown pulled off the street and into the lot of a Union 76 station. He parked near the restrooms and got out. He walked around to the rear of the truck and opened the door. Ardath got out slowly, still holding his arm.

"Jesus Christ." Dan Brown said. His voice sounded flat and far away in the empty lot. Dean stared into the metal wall before him. He heard Ardath scream and turned to see Dan Brown inspecting his arm. "Chuck," Dan said. "Come here and check this shit out, man."

The bearded man groaned and shook his head. He got out of the truck and walked around to the back. Dan Brown was laughing. "He thinks it's broken," Dean heard Dan Brown say. "The motherfucking bone is sticking out of the motherfucking skin." Dean thought of looking himself, then thought better of it. Then he thought of something else. He was, for the second time in less than an hour, alone in the truck. This time the engine was still running. When he looked toward the dash the ruby eyes of the suicide knob winked at him in the station's pale fluorescent light. Dan Brown's keys dangled from the ignition. The engine idled smoothly. Dean's head throbbed in time with the engine. He looked toward the lot from the open door. Ardath had begun to pace, still clutching his arm. He was moving away from the van, toward a lone phone booth. The other two men moved with him, their backs to the van. It was a motherfucking invitation is what it was and Earl Dean knew an invitation when he saw one. Many came, he thought, few were chosen. He moved between the bucket seats and eased himself behind the wheel. He eased the truck into gear. And he dumped the clutch.

He was watching them in the rearview mirror. They never even looked until he hit the brakes at the driveway, slamming that rear door the way Dan had done it on the freeway. And then they had all looked at once. Faces twisted in the moonlight, framed by the night, like something out of Goya, faces in *The Deaf Man's House*. And then Dean was gone. He blew the traffic light at Kingsley and Gary and just kept going. He was three blocks away and headed toward the heart of Pomona before it occurred to him that he had just stolen Dan Brown's panel, that he had no clear idea of what, exactly, he should do with it, and that, after this, he really couldn't live here anymore. He could go to the cops. That might buy him a couple of days. But, as far as he knew, the man hadn't really done anything that was going to send him away for a long time. He'd failed to report the death of his brother. What was that good for? Dean hadn't a clue. His belief was that it would not be enough. Coupled with that uncertainty was the unsavory prospect of dealing with some constipated bureaucrat, of answering official questions. He would no doubt be called upon to fill out some kind of form. His life would be further entangled with the lives of the Browns. At which point he thought once more of the girl, the one with the knife. What of her if he went to the cops? What of her if he didn't?

At the intersection of Fifth and Gary, in front of the Golden Ox, he made the ridiculous observation that he was a thief for the second time in his life. It was of course an absurd thing to think of but there it was. Perhaps he was simply looking for some way around the more pressing questions of the moment. His head still rang from the biker's punches. He was giddy with adrenaline. There was an uncomfortable tightness about his chest, a faint pain in his left arm. Perhaps he was in some danger. He considered seeing a doctor. He ran a second stoplight, cut the corner at Park and Kingsley, putting two tires up over the curb and nearly running over a young black girl selling flowers from a plastic bucket. At the moment in which he narrowly avoided taking her life it seemed to him that their eyes met. Hers were wide with terror. She literally threw the bouquet in her hand toward the sky, deserting her bucket altogether. Dean hit the bucket. Plastic popped beneath his tires. Colored paper and yellow chrysanthemums flew before the night. And then she was gone, but there were more to come.

At every intersection there was someone selling something. There were white kids and black kids and Mexican kids. They had their flowers and their bagged oranges. One went far enough along Fifth and one found the hookers, with their leather miniskirts and spike heels. In the valley of the Quick Decline they were selling it on the street. "We sell the earth" was the phrase that came to mind. It was out of Brackett. Dean made an effort at calming his racing heart. He sought an angle of repose. He thought of the book. He'd discovered it in the special collections room of the Pomona Public Library. He would have checked it out but it was a reference book. There were additional complications. Fluorescent lights gave him headaches. In the end he had managed to lift the thing. It was not easily done. The book was a large, ungainly item. The cover was bright red. Among the book's many biographical sketches, two pages had been devoted to W. T. McCauly. "Pomona has been fortunate," the sketch began, "in the quality of citizens who have chosen this beautiful Valley as their homesite. . . . Among these may be mentioned William Tacompsy McCauly, so recently gone to his reward." Of the particulars of that passing F. P. Brackett had remained quite mute. He spoke instead of how William had come west to settle in the Pomona Valley, of how he had purchased a dozen acres of land on North San Antonio Avenue, which he had planted to navel oranges and prunes, later changing to navel and Valencia oranges. Still later he had acquired an additional ten acres and planted these to navels and Valencias as well. He had served as president of the California Produce Company, as a director of the Kingsley Water Company, as director and stockholder in the Fraternal Aid Association which erected the opera house at Pomona. It was,

Dean thought, an impressive list of accomplishments, though perhaps incomplete. Dean would have added that the man had also attended the burning of Chinatown, where he had contrived to have himself shot. That in lieu of seeking help he had elected to try for home and so made possible a private passing in some dark grove where in the very end he had managed to irrigate the property with his own bodily fluids.

Eventually, Mr. Brackett had commented upon the destruction of Chinatown. He did so beneath the heading THE CHINESE PROBLEM. Amazingly, Dean found that the death of his great-grandfather had been omitted. Apparently, in the mind of the author, there was no connection between the passing of the McCauly patriarch and the eventual handling of the Chinese Problem. In fact the amount of space given over to the handling of the Chinese Problem was even more scant than that given to William McCauly. Brackett began his account with the words "The town of Pomona was much excited over the presence in its midst of the heathen Chinese," and concluded the episode thus: "The unreasoning prejudice against Orientals as a class had its own way in Pomona. . . . Few seemed to have learned to discriminate between the Chinese merchant or laundryman or vegetable man who is always honest and reliable, on the one hand, and the Japanese speculator . . . who can not be trusted in private or legal matters. . . ." The book, Dean had discovered, was filled with such gems. In fact, he couldn't leave it alone. The thing was eight hundred and eighteen pages long. Dean read it the first time around in perhaps half a dozen sittings, and when he had he knew more of the history of the valley than anyone else at Emerson Junior High School. In the valley of the Quick Decline they were not big on local history. Most of it had been so effectively erased one might almost imagine that what was there had more or less grown by itself, materializing full-blown like some new and virulent disease. Dean knew better. He knew the name of the first constable. He knew about the willows and the stream at the eastern edge of the hills. He knew that the first orange trees were planted by moonlight. He knew about the squat fat Indians and the heathen Chinese. Of his great-grandfather, and the mystery which had haunted his family for three generations, he knew no more than when he started.

Dean thought once again, now, of that moment in time, that instant in which the old man had turned his horse, not toward the north, but toward the south, and galloped off through the gathering darkness. Was the man a hero or a fool? Was the act evidence of virtue or of vice? Or perhaps simple curiosity? No one had ever been able to say. Dean had read his eight hundred and eighteen pages and couldn't say either. Maybe the man had just fucked up. People did that. Dean drove now along the south side of town, bound for the homes of Clear Lake. Looking north, above the run-down bungalows of south Pomona, he found that he could just make out the tops of the palms which bordered Second Street. He found their fronds lit by the white floodlights which issued from that monolithic slag heap of concrete and blue tile someone with high hopes had plunked down on the two-block strip of land that had once supported the shacks of the Chinamen with their fronts of colored paper, their hieroglyphics of red and gold.

Dean hadn't bothered to tell Dan Brown, but he had done his research. He had read his Brackett. In Pomona's little Chinatown there were no women. The men were gardeners, launderers, vegetable peddlers, and probably just as hard up for pussy as the next man. For though Dean had said nothing of it at the time, Dan Brown was not the first to entertain such a notion.

Dean drove past the Montclair Cinema. He stopped at a light. A skinny black girl waved at him with what appeared to be her shoe. Trash scooted along the gutter, pushed by a dark wind as a white marquee showered the night with its harsh brilliance. Dean supposed upon reflection that informing Dan Brown of this detail would have given him little satisfaction. The man's mind would have leaped no doubt to other conclusions. . . . The Chinese laundryman, he have one son, you know, and such a sweet boy. . . . A lowered Chevy Impala cruised slowly by, taking away his view of the black girl. He supposed that if Brackett had not told him anything concrete concerning his grandfather, the book's voice had fascinated him nonetheless. For it seemed to him that what was most mysterious about the past was not to be found in the details of what had gone down, but rather in the dark terrain of hearts long dead, in thoughts and feelings destined to remain forever beyond memory's grasp. And it seemed to him that one caught glimpses of just such items, in this bulging history, between the lines of course, in the rhythms of a voice so clearly of another age, with its overweight Indians, its lecherous Japanese, its facile optimism through which one might so easily see the grinning skull of the future.

Dean turned off Fifth Street, which was a major boulevard, and drove south on Romona. He rolled down a window. It was the first time he had thought to do so. The night air whipped through the fetid bowels of the panel, cooling him with her fan. He drove toward Clear Lake, toward the Homes of Tomorrow. "Nature," F. P. Brackett had once written, "has ordained that the way of the future, like that of the past, shall lie in agriculture. . . . She invites especially those who would learn to receive her more immediate gifts of fruits and field. . . ." He passed the last Mexican with a bag of oranges. He passed the last black boy with tulips. He passed the last hooker with her golden smile, her leather purse. He passed the last dealer basking in the last halo of the last street lamp. "Some who are not invited," Brackett had warned, "will continue to come . . . the grafters who find it easier here than elsewhere to live the life of a leech upon mankind, the foreigners who will not become assimilated as loyal Americans, the hobos and the criminals of worse ilk. . . ." Well, what could one say? The future had clearly gotten out of hand. Nature had thrown a spitball. The sad part was that the cheerful and indefatigable Mr. Basett was no longer among the living, what with his lovable, hustling ways. If selling the earth was what had given him a hard-on, Dean could have taken him on the grand tour. The man could have ridden shotgun in Dan Brown's panel truck. He could have seen what the selling of the earth was all about. He could have scored himself some crystal meth, nailed himself some black pussy. Dan Brown's daughter could have given him the high enema with a Cyclone Air Purifier and he could have died with a smile on his face, the hose still up his ass, the scent of mountain pine ventilating his large intestine. They could have put him on ice and buried him on the last acre of citrus in the Pomona Valley.

When Dean reached the entrance to Dan Brown's cul-de-sac, he stopped. He pulled up in the shadow of an old pepper tree and sat looking down the dark street. He consulted his watch. It was eleven thirty-five. Two and a half hours had passed since he'd last seen the house. It had been four hours since his arrival. It felt like a lifetime. He didn't want to think about having stolen the car. He wanted to put it back in the carport, get the Falcon, and get out, preferably a long way out. In the time it had taken him to get from Fifth to Clear Lake he had begun to wonder if

Carl was still good for the money he had offered. He had begun to think about something he had not thought of in a long time. There was a train that ran from Pomona to New Orleans. Or at least there had been, twenty years ago. Twenty years ago he and his friends had spent considerable time in that part of town. They'd shoot a little snooker at Kessner's, then cross the tracks to sit at the counter at the depot, talk about riding that train to New Orleans for Mardi Gras. He'd liked that part of town then; the depot sat next to the Greyhound bus station, across the street from Continental Trailways. It was a fine place for an eighteen-year-old high on Jack Kerouac. Infinitely more interesting than those freshly scrubbed tract houses every one of his friends called home. A man could soil himself in some fundamentally important way downtown. He could sit out on those hard wooden benches where the lights of the station lit the rails, drink beer with one or two like-minded companions, all extolling the song of some highway not one of them had done more than dream about.

There had been a time when he had thought to make the trip with a certain red-haired girl. It hadn't happened, of course. One more road not taken. In the end she had gone alone, not to New Orleans but to points farther north and finally to points on a compass all her own. She may as well have ridden to Chinatown and had herself shot. And there were times when he wondered if she was even the person it had long pleased him to believe in. Perhaps he had only invented her, built her out of spare parts in some secret workshop of the heart, but that was a chilling thought and not, at the moment, in his best interests to pursue. . . . Gotta do something for me, Doc, been pursuing bad trains of thought, give myself a case of the heebie-jeebies. . . . It was of course a pathetic little picture. Armed with it, he put the truck in gear and exited the shadows.

Dan Brown's house looked now much as it had when Dean first arrived on the scene. There appeared to be a light on in a back bedroom. Other than that, the house was dark. The carport was empty. The bikes still sat on the ragged lawn. Ardath's tools lay scattered where he had left them when Dan Brown had kicked him in the foot to get him out from under his bike.

Dean turned off his lights. He killed the engine, allowing the heavy panel to roll silently up into the drive, beneath the roof of the carport. He had in mind jumping out quickly and running across the street to the Falcon. It worked as planned. He moved quickly but carefully, his shoes making almost no sound on the street. He withdrew his keys, slipped one into the handle of the Falcon's door, and turned. The door opened. He slid behind the wheel, pumped the gas pedal twice as he was sliding his key into the ignition, and then gave it the appropriate turn. There was no response. Dean stared into the moonlight that lay upon a cold metal hood. He tried the key again. The moon continued to float above him, high and white, apparently unconcerned that Dean should find his destiny modeled in such steaming cow fop.

He was about to try the key for a third time when he felt something scrape his leg, touching the skin through one of the tears in his slacks, and looked down to see a number of loose wires, which had been ripped from the back of his ignition switch. He had bent to examine them when something tapped at the glass near his head. He dropped the wires as if he had received a shock and looked toward the street, his heart hammering erratically, and found himself face to face with a pale apparition in a purple top.

Dan Brown's daughter was peering at him through the glass, her face framed by the night, the dark bandanna still wrapped about her head. Upon sitting up, he noticed that she had traded the black jeans for a pair of faded jeans that had been cut off just above the knee. The girl tapped at the glass once more with her knuckles. Dean rolled down the window.

"I tried to hot-wire it," she said. "I couldn't get the fucker to go."

Dean nodded, as if this were quite right and proper.

"Some bastard stole my Cyclone," she added. "And I want it back."

Dean continued to sit behind the wheel. For some reason he was finding it difficult to focus.

The girl stared at him. "I said, some fuckhead stole my Cyclone. He took yours too."

Dean turned to look into the rear of the Falcon. The girl was right. The car was empty.

"This guy," Dean asked. "What did he look like?"

"Fucking Mexican. Harelip, bad ears. Asshole had something wrong with his voice." The girl was silent for a moment. "I was gonna kick the fucker in the balls—"

"But he pushed you down. You hit your chin."

The girl just looked at him.

"I was at the bar, remember."

The girl nodded. She gave Dean a long look, as if it had suddenly occurred to her that something was wrong with this picture.

"What happened?" she asked rather abruptly. "You didn't try to run away again?"

"I did run away."

The girl turned toward the panel in the carport, appearing to notice for the first time that Johnny Magic had come home alone. "Well, how . . ." she began and then let her voice trail away. When she looked back at Dean her lips were slightly parted. Her breath seemed to hang on the air. It seemed to Dean that he was aware of something else as well, the rapid beating of her heart perhaps, as it labored in the darkness beneath her small breast. In fact, and to his great surprise, he found that all at once he could imagine it quite vividly, beneath his hand, the warm skin, the delicate ribs, the hurried pulse of a small animal. "Are you trying to tell me you ripped off the fucking truck?" the girl asked him.

Dean nodded.

"Buddy . . ."

"Fell out the back on the freeway."

The girl's laughter rang in the street. "Man, you fucked up," she said. Her words, however, were without scorn.

"Yeah. Now I'd like to get out of here before they come back." He didn't know why he felt he could confide in this girl. But for some reason he did.

The girl smiled. "That's cool," she said. "But guess what?"

Dean waited.

"I've got your fucking distributor cap."

Dean and the girl looked at each other. Her eyes were small and black, like her father's.

"Your car was pissin' me off," she said.

Dean waited one more time. He was sure she would have an answer.

The girl looked into the street, as if considering something. "Listen," she said. "I'll make you a deal. You promise to score me another Cyclone, I'll give you back your stupid cap."

Dean considered her offer. It seemed to him one more in a growing list, exactly the kind he had been entertaining since his return to the valley of promise. He could hear in it the echoes of Dan Brown, of Carl and Alice. He turned a palm to the moonlight. "Let's be fast about it," he told her.

*   *   *

While the girl retrieved the cap, Dean busied himself with the wiring. Fortunately, in a vehicle as simple-minded as the Falcon, it was a process he knew something about. There were really only three wires to address. He twisted two of these together and waited for the girl. He could see her outside. She had the hood up and she was leaning over a fender. He could see her hips pressed against the metal, her small, rounded ass turned toward the street.

When she had finished with the cap she slammed the hood and got in. Dean touched the wire running from his solenoid to the two he'd already braided. The car jumped to life. The girl sat up on the edge of her seat. "Hey," she said. "You were supposed to wait. I wanted to see how you did that." "I'll show you later," Dean told her.

"Yeah?" She seemed pleased. "I had a guy show me once. But it was on a different kind of car. With this thing . . . I was sort of afraid I was going to electrocute myself." The girl slapped the dashboard with the palm of her hand. It seemed difficult for her to sit long in one place. "Come on," she said suddenly. "Let's go."

Dean nodded. It had been his intention all along. She was clearly her father's girl, he thought, and was again surprised that he had not noticed it at once. She had the blood, and most likely the nerve to go with it. He supposed she could no doubt be quite ferocious if cornered. She was single-minded and determined and, perhaps, if she was a little bit lucky, not unduly bright. But then these were all fine qualities, he thought. They would serve her well in the coming darkness.

"This car is really a piece of shit," the girl said. She had remained on the edge of the seat, fiddling with the radio. "Sometimes it works," Dean told her. "You just never know." The girl gave the knob a final twist, then heaved herself back into the seat. Having given up on the radio, she seemed to fold in upon herself, as if nothing else in the car was of interest. She wrapped her arms tightly against her chest and turned her face toward the darkness beyond the glass. Dean found himself examining once more the scar on her shoulder. The markings, he thought, seemed to have taken on a faint glow in the light of the dashboard.

They were by now on Central Boulevard, headed for Dean's office. It was crazy of course. Swollen nose and all, he certainly could have stopped somewhere, anywhere really, and shoved this scarred runt from the car—the course no doubt of prudent behavior. And yet there were a couple of things that argued against this. It would not do to try it too close to home, on the streets of Clear Lake, where there was a very real possibility that Dan Brown would show up at any time. The girl would no doubt put up some sort of fight. It might well be an ugly little scene and not something one would want her father stumbling upon. Conversely, to dump her too far from home, on the streets of Pomona at midnight, would not do either. He had no desire to throw her to the sharks. The fact of the matter was, he liked her in a way. It was a pathetic sort of admission, but there it was. Maybe he would even score her a Cyclone. Maybe he would keep his word. She'd kept hers. He had his distributor cap.

At the very least, he could leave her at the office, if there was anyone there. At this time of night it was impossible to say; just depended on how the boys in the field had done. It was possible Betty would still be there. Perhaps his Cyclones would be there too. He had a fairly good idea of who had come after them.

In point of fact, the Mexican was really a pretty

clever idea on the part of Bill. The Mexican was part of Dean's graduating class, a former professional boxer who'd once done time as a sparring partner for Mando Ramos. It was the high point of a career that had left him with bad ears and a funny voice, left him the father of six kids and looking to sell Cyclone Air Purifiers as his third job. As far as Dean knew, the new career was not flourishing. The office was already into him to the tune of nearly two hundred dollars for the dollhouses given free to the customers but paid for by the salesmen. Dean wondered what kind of incentive Bill had offered to get the guy over to Dan Brown's place in the middle of the night. He was certainly the only guy in the office who might actually stand a chance taking something away from Dan Brown, though in a way Dean was glad the Mexican had called when the man of the house was out. It would not have been a pretty scene. Dean liked the man and felt a sudden pang of guilt that he could not recall his name. It then occurred to him, and it came as something of a shock, that in point of fact, he could not remember the name of one man in his graduating class, and there were only four, besides himself and the Mexican. It was absolutely true. He could not remember one name. The thought frightened him and he sought to make conversation with the girl.

"Did you know," he asked her, "that road over there was named after Patrick Tonner? He was the first schoolteacher in the Valley."

The girl did not bother to look. "I used to mug teachers," she said.

"This guy might have given you a fight," Dean said. "He was a big Irishman. He'd been trained as a Jesuit in the East. He wound up in Los Angeles, then lost his job for kicking some student's ass. He came to Pomona. When he wasn't teaching he was generally in a bar somewhere, reciting poetry and drinking himself into a stupor. Some mornings the kids used to have to go downtown to find him. They'd find him out in the street somewhere, put him in a wheelbarrow, and wheel him back to class."

"Shit. I would've left him there."

Dean looked at the girl's scar.

"What's with the scar?" he asked her. He found that he was still afraid.

The girl examined her own shoulder. "A friend of mine did it for me." They rode for a moment in silence, the girl continuing to study the strange markings. "It was sort of crazy. Danny didn't want us doing it at the house. Then we were going to do it at my friend's house. We had the razors and the alcohol. We were all set, then my friend's mother checks us out and she freaks. We wound up down there in the wash by Ganesha Park about two o'clock in the morning."

"I'm curious," Dean said. "Why didn't Danny want you doing it at the house?" In fact, he found this nothing short of astonishing.

"Who knows?" the girl said. She looked out a window. They rode again in silence. Dean thought about Dan Brown not wanting his daughter to have a scar tattoo. He thought about the daughter getting one anyway. She always, he noted, spoke of her father by his first name. He considered asking her about this. He asked her instead about the scar. He asked her what it meant. She turned to look at him.

"You mean is it a symbol, or something?"

Dean nodded.

"I don't know," she said. She said it as if the idea of not knowing amused her in some way. "What I think," she said, "I think someday I'll travel to another country, like India or someplace, and someone will be there who will know what it means. Only, like . . ." the girl paused. It seemed clear that she had given the matter some thought. "I won't know . . . if it's good or bad. It will either make me a queen or get me killed." The girl laughed.

Dean laughed as well. It seemed to him that this exchange had suddenly and for no good reason that he could think of lifted his spirits.

"You know something," he said. "I don't even know your name."

"Diana," the girl said. "What was that stuff Danny was reading in your wallet, Earl J. Dean, or something?"

Dean glanced at Diana Brown. He was surprised that she had remembered. Perhaps he had misjudged her. "That's my name," he said. "Earl Dean."

Diana laughed once more. She repeated his name softly, staring from a window. "I can see why you went with Johnny Magic," she said.

Dean pulled off the expressway and onto Gary Avenue. The fear that had washed over him seemed to have passed and they drove the rest of the way to the office in silence. The place was obviously shut down for the night. The windows were dark, the door locked. The parking lot was empty save for a couple of lowered minitrucks around which several young black guys stood listening to a ghetto blaster. Dean and the girl sat in the car, the strains of rap music drifting to them across the ragged black asphalt.

Perhaps, Dean thought, if he could find a phone book, he could remember the Mexican's name. There was a booth at one end of the lot, near a now defunct gas station, and Dean went for it. He drove, not wanting to pass the minitrucks alone, on foot. The booth, however, had been gutted. There was still a phone there. Everything else had been ripped out. The Plexiglas sides had been cracked and covered with graffiti.

Dean stood at the side of the pillaged booth. He was

aware of Diana Brown watching him from the front seat of the Falcon. He'd pulled the car right up to the side of the booth. He was aware of the black kids by the trucks. They were watching him now too, about five of them altogether. To linger, Dean thought, on this barren ground, would not be the wisest move. He looked toward the street. He was somewhat anxious to recover the Cyclones and dollhouses. He'd signed for the Cyclones and paid ten bucks apiece for the dollhouses. He would like to be sure it was the Mexican from his office who had taken them. It would be nice, he thought, to be sure about something. As he continued to stare into the street a third minitruck pulled into the lot and joined the other two and it was time, he thought, to be going.

They tried two more shopping centers and a liquor store. In each case it was the same. The booths had all been boned and gutted. Apparently it was the new thing. Cockfighting and horseracing had been replaced by booth bashing, amongst other things. The activity no doubt had its pleasures. And so, with the hour growing late, and the girl growing impatient, Dean made a left on San Bernardino Boulevard and headed for San Antonio. The search for a phone had led them to within a mile of the place and he saw no reason not to go. Johnny Carson would be on the tube and Alice and Carl would be watching. At least they would be up. They would be in possession of a phone book. Besides that, Dean owned the joint, just like William Tacompsy McCauly had owned it before him.

EIGHT

This setting in which the Burdicks found themselves would not be complete without some reference to the Indians, by this time no longer a serious menace to civilized people.... There were however, sometimes bad Indians among them, maltidos, as Ramon Vejar calls them.... Once, when the Alvarados were sleeping, a Coahuilla Indian who had been working for them attacked them with an ax.... Manuel Alvarado and others hunted till they found him, and hanged him from the limb of a Sycamore. While they were stringing him up, a certain Juan Garcia tried to persuade him to repent and pray for forgiveness, but he picked up a rock and smote his solicitous intercessor a savage blow on the side of the head. Yes, he was a maltido.

—F. P. Brackett

One smoggy September afternoon in about 1975, a trio of youths—the oldest was sixteen—made their way along the rutted drive that led from San Antonio Boulevard to the house of William Tacompsy McCauly. There were no fences then. The boys simply turned off the sidewalk on their way home from Emerson Junior High School and walked along the narrow dirt drive, past the roses and ragged trees, up the steps, and into the house. They were seeing themselves back out when Dean's grandmother noticed she had company. She also noticed the youths had elected to take her color television set with them.

In the ensuing struggle—for Milly had chosen to engage the young men with her cane—the old woman sustained a badly broken hip and a serious concussion. As might be said for what went down upon the death of the patriarch himself, it was all downhill from there.

The hip healed poorly. Unable to tend her gardens, Melissa McCauly sat behind the dust-filled screens on the wide porch where she and her sister had, as young girls, posed for pictures in their summer dresses, and she watched her flowers go the way of the grove that ringed them. She saw them turn brittle and gray. She watched as their naked limbs reached among the weeds to scratch upon a smog-choked sky—a crippled dog scratching at the door—begging entrance to another time.

By the time Dean drove home to claim his inheritance the old house had taken on all the charm of a fort. Seven-foot chain-link fences surrounded the entire property. No trespassing signs sprouted like mutant growth among the dead trees and thorny weeds. Where windows or screens had been broken or lost, plywood had taken their place. Wrought-iron bars covered all the first-floor windows. The sight had taken his breath away and he had sat for some time in the sun-baked street, behind the wheel of the Falcon, as the last strains of The Prisoner's Song played out on the tape deck in the seat next to him and he'd watched the sunlight glinting off the metal sides of Carl's Winnebago, its brightly painted metal nearly touching the faded paint of the house, and the sight had broken his heart.

In fact, each time he looked at the place it hurt. The old man's groves. His grandmother's gardens. His story. A narrative of rotting wood and peeling paint. A legacy of decay.

"Where the fuck are we?" Diana asked. They were parked in front of the house.

"Home," Dean told her.

The girl looked toward the drive. "You live here?"

"Not exactly," Dean said. "But it's mine." He got

out of the car and unlocked the chain-link gate. When he had pulled the car off the street he got out again and locked the gate behind him. This time when he got out the girl followed him. She stood at his back, in the darkness, as he fooled with the lock.

"You know something," she said. "Someone could think you were weird, bringing me out here. This is a weird-looking place."

Dean nodded. What the girl said was true; someone probably could. When he started down the drive, however, she was right behind him, and he supposed that weirdness, given her upbringing, was not something of which she was particularly frightened.

They went in single file. Carl's Winnebago made this necessary. The foolish thing filled the entire drive and getting past it meant negotiating a gauntlet of brittle tree limbs and waist-high weeds. Dean could hear Dan Brown's daughter cursing behind him. As they approached the porch, it became clear to him his parents were indeed still awake. There were lights on the first floor. There were also voices, harsh and brittle as dead branches issuing from the fetid shadows, and raised, one would assume, in anger.

"They're fighting," he told the girl.

She said, "Oh, boy," in a bored sort of way that seemed, to Dean, about right. For Dean the sounds served only to stir unwelcome memories, to bring back the hateful years. Their return was as the return of some loathsome disease—one of those viruses splice themselves right into the DNA, always come back when least wanted, just to kick a man when he was down. He reminded himself it was a virus that had taken the trees. At which point it occurred to him in a sudden flash of illumination that Professor Brackett had been right after all. Nature had ordained the way of the future. She had given them the Quick Decline, the AIDS of the citrus industry, sent down from above, on the wings of the aphid.

Dean's mother was in the kitchen. Carl was on the porch, getting a beer from the refrigerator. When Dean's mother saw Dean in the hallway, a young woman in tow, she said, "I don't know, Earl. I do what I can." Just as if she had fully expected to find her only son standing there in front of her, his nose swollen, a dark-eyed stranger at his side. Carl registered more surprise. "What the hell is he doing here?" he asked.

"It's his house," Dean's mother said. Her tone, Dean thought, was openly defiant. "Or had you forgotten?"

Dean's mother was dressed in a faded terry-cloth bathrobe. She had red house slippers on her feet. Her dark hair lay in a pile of unruly curls about her face. Her legs, protruding from the bottom of the bathrobe, looked white and frail. Dean suddenly found himself trying to remember exactly how old she was, or if she was well. He didn't know. He didn't know if his mother was well or not. He could not recall the name of a single man in his graduating class. What was wrong with him? It was life, he thought. It was withering before his eyes, leaking through some breach. He found himself set upon by such an overwhelming feeling of depression, he thought for a moment he might cave in beneath it, broken, like the spine of the old barn hunkering in the moonlight.

"Don't start," Carl said, then moved a step forward, for a better look at Dean. "For Christ's sake," he said, addressing himself momentarily to Dean. "You been in a fight, or what?"

Carl was dressed for bed in a sleeveless white undershirt and striped pajama bottoms. It was the way he had been dressing for bed for as long as Dean had known him. His ankles, which stuck out from the bottom of his pajamas, looked about as big around as Dean's mother's, and just as white. He wore a pair of the same red slippers as well. Dean's depression included something akin to shame. These were his people. And here they were, the remains of the McCauly clan, standing in the ruins of the old man's house, up late and pissed off, half in the bag, haunted by old wounds and canceled promises, and it might as well have been yesterday. The scenes of Dean's youth seemed to flutter about the room like stricken bats.

Dean looked from Carl to his mother. He could see that she had been crying. He looked out a darkened window, into the dead groves. "Jesus," he said.

"What?" Carl asked him. "What was that?" He turned to Dean's mother. "What did he say?"

"Listen," Dean said. "You made me an offer once, on the house. Do you remember it?"

Carl just stood there, a tall can of Old English 800 sweating in his hand. Dean was forced to repeat the question. Carl turned to Dean's mother. "Can you believe this?" he asked her. "What did I tell you?" He took the beer and went to the kitchen table.

Dean's mother crossed the floor and seated herself at the table as well. "He doesn't have it," she said. She seemed to be saying this to Dean and he assumed she was talking about the money. Carl took a drink of beer. "You shoulda taken it when you could," he said. "Shit, I don't see why I should pay you anything. I'm gonna wind up with it anyway."

Dean's mother shook her head. "Yeah, if you can make the payments—"

"I'll make the payments." Carl cut her off in such a way as to suggest he might not make the payments after all.

"If you hadn't gone out and bought that stupid house car . . ." Dean's mother began, then fell silent once more, as Carl slammed his can down on the table and stood up. It was all Dean could do to keep from breaking into some stupid laugh. Carl extends himself on a new Winnebago. A bank forecloses on what was left of the old man's empire. "You know," Alice Dean was saying, "if we could all just work together on this thing . . ."

Dean looked closely at his mother. It was the second time since he walked in the door that she had voiced some show of support for him.

Carl took a drink of malt liquor, then made a kind of shrugging motion, as if to say this was, after all, a possibility. Dean could not quite believe it. Carl, Alice, and Dean, partners on the old man's land. The concept boggled the mind.

One could see, however, that Carl was not a happy man. He continued to work on his malt liquor in silence, his eyes fixed upon the floor.

"There was some man here," Dean's mother said at last. "He had some of those things you've been selling."

"A Mexican, with bad ears?"

Dean's mother nodded.

Dean could not at once figure out how anyone at the office had gotten this address. Then he remembered that the night he applied for the job, he still didn't have a phone. He must have given them this address along with the number.

"What did you tell him?"

Alice looked at Carl. "We told him he could put them in the barn," she said. Carl said nothing. Alice Dean smiled at her son. "He says you're quite a salesman," she added. "Says you've sold more of these units than anyone else in the office. Says if you keep going you get this free trip to Hawaii."

This time Dean did laugh out loud. He couldn't quite help himself. The Cyclones had not been stolen.

Not only had they not been stolen, they had thought highly enough of him at the office to make sure he got them back. In fact, he suddenly saw Bill's strategy in a new light. The man must have figured Dean had walked into something down in Clear Lake. And yet he probably felt that he could not be sure, that calling the cops might be a little drastic. He had opted instead for the Mexican. It was really not a bad move. Upon hearing that the Cyclones had been recovered, he had then seen to it that they were returned. Dean thought once more of the Mexican with the bad ears, taking the time to stop here on his way back to his house and his six kids and his wife and his two other jobs, and it occurred to him that the man had done him quite a favor, unknowingly perhaps, but a favor nonetheless, a favor over and above that for which he had been paid. He had put the fear of God into Carl and Alice. Or rather the fear of the almighty dollar, which was probably even better. Carl had fucked up in some way. They might not be able to hold the land after all and now their only son had mutated into some sort of super salesman of the month, kind of high roller might just stop long enough between trips to Hawaii to have his aging parents thrown into the street. It was clearly too much for Carl. The man stood and, without looking at Dean, walked from the room.

Dean went to the refrigerator and helped himself to a can of Old English 800. The malt liquor was deplorable stuff but under the circumstances a drink seemed called for. As he opened the door of the refrigerator he suddenly remembered Diana Brown. She had been standing still for all of this in the hallway that led from the back door to the kitchen. "You want something to drink?" Dean asked her. She nodded at the can in Dean's hand and laughed. "That stuff? Give me a break."

Dean laughed as well. He was suddenly feeling rather festive, in spite of his nose.

Alice looked at the girl. "Who's your friend?" she asked.

But the girl was already outside. Dean followed her out to the porch. It was dark and cool there. The night smelled faintly of rotting wood. The moon lent a silver light to the dark silhouette of the old barn as Dean stood before the remains of his inheritance, on the wooden porch where his great-grandfather had stood before him, in the gathering dusk of a distant evening. It would have looked quite different then, of course. The evening Dean had in mind would have been in the spring. The groves would have been young and in bloom. The mountains would have begun to color in the last light. Perhaps the man had stood just where Dean stood now, at the very edge of the step, supporting himself on the rail. Perhaps he had watched his eldest daughter at play in the yard. Perhaps he had called her and caught her to him and held her for a moment, taken suddenly by some vague premonition that all was not exactly as it seemed, that something was wrong with the day. Perhaps he had sensed a shadow in the wind, a passing darkness, a sudden chill. Perhaps he had sensed nothing at all. Dean had, after all, the benefit of hindsight, the psychic powers to be found in a tall can of Old English 800. On either side of him were the remains of Milly's roses, reduced now to a tangle of vines and weeds. His grandmother had once tended them for hours on end, in her bright yellow gloves, in the rubber boots she favored for tramping about her acre of citrus. Dean treated himself to a healthy sampling of the malt liquor, then set himself to looking for the girl.

He was about to conclude he had lost her when some small sound drew his attention and he caught sight of her tank top, shimmering in the shadows of the fumigation equipment the old man had left at the side of the barn. The stuff hadn't been moved in close to a hundred years. It was magical stuff really, all rusted gears and gauges and rotting pipes. It had served him well as a boy. He'd orchestrated great battles from the decks of those wagons, littered the barnyard with the bodies of the dead. Dean left the porch and crossed the dirt.

The girl was on the wagon now, inspecting the piece of machinery that occupied most of the space in the wagon's bed.

"What's this?" the girl wanted to know.

Dean looked into the tangle of machinery.

"Fumigation equipment," he told her. It was all he knew. There was an engine with a wheel attached to it, a coil of hoses, a pair of wooden handles. "I used to play with this stuff when I was a kid," he said. The girl banged the side of the engine with the metal bar. He had played with it. Later he'd learned the stuff had been used to pipe cyanide gas to tented trees. In an age of greater ecological awareness, he supposed that even playing with the stuff had increased his risks of cancer or at least some form of chemically induced psychosis. Now the girl was swinging a metal bar around in the moonlight and he wondered briefly if some poisonous residue might not linger still, in the bowels of the old equipment—potent enough to kill the scale, but powerless against the Quick Decline, which had devastated the industry, effectively closing the door on the days of orange blossom and sage, on the civilization that had grown up around it.

The old man had missed the Quick Decline. He had weathered killing frosts and desert winds, the machinations of greedy packers, the loss of a limb, only to achieve his own quick decline on the streets of Chinatown, two decades before the arrival of the virus.

The virus, like one more exotic dance, was first noticed in Argentina, later in Brazil, where it was given the name Tristeza, a Portuguese word meaning sadness or melancholy. In California they called it the Quick Decline. By the 1940s it had spread to trees within the Pomona Valley, placing them on a quarantine list. The disease, it seems, had the mind of a boxer. Kill the body, the head follows. The virus attacked the root systems of the trees, robbing them of starch. The branches followed suit and the trees died, at least visibly, from the top down. Entire groves were lost within months, growers powerless to stop it, or even, in the beginning, to identify what was killing them, so that, in some ways, the urban development spreading east from Los Angeles came as a kind of blessing. Declining groves, suddenly of little value, could be sold to developers. The march of the tract homes had begun. They did them up in pale pastels, covered them with tarpaper roofs and colored rocks. They lined the streets with tiny Chinese elm, one in front of each house, and soon enough tiny white blossoms lay like snow on the freshly fertilized patches of grass, the freshly poured asphalt, borne upon the same westerly breezes already pushing an unsightly brown haze into the skies above the valley.

The haze thickened with each passing year. And then there was the coming of the San Bernardino freeway, the end of the Korean War, the loss of jobs at the local defense plant. Suddenly many of the jerrybuilt tract homes were standing empty behind weedchoked yards and dying elms. Lenders had foreclosed. Buyers were needed. At which point there came the Watts riots, the Great Society housing programs. Black families intent upon escaping the ravages of south cen-

tral Los Angeles could suddenly move to a tract home
in Pomona for no money down. The white folk headed
north. It was, in retrospect, the last act in a veritable
shit storm of change begun just prior to the Second
World War. And it ended here. It was what Earl Dean
had driven five hundred miles to stand knee deep in
and it was nothing at all like that carpet of wildflowers
and sage that had blossomed before the eyes of the
Spanish explorers. Nor did it bear much resemblance
to what his great-grandfather had found at the end of
a transcontinental train trip, or to what he had left
behind. Within forty years of his death it was gone,
defoliated, smogged, ransacked. There were iron bars
on the windows of the Cinderella tract. It was breathtaking, really. It was the story of the state, possibly the
story of man. Even Dan Brown, cruising out there in
the night, seemed suddenly of a dying breed. He was
out for blood but at least it was personal. It was family.
Out there with him, sharing the streets, were the
gangbangers, the shooters, the rock-cocaine houses.
There were children with guns and there was violence
that seemed to exist only to beget violence.

Above Dean's head, the girl banged once more on
the side of the tank, or perhaps she had been banging
all along. For it seemed to him as if the dead groves
were fairly ringing—great clangorous gongs advancing
in waves, a delicate veil of cyanide crystals spreading
in their wake. Sunday in the park. He considered telling her to cut it out, she would wake the neighbors.
But then she seemed to be enjoying herself.

She also seemed to be irritating Carl. The man had
come to the back porch and was yelling something at
Diana Brown. It was difficult to hear what he was
saying. Diana was making too much noise. But Dean
could see his jaws working in the moonlight. His
candy-striped pajama bottoms shimmered before the
faded paint of the house. He gripped the rail with one

hand, a can of Old English 800 with the other. Perhaps the fool would call the cops. Dean would be forced to meet them at the gate, to contrive some explanation. He would wring his hands. He would affect an expression of concern. He would agree that the noise was of course most unfortunate, not to mention the possible threat to the environment. . . . It was just granddad again, however. . . . Seems the old beggar got his foolish ass caught in a tent, along with a contaminated tree. . . . 1926, or thereabouts. . . . Should have killed him of course. Funny thing though, left the body, destroyed the mind. . . . Yes, yes, a sad case. Not without its humorous aspects, however. Seems the old fart has been reading too much of the local news, gotten to believing the bug that killed his trees is still with us . . . mutated by now of course, no longer carried by the aphids. It's these black boys do the carrying now, the virus itself having mutated into some kind of illicit chemical substance known to promote random violence. So granddad figures, you fire up the old equipment, make a few changes here and there, pull it up to the back of one of these rock-cocaine houses, stick a hose through the wall, and gas the whole lot. Soon enough, who the fuck knows? Just maybe you get it all back. The tree-lined streets. Saturdays in the park. The scent of orange blossom wafting on air so clean you'd swear it just blew in off the Pacific . . . yes, yes, Pacific we had out there before they mucked it up with oil rigs and DDT, and so on and so forth. . . . Each man beneath his own vine and fig . . . his own brace of pussy . . . river of Old English 800 flowing gently across his grandmother's paisley shawl. . . . Earl Dean chugged what was left in his can, thought for a moment his stomach might reject the offering, gagged briefly on his own bile, then realized the girl and Carl were now in direct communication.

It was not a pretty sight. His stepfather had come off the porch in an effort no doubt to make himself heard. He had a beer in one hand. Dean's mother had him by an arm. She appeared to be warning him about something . . . his heart for Christ's sake . . . as, meanwhile, the content of the shouting match continued to deteriorate until finally the two, Carl and the girl, were simply yelling fuck you at each other. The girl of course had the advantage of being able to punctuate her fuck yous with a good rap on the tank, while Carl was only able to shake his beer can. At last, however, even as Dean watched, the girl seemed to tire of the fight, for she suddenly tossed the bar into the wagon at her feet and looked at Dean.

"So, dude," Diana Brown said. Her voice was by now slightly hoarse. "Where's the Cyclones?"

Dean allowed himself a moment or two of simply staring at this waif, up there in the moonlight, tiny breasts making little points of light in the sleeveless purple top. It occurred to him that the aging cyanide victim would of course need an assistant, nubile young thing no doubt. . . . Dean belched. The center of his face seemed to have been effectively numbed by Carl's malt liquor, as if in the end there was some point to the stuff after all. The Cyclones, Dean heard himself telling her, were in the barn. And suddenly she was scampering away from him once more, this time disappearing into the doorway of the old barn as it sat there before him, with its sagging doors, its broken back yawning in his face like some toothless old fuck of a future one would do best to avoid.

The barn's roof was filled with cracks. There were missing shingles. The moonlight came through in ragged dusty patches. The girl must have been equipped with some sort of homing device—electronic corner duster hidden up her ass—drawing her home. She went straight for the Cyclones and by the time Dean got to the barn's single light, a lone bulb suspended upon a wire strung between a pair of posts, she was already poking through the boxes. "You've even got more of these stupid dollhouses," she said. "What a rip."

The funny part was, he really couldn't decide to what extent she was consciously trying to rip him off and to what extent she really did believe herself entitled to a Cyclone Air Purifier because she had agreed to let someone come out and show her one. It was difficult in fact to know just how smart she was.

"You know something," Dean told her. "These aren't free. You know how much these cost?"

"Don't give me that shit. I let you come to the house."

"That was so I could show you the thing. Then you decide if you want to buy it or not. The dollhouse is what you get. That's the free gift."

"You mean you're not even going to give me one of these fuckers . . ."

Dean laughed. "Tell you the truth," he said, "I don't know if I am or not." In fact he thought that he would. The sight of Carl and Alice on the run had raised the tone of his mood a notch or two. This, combined with the onset of the Old English 800, even had him thinking about sticking around, as if his fear of Dan Brown's wrath had been deadened along with his nose. He just didn't want Diana Brown to think she was putting one over on him.

She was standing in front of him now, her hands on her hips. "Then what the fuck are we doing here?" she asked.

"You had my distributor cap . . ."

"You're a fucking liar," the girl said. Dean's first thought was that she meant to swing on him. She came a half-step forward, then swung abruptly and put one of her purple high-topped sneakers into the nearest dollhouse. SOS pads, rubber gloves, together with other assorted items one might use around the home spilled across the dirt. Dean laughed. He didn't seem to be able to help himself. The girl looked like some sort of bird. She probably did think he'd brought her out here to rape her or something. She was going to have to fuck him for a Cyclone. He would do terrible things to her with his attachments. . . .

Diana reached into her pocket. She came back out with some sort of knife, a silver scissorblade. With an expert flick of the wrist she produced the blade. "I know how to use this," she said. "Danny showed me."

Dean did not doubt her. Danny would. He walked across the dirt to an old wooden crate, then sat on it, facing the girl once more. "Jesus Christ," he asked her. "You think I'm that desperate?"

"Yes."

Dean dragged a hand through what was left of his hair. It was clear he would soon be in need of more Old English 800.

"It may interest you to know," he said, "that you can have one of those stupid Cyclones. For free. No strings attached. Now what do you say to that?"

Diana just looked at him.

"I'm serious," Dean said. "On the house, courtesy of the Cyclone Salesman of the Month."

"You're just scared of Danny."

Dean found that he did not like being reminded of Danny. This high he had stumbled into was a delicate thing, he knew, even as he rode it out. Beneath him yawed the abyss. "Of course I'm scared of Danny," he said. He was about to head for the refrigerator. "Guy's a fucking homicidal maniac. No offense." Dean smiled. Diana Brown, apparently satisfied as to her immediate safety, remained unmoved. The knife went back into her jeans. She turned to inspect her unit.

Dean watched her from his crate. She had now seen a Cyclone Air Purifier in action and it was clear she wasn't going anywhere with one of these until she had taken a head count of attachments. She was standing about three yards from Dean, bent at the waist, a position in which her small, hard ass pushed for all it was worth at the seams of her cutoffs. Her tank top was hiked up over her hips, exposing the flesh of her back, which was as smooth and white as the rest of her. Well, maybe fucking her for a Cyclone was not the worst of ideas. He would buy the ticket to New Orleans after all. She would come with him. He would discover that she was smarter than she seemed, a veritable diamond in the rough. There would be a flat in the French Quarter, room to paint, a modest income. Her love would lend a measure of grace to his declining years. He would wear a white suit and carry a cane. He would buy her clothes. . . . It was difficult, really, to say just how long Dean pursued this train of thought, shamelessly mesmerized by skin as pure and soft as the driven snow, before his awareness spread out to include something else, something besides that strip of bare white flesh, something that, like her skin, had till now been hidden by the loose bottom of the purple top. What he saw was a strip of foil. There was perhaps an inch of the stuff sticking out of a hip pocket. The interesting part, however, was that it was not just any kind of foil. It was of a particular violet shade. Perhaps, he thought, if she had not just pulled a knife on him, if he had not so recently heard, by her own admission, that there was this particular way of holding it. But then she had and he had and it was, after all, the second time that night he'd run across the shade.

*　　*　　*

Diana Brown called to him as he started for the door. She wanted to know where he was going. "I'm going to get you a cab," Dean told her. Diana said nothing. "Well, you don't think I'm going back there, do you? I'll get you a cab. I'll even pay for it. You can ride home in style." Dean forced a smile.

"Look," the girl said. "I'm sorry . . ."

Dean stared at her for a moment. Her words seemed so far out of character they struck him as being somewhat comical. He smiled once more.

"It's okay," he told her. "I might just be that desperate. Believe me."

The girl never batted an eye. Dean stared into the dark interior of the barn. He could see the stable from where he stood, the remains of ancient feed bags. He could see the very place he'd made love to Rayann for the first time. Her scent still lingered here, he thought suddenly, amid the cobwebs, the rotting wood. It mingled with the long-ago scent of his own spilt seed. He felt once more the backs of her thighs, streaked with sweat and the fine gray dust of the barn, pressing against his chest and shoulders. It was here that he'd seen that dark light in her eyes for the first time, and imagined that it was something to which he might lay claim. He had taken it for a storm down in the soul. It was the thing toward which he had pressed. In the end it had eluded him and he found his mind returning to the thought that had come to him earlier in the evening, at the entrance to Dan Brown's street, at the wheel of the stolen van, that he had, after all, not known her as he might. She had been taken from him after so little time. To remember her as he did was to invent her afresh each day. Everything, it seemed, required some leap of faith. There was really so little one could know.

*   *   *

Dean walked directly into the house and picked up a phone. He dialed four, one, one, and asked for the number of the Mid-Dump. When he dialed that number Debbie answered on the second ring. She said, "Yeah."

Dean told her it was Dean.

"Jesus Christ. You all right?"

"I'm all right. Listen, Debbie. I want you to tell me something. The girl Buddy was arguing with today. That wasn't just some chick from the band. That was Brown's kid, wasn't it?"

In the silence that followed Dean could hear the noises of the Mid-Dump, the rap of glass on wood, what sounded like the Destroyers on the jukebox.

"I'm sure I wouldn't know," Debbie said at last. "I wasn't there, remember."

Dean felt himself nodding, as if this was quite right and proper. He could see how it was going to be. He was also aware that his mother had entered the room. Or at least that she had come to the door, still sporting the blue bathrobe, one of Carl's malt liquors in her hand. She was propped against a doorjamb, backlit by the flickering light of a television in a dark room.

"Tell me this," Dean said. "The girl sells flowers, doesn't she? She's one of those kids I've been seeing all over town. She must have a spot up there somewhere—"

Debbie cut him off. "Dean. I want you to listen to me for a minute, okay? I don't know what you're getting yourself into, but if I was you, I'd stay out of it."

Dean allowed himself a moment of reflection. The plaintive strains of "Bad to the Bone" were coming to him out of the night, curtesy of Ma Bell.

"Debbie," Dean said. "I was in the bathroom. I saw the flowers. They had blood on them, and dirt. Someone went out there and picked them up, and threw them away, and covered them so no one else would

see them. The flowers had foil on them. Diana Brown's
got the same kind of foil on her." Dean paused. An
image had come to him, the girl in the unpleasant light
of her kitchen, one pink glove on her hand, as if the
gloves were something she could use, he had thought.
"She wanted the gloves," he said aloud. He was thinking of his grandmother, trimming her roses in her yellow gloves. He was thinking too of the glove he had
seen in the front seat of the girl's car, like the tongue of
an animal. She had come, he thought, to do something
about the flowers. "She has a knife," Dean said.

"Dean." Debbie said. "Did you hear what I just
said? This is Dan Brown's family you're talking about.
Jesus Christ. You know this guy. You know what he's
like. Are you crazy or what?"

Dean said nothing.

"I'll tell you something else," Debbie went on.
"You've been away, Dean. The man is worse than
ever. Fucker's dusted half the time. I saw him knife
some guy himself, right here at the fucking bar. The
guy is a killer. His friends are killers. These guys will
fuck you up for looking at them wrong. Now you want
to tell the guy his little girl killed his brother, be my
guest, just leave me the fuck out. I don't want any
part of it. We communicating here?"

Dean said that they were. Everyone else would of
course want to be left out as well. And who could
blame them? It was after all the course of prudent
behavior. Debbie was absolutely right. A pair of
images flashed before Dean's mind. One was of Dan
Brown, as Dean had seen him earlier that evening,
beneath the light of the ruined chandelier, above the
coffin of his brother. "Family," Dan Brown had said.

The second was that of Dan Brown swinging a burrito around in his truck and then blaming the mess on
Dean. Dan Brown didn't like one man's reality, he simply invented another. Friends were invited to partici-

pate. Messengers bearing bad news would be boned and gutted. Buddy Brown would be properly laid to rest and Dan Brown would have his pound of flesh. What occurred to Dean now, standing in the shabby confines of his inheritance, was that he was undoubtedly the last to know. Everyone else had known all along. Perhaps it was what lay behind Ardath's rude behavior, Chuck's silent, wistful gazes. Perhaps it accounted for the particular brand of electricity charging the stale air of the Mid-Dump. Everyone knew, and everyone was waiting, or casting about for some serviceable set of circumstances available for a substitute reality. And, in the course of the evening . . . lo, a vision had been made manifest, a story had begun to take shape. A girl had come to the bar, a blond-haired amazon with tattoos and dreadlocks. . . .

"And this girl with the band?" Dean was staring from a window now, in the direction of Pomona, toward a sky too dark to suggest a town. "I mean what's that all about? Everyone just decides to give her to Dan Brown."

"Hey," Debbie said, "I wouldn't know. Okay. I wasn't there."

"Convenient."

"Hey, Dean, back off, okay. For all I know, this girl could have stabbed him. She was there. There was an argument. There was a fight. The Stench says he saw this chick running along the side of the road—"

"But Diana Brown was there too, wasn't she? Dan Brown's kid was there. And you hid the flowers." This seemed obvious to him all at once. The girl had come to get rid of something that might be incriminating, but somebody had already done it for her.

Debbie had nothing to say. Dean listened to the noises of the bar.

"Listen," Debbie said at last. "Nobody saw what happened. The only guy who knows is Buddy Brown and he's not talking. You know what I mean? Whatever happens . . . it's out of my hands. It's out of your hands too. I mean what do you think you're going to do about any of this anyway? And what's this girl to you?"

It was Dean's opinion that somebody should at least tell the girl she had been given up for vengeance. It seemed to him that she should know at least that much. As for the rest of it, as for what she was to Earl Dean, or what she had managed to become for him in the course of the evening . . . The thing clearly did not explain well and Dean thought it better not to try.

"You don't think someone ought to at least tell this girl what's going down?"

"You think she doesn't know?"

"I wouldn't know. Do you?"

"Dean. The bitch is Diana's girlfriend. Now. Do you get the picture?"

Dean was working on the picture. All he could say for certain was that the New Orleans fantasy stood suddenly in need of revision.

"Dean?"

"Yeah."

"No one here is going to cop to seeing Dan Brown's kid. The Stench saw a blonde arguing with Buddy. Later he saw her running down the road. That's it. End of story. It's their problem, Dean. Let 'em work it out."

"Okay," Dean said at last. "Just tell me one more thing. The flier, what did it say?"

Debbie heaved a sigh of exasperation.

"Debbie . . ."

"I don't know what you're thinking of, Dean, but I'll tell you this, you manage to stop what's going down before D. B. gets his, I mean you call in the pigs or some such shit . . . they ain't gonna hold him long. Shit, you know that. The fucker hasn't done anything yet. He gets out, he's gonna be crazier than ever. He's also gonna wanna know who messed up his plans. And I live here, you know what I mean?" There was a moment of silence on the line. "I'll tell you something else, you try to get the cops in on this thing, no one is going to cop to shit. I mean it, Dean. And you and I never had this conversation."

"Hey, Debbie . . . Look, get hold of yourself, okay. Who said anything about going to the cops? I just figure this girl didn't do anything, somebody ought to tell her there's some lunatic out there planning on cutting her heart out. She wants to go to the cops, that's her business." Dean paused. Debbie had nothing to say. "I'm just trying to figure out what went down."

"Why?"

"For Christ's sake, Debbie. What if the girl didn't do it? You think you don't owe her a fucking thing?"

Debbie sighed once more. "No pigs, Dean. I want your word, right now, no pigs or I'm hangin' up."

"No pigs," Dean said.

"Look in the paper," Debbie told him. "Entertainment section. That's all I got to say."

"Hey Debbie, look, one more thing, then that's it, I swear it."

Dean could hear her sigh. She said nothing.

"This girl," Dean said. "Pomona Queen. Do you know anything about her?"

"Jesus. Pomona Queen is the name of the band. And no, I don't know anything about her. I saw her play once, out at the fairgrounds."

"Was she good?"

"How would I know? Shit she plays is too loud to hear."

"Come on, Debbie. You've heard enough musicians in your day. You dug the way Rayann played."

"Dean . . ." Debbie said, and there was something in the way she said it, the way her voice trailed away.

Dean realized that he had perhaps gone too far, that his naked need had perhaps shown itself, as some deformity one would do better to hide. "Okay," Debbie said. "Okay. Maybe I'm beginning to see why. Jesus. It doesn't work that way, Dean. You know what I mean?"

He knew what she meant.

"I'll tell you one thing," Debbie said. "I've never heard a chick play guitar like her. And I'll tell you something else, too. From what I hear, she's crazy. She has anything to do with the Brown girl, she has to be crazy."

"The good ones always are," Dean said.

"I'm hangin' up, Johnny. It was good seein' you. Hang loose, hang tight, be cool. Whatever happens, happens. Am I right?" The line went dead. Dean stood looking into the darkness covering the yard.

"What was all that about?" The voice belonged to his mother.

"Nothing," Dean told her.

"Nothing? You're telling somebody no cops, no pigs, and you tell me it's nothing . . ."

Dean looked in her direction. Diana Brown had returned to the house. She stood just behind Dean's mother, in the shadows. He had no idea how long she had been there. He turned and started from the room. His mother fell in behind him.

"You're in some kind of trouble, aren't you?" she demanded. It was just like old times.

NINE

After the Burdicks settled on their ranch, the question of how their children were to be educated became a serious one. . . . Mr. Burdick went to Los Angeles. . . . There he learned of a young man who seemed to be well qualified. . . . In fact he had been educated for the priesthood in the Catholic Church. . . . The young pedagogue with the Irish brogue and the shock of red hair was C. P. Tonner, a man who was to be for twenty years the most striking character in the new town. . . . But the responsibilities of his office rested lightly on his shoulders and the lure of the out-of-doors, in this wonderful new country was very attractive. And more than this, the wine of the tippler was in his veins.

—F. P. Brackett

The paper was in the television room with Carl, strewn across the coffee table and floor, among the litter of empty cans.

"He's in some kind of trouble," Dean's mother announced. She had followed Dean into the room.

"So what else is new?" Carl wanted to know. Carl had once been forced to bail Dean out of jail when he was nineteen years old and the man had never forgiven him. To hear Carl tell it, he had been made stepfather to the Son of Sam. "You know something," Dean told him. "You really are full of shit." He found that saying it gave him some small satisfaction. Carl made a vaguely threatening gesture but his ass never left the couch. He pulled hard on his can of Old English 800 and kicked up the volume on the television set. He was enmeshed in an episode of "Night Court."

Dean found the entertainment section of the paper.

It was all on one page, a handful of theater listings, a few local clubs. It didn't take long for Dean to find what he was after. The thing fairly leaped off the page at him. In black-and-white updated speed-metal fashion, someone's interpretation of his great-grandfather's label. POMONA QUEEN. Only now the letters were throwing off steam, as in some horror-movie poster, and the dark-eyed girl with the flapper's locks had been replaced by the black-and-white photograph of some neo-proto-heavy-metal facsimile thereof. Dean took her to be his sword maiden. Though perhaps now she was not his sword maiden after all, not if Diana Brown had held the knife. The girl in the picture came to him out of blackness, the photographer having positioned himself above her so that she seemed to be headed his way from the depths. She was sighting more or less up the neck of what Dean took to be an S. G. Telecaster. There were bracelets on her wrists and tattoos across one shoulder and one forearm and one could see her lower teeth and the whites of her eyes below the iris. The photograph was surrounded by blocks of writing. "An Inferno of Womanhood," read one, "complete with terrifying rhythm section." Another referred to her as "The Mistress of the Deadly Decibels." At the top of the ad there was the name of a club, the Club Alibi, on the Pomona Mall, together with a pair of dates, September 7th and 8th.

.It was, Dean noted, the 8th of September, and if he wanted to see for himself just what this inferno of womanhood might look like in the flesh, he had just about two hours left to do it in. Dan Brown, if he had not done so already, would have the same two hours. It was food for thought.

"You're crazy if you go there," a thin voice croaked from the shadows. Dean turned to find Diana standing almost directly behind him. She appeared to be reading the paper over his shoulder. His mother was behind her. The girl had soot from the barn across one cheek. His mother's upper lip was beaded with sweat. It occurred to him that he had forgotten to call a cab.

"Where's he going?" Dean's mother asked.

"I'm going to call her a cab," Dean said.

"Far out," Diana Brown said.

"I'm going to pay the guy to take her as far as Clear Lake."

Diana Brown laughed. "No way, dude. You're going downtown, so am I."

Dean just looked at her.

"I didn't know where they were," Diana said. "No one would tell me. We didn't have a fucking paper."

"You're not afraid your old man will show up? He knows about it, you know. He knows about the gig."

"You're the one lost Buddy," Diana said.

"I want to know where he's going," Dean's mother demanded once more. Dean stared at Diana Brown. It seemed to him the girl was smiling at him. He found himself mildly irritated that his mother continued to refer to him in his presence in the third person. They had done that to him as a child. "You can't talk to him," one would say to the other. "He doesn't listen." In fact he had, then discovered there was no percentage in it.

Alice appealed to Carl. "You ask him," she said. Carl responded with his remote control box, jacking up the volume one more time, his eyes glued to the vaguely distinguished-looking old fuck in black robes, himself embroiled in heated debate with some sorry collection of white trash sweating uncomfortably before him. It seemed someone's cat had been defecating in a neighbor's yard. The neighbor didn't like it. You had, Dean paused, allowing himself the simple pleasure of reflection upon problems not his, to feel just a little bit sorry for the guy with the yard. There he was on the tube, fat and bearded, sporting a Raiders T-shirt and a CAT tractor hat, eyeball deep in debt, piles falling, the wife putting on a few pounds, kids getting old enough to tell him to go fuck himself, the alcohol necessary to cope with it all tearing a hole in his gut. . . . And now, on top of this growing list of obscene jokes, comes the coup de grâce: The man is required to shovel cat shit not rightfully his. It becomes too fucking much and he is forced to blow the offending creature into a million scarlet threads with a Moseburg riot gun.

At some point in this reverie it became apparent to Dean that his mother had begun to shout, trying valiantly to make herself heard above the judge—his honor allowing that the destruction of the feline in question was a definite no-no. Dean supposed his mother was looking to Carl for some show of support. Carl wasn't having any. The man was dug in, thumb on the box, eye on the tube. It would perhaps require artillery to dislodge him. Dean turned to leave the room.

Alice, however, was not quite ready to throw in the towel. She assailed the girl now waiting as Dean stepped into the hall. "You," Alice Dean said. His mother was perhaps an inch shorter than the girl. "You," she said again. "You said he lost Buddy. Now what in hell is that supposed to mean?"

For a moment the two women stood facing one another in the hallway. Dean was trying for his old room at the opposite end of the house but he heard Diana's response. "He had a body in his car," Diana Brown said. "It fell out on the freeway."

Dean stopped and faced his mother. The woman looked as if she had just been kicked in the stomach. In the room behind her the shadows danced in blue light upon the papered walls. The television howled. "Actually," Dean said, "it's not as bad as it sounds."

His mother just looked at him. Dean made once more for his room. Upon reaching it he found that, not surprisingly, he had been followed by Diana Brown.

"You don't know what you're doing," the girl told him.

"I'm gonna take a shower," Dean told her. "I'm gonna put on some other clothes, then I'm going downtown." In fact Dean was not absolutely certain he was going to do this, but the idea did have a certain grotesque appeal.

"Why?"

"Your father thinks this girl killed his brother. Unless someone tells him differently, or warns her, he's going to kill her."

The girl continued to stare at him. It seemed to Dean that a certain knowledge passed between them, that the room was occupied by a silence in which words were rendered unnecessary. At last, however, she fixed him with a knowing sneer. "So what are you going to do about it?" she asked. Her voice was, for the first time that night, filled with scorn.

"I don't know," Dean told her.

In point of fact he didn't. It was what he reflected upon as the water hit him squarely in the center of his head. He really didn't know what he was going to do, about the girl, about his job, about Dan Brown, about the land. It seemed to him in the steaming confines of the shower that he did not know what he was going to do about anything. He was at such a loss it was almost exhilarating. It was either exhilarating or terminally depressing. Debbie had warned him out of it. She wanted out of it herself. Anyone would. Everyone always did. It was as good a reason as he could think of for wanting in. When he understood this, he turned off the water. In part it was that simple. As for the other parts, for it seemed to him there were many, it was harder to say, certainly nothing one would ever want to get stuck trying to explain in a court of law. He felt a sudden kinship with the bearded galoot on television, burning with righteous fury, mute as a box of rocks. The thing was, Dean wanted to see this girl, the one who had thought to name her band after his great-grandfather's label. It was after all modus operandi among those select few willing to work in the realm of the incomprehensible.

Played off against that there was, of course, the course of prudent behavior. His mother had offered, apparently, to cut a deal. Added to which, Carl was clearly ripe for the taking. Not to mention the fact that Dean's job was still intact, his Cyclones returned. And yet somehow it had already begun to sour, this peculiar task of salvaging what he could of another man's dreams. The house after all was nothing more than a shambles, a crumbling stockade ringed by dead trees, hostile neighbors. To make it his he would have to continue with the deadening jobs. He would be forced to breathe the bad air. The place was just too far gone. The valley of promise had been laid to waste, claimed by the barbarians. And now, on top of all this, he had made an enemy of this phantom from his youth; he had, as Diana pointed out, lost Buddy. The flat truth was, it just wasn't worth it. At least that was what he told himself, drying in the misty yellow light, just as if the motives that actually drove his life were no less vague and elusive than the past.

One should, however, Dean decided, at least make a head nod at reason. No matter how badly one explained. One could, for instance, have a plan. Now you take the sad remains of old Buddy Brown there, spilled in such unceremonious fashion onto the San Bernardino freeway. Probably the cops had already made him, though Dean could not know this for sure. It was hard to say just how much of Buddy there had been left to recognize. So what if Dean called? What if he gave them a tip, a description, let's say, of Dan Brown's panel? He was certain the Pomona cops knew the Browns, that if they weren't looking already, they soon would be. And if Buddy was what they picked him up for, Dan would have no reason to suspect anyone from the Mid-Dump had tipped the cops about his plans for the girl. With any luck, the man might be picked up before he ever got to the Alibi. In fact, with any luck at all, he already had been. Fueled by such optimism, a fevered plan began to form.

Dean would call the cops, no need to mention the club. He had after all given Debbie his word, just make sure Pomona's finest knew it was Buddy Brown spread across the on ramp. Inspired, he went on. There was, for instance, the matter of this money he'd made selling Cyclones. Why not buy a couple of tickets downtown for that train to New Orleans? He could warn the girl. He could, depending on how that worked out, even offer her a ticket. She didn't want it, fine, he'd done his thing. He could take off himself. Cash in the second ticket. Once in New Orleans, he would strike a bargain with Carl. He could count on his mother for that at least. He found the absurdity of the plan vaguely satisfying.

There had been a time in Dean's life, when he was quite young, in his father's absence and before the coming of Carl, during which Alice Dean had read to him each night from the Bible. She had read to him at bedtime. As a consequence, the dragon with the keys to the abyss had walked often in his dreams. Birds of prey had gathered over the valley of dry bones. Later, when he had begun to run with what his mother took to be a "bad crowd," she had instructed him in the dangers of that broad and spacious highway, the one leading off into destruction. It struck him now as quite ironic that the Scripture should become a tenet of his own faith. And yet it had. It seemed quite clear to him, really. It was the highway of reason one had to mistrust, the middle roads of moderation and common sense. In their absence it was clearly every man for himself.

Dean had developed an interest in secret signs, a magical universe. In certain respects he had become something of a Reichian: "You know, Peeps," the good doctor had once told his son. "Hundreds of years ago there was a sickness called the Black Plague. It went all over Europe killing thousands and thousands of people. Today, I have discovered a new kind of plague. . . ." In fact, Dean had discovered one himself. Heidegger's "will to will," Burroughs's "Virus Power," the Quick Decline. Mutations on a basic strain. It seemed plain enough to Dean, and never more so than now. The Quick Decline had surely arrived upon the scene, the manifestation, both physical and prophetic, of a much grander malaise. The virus attacked the root system. The tree, cut off as it were from the ground of its being, died quickly, often within days. One could see how it worked. The Old English 800 helped.

What was less clear was what, exactly, one was to do, for the fact of the matter was, Dean carried the virus himself. He was quite sure of this. He could feel it there on a bad night, at the base of the skull, a bad thing in the shadows. He believed it had something to do with the fact that he did not know if his mother was well, that he could not remember the name of a single desperate man in his Cyclone class. Root system's shot, Doc, I got the heebie-jeebies. Doc prescribes malt liquor and lots of it. Further, Doc prescribes the rash act, the crooked path, extreme anxiety. . . .

Dean had no idea what the growers had done, finally, about the Quick Decline. But he had a theory about advanced mutated strains. They suffered if traumatized. It was only amid the heat generated by the heart's rash act that one might expect the fog to lift, that one might glimpse, if only for a moment, what lay beyond, the gleaming untraveled road, the harmonious design. There was, for instance, the location of this girl's gig. The Alibi was located at the west end of the mall and when the girl had said you're crazy if you go there and his mother had wanted to know where, Dean could have sworn there was a voice in the room. Just to whom it might belong, he could not say and yet it had answered his mother with a familiar line. The line itself was from a film. Dean was, however, all things considered, quite willing to accept it as the voice of the patriarch speaking to him across the curvature of time, as if somewhere in the magical stream of things the old man's spirit had caught a flick or two, remembered a line. . . . "Jesus," the voice had whispered, "that's in Chinatown."

And people thought it all formlessness and waste. In fact, Earl Dean would on this very night follow the path William Tacompsy McCauly had followed upon the night of his death. You wanted to talk about harmonious designs. . . . Ostensibly he would go to a girl in need of warning. It was not a bad reason. On some other level he would go for reasons all his own, which did not explain well. He would go for a red-haired girl, dead young, a reader of hearts. It only bothered him to think that Debbie had come so close to unmasking him. "Okay," she had said. "Okay. Now I know why." Well, if she knew why then she knew more than Dean . . . still, such perception. Who would have thought it of the old sow? Unless he explained, at some fundamental level, a good deal more easily than he imagined. But that was a depressing thought and he dropped it. He preferred karmic closures,

angelic cryptography. In point of fact, preference was
something of a euphemism. He preferred them like an
addict prefers junk and he did not imagine he would
tote his load much further without them.

Dean, alone in the room, made his call. Someone
was still talking to him when he hung up. They were
asking him for a name. Well, they could ask all they
wanted to. He had done his thing. He had given them
a name. It was a long shot, he knew. But there you
were. Something to hope for. It was the first piece of
an old equation: something to hope for, something to
do, and someone to love. One down. And he had,
only moments before, carved out for himself something to do. There remained someone to love but he
would think about that later. There would always be
time to think about that. It was what you thought
about when the soldiering on had come to mean nothing more than the marshaling of one's resources for
the long retreat.

With that in mind, he pulled on a fresh T-shirt. He
was about to leave the room when something else
occurred to him. Perhaps the shower had sobered him
more than he would have liked, got him thinking
about the possibilities of crossing paths with Dan
Brown one more time. The implications of such shit.
Clearly more Old English would be called for. In the
meantime, he elected to make a second call.

He called the Alibi. He had two things in mind.
First, he would have them page Dan Brown. Secondly,
whether the man was there or not, he would page the
girl. He would tell her he had to talk to her, tell her
to meet him in back. With any luck, he could talk to
her in the parking lot, without ever getting out of his
car. The phone rang, half a dozen times it seemed. At
last there was a soft click, and then a voice, on tape.
The voice spoke of club dates, the names of bands. In

the background he could hear music, loud, speed-metal fast. The recording ended with a beep. Dean stood in the ensuing silence, the phone still in his hand. It appeared that if he went ahead with this, he was going in blind. It was, he supposed, a moment of truth. Just how badly did he want to see this girl? How many checks, he wondered, could a man dodge in this life and still call it a life? Beyond the window a quarter moon had come to rest in the branches of a tree. The house seemed to groan beneath him. Perhaps it was only the motion of the planet, the inexorable roll toward winter. Dean went to the door. His mother was nowhere to be seen. He imagined that she had rejoined Carl with his television, that she had fallen once more beneath its spell. The girl was there of course, Diana Brown, stubborn as some new and virulent strain of the clap. But then why wouldn't she be, if Debbie had called it, that is? If Debbie had called it, Dean and Diana Brown had something in common. They shared one ax mistress of the heart, as rivals or as allies. It remained to be seen. Dean headed for the kitchen, the girl at his heels.

Although refusing to look at him, Diana Brown had, at some point along the descent into the dark heart of downtown Pomona, and perhaps for reasons no clearer to her than Dean's were to him, launched into a tale of lust, greed, revenge, and mistaken identity convoluted enough to make any soap-opera addict weak with envy. Dean, once more in the throes of Old English 800 dementia, followed as best he could. "The fucker tricked me into ripping off my mom," the girl said. "He wanted this ride." Dean assumed she was talking about her uncle, so recently gone to his reward. She shook her head in disgust. "He's so stupid." Dean thought of telling her the man was no longer among the living but decided to let it pass. The girl had her story. He had his. He stared across the hood of the Falcon into the darkness covering Pomona.

For Dean the place was rife with ghosts, canceled promises, missed opportunities, so that beneath the visible town, there was always the other. There was the town as it must have appeared to his great-grandfather, with its wide dirt streets, its fine Victorian houses, its towering eucalyptus.

"Pomona was the center of things then," an old grower had once told Dean. He was speaking of his own youth, talking with watery old eyes about how, when he was a boy, Pomona was the place to be. He had talked of how people had come from miles around to drive the wide streets, to observe the fine houses, to shop in the stores. Dean had gone to the man's house because the old grower was a collector of orange-crate labels and Dean had thought to make a sale of one of his Pomona Queens. The man, had, on the afternoon in question, been on his way out to Riverside for a meeting of retired growers. He had invited Dean to go along. The man's wife had advised against it. "It'll bore you to death," the woman had told him. "Just a handful of old geezers sitting around talking about the old days." In the end, Dean had declined the old man's offer. He had made a sale of one of his labels, then gone downtown to meet a friend in a bar. Sitting now, at the intersection of Holt and Palomares, Dean found himself wishing he had gone. Perhaps he would have run across someone who had known his great-grandfather. Perhaps he would have learned something. But then Dean had not been as interested in all of that then, not yet a seeker of hidden paths.

At his side, Diana was still talking. "He wouldn't tell me where we were going. He just said we had to make this stop. Okay. So I'm sitting there, outside this house. Buddy goes inside. Pretty soon he comes out carrying this television set. He puts it in the back seat of my Bug. Says wait here. Then he comes out carrying this stereo system. . . . What I find out is, he's ripping off my mom. That was my mom's house."

It seemed to Dean there was some note of genuine wonder in her voice. He stared across the street, into the parking lot of Mel's. The place had been more or less a family burger joint in Dean's youth. Tonight there were lowered minitrucks in the parking lot. Blasting rap. Hostile vibes.

"Then I find the asshole's jacket in my car. So I sold it."

"To the girl in the band."

"The thing is," Diana told him, "I didn't know that was my mom's house." The girl paused. "She couldn't let Danny know where she was. That was the reason. She was afraid. So I didn't know either. I didn't even know she was still alive."

Dean looked at the girl. She was staring out the window. She had one hand on the arm rest. The other lay in the seat between her and Dean, absently widening a small tear in Dean's upholstery.

"I wouldn't even have taken the jerk there if I had known. I mean it's not like she doesn't need that stuff. That's why I sold the asshole's jacket. I was going to give the money to her."

Dean watched a light turn green. He drove through the intersection, past the gangbangers at Mel's, headed toward the darkness at the heart of town. "I was supposed to meet this chick there today," Diana said at last. Dean saw that she was watching him in the darkness.

"At the bar," he said. It seemed to him that some reply was called for. Diana nodded. "I sell flowers off that corner up there. She told me to meet her at the Mid-Dump, she would give me the money for the jacket. How did I know Buddy was going to be there?"

She had a point, Dean thought, how would she know. "Absolutely no way," he told her. She looked at him once again, as if to gauge his sincerity. "Right on," she said at last.

"He sees you there. He sees the jacket. The guy freaks. You pull the knife to scare him. . . ." Dean could see it clearly, the girl pulling the knife, just as she had pulled it on him in the barn, holding it just the way her father had shown her. He stopped when he realized the girl was looking at him as if he were talking gibberish.

"Dude," the girl said, "Jamel had the knife."

Dean nodded. He supposed it was too much to ask that she should cop to the act, in front of him, or anybody else for that matter.

"Jamel? That's the name of the girl in the band?"

Diana folded her arms across her thin chest and looked out the window.

Dean stared into the night, content that she was lying. He had no idea why she had bothered to tell him any of it, the whole elaborate business about the television set, the jacket, the estranged mother. Somehow he had the idea that she was probably lying about most of it, perhaps trying for a story she could use later. "So why are you even here?" he asked her. "You're going to let everyone think she did it, what are you after?"

"I'm after my seventy-five bucks," Diana said. "She happens to owe it to me." At which point she turned away and spoke more softly into the window at her side. "Besides," she said, her voice barely above a whisper, her words fogging the glass, "he knows who did it."

Dean thought to press her. He then remembered what Debbie had told him, that the girls had been lovers. If it were true there would be of course a whole other dimension to the thing, a place where reason mattered little. "The heart is treacherous," the prophet had said, "and desperate. Who can know it?" As near as Dean could tell, none could. His conviction was such that it seemed suddenly pointless to ask her for more. She had her story, he had his.

As he drove south along Palomares, it occurred to him that the birth of the town had begun with a deception of sorts as well. According to his beloved Brackett, those who had ridden out from Los Angeles to attend the land auction in 1878 found streams of water flowing in open ditches along the streets. By morning, however, upon completion of the land sales, the water was back in the San Jose Creek where it belonged and the ditches were dry as the cattle bones destined to fill them in the coming years of drought, leaving one to speculate that perhaps affairs of the heart and affairs of real estate had more in common than one might at first suspect.

They were at the intersection of Palomares and First now, still immersed in this mutually agreed-upon silence that had followed Diana's story. Dean turned left and drove along the side of the old Southern Pacific railroad tracks, the same he had once imagined carrying him as far as New Orleans. The tracks were dark, streaked here and there with patches of reflected light. North of the tracks a handful of old packing-houses, long gone to ruin, sat gaping at the remains of the town. Dean and the girl were in fact just set to enter the mall, the very heart of the old downtown district. The monstrosity that was Buffums rose like a blue-tiled monolith before a starless sky. Its walls, circled by chainlink fencing, were washed in floodlights. Dean stared past the huge building that occupied all of what had once been Chinatown. Somewhere in the darkness before him stood the Club Alibi. Somewhere on these streets his great-grandfather had once lain bleeding in the dust. He stared into this darkened arm-pit of history for some time before becoming aware once more of the girl at his side. He believed she was staring at him, at which point it occurred to him that he was parked at a four-way stop. He could proceed at any time. He looked at the girl with exaggerated embarrassment. It was a gesture intended for comic effect. Diana Brown remained unmoved. Dean allowed the car to roll forward, made a left turn, and entered the mall.

The mall was really the town's last desperate attempt to save itself. Set upon by white flight and parking problems, suddenly in competition with abor-tions like the Sear's shopping center, Pomona's old downtown district was, by Dean's high school years, in an acute stage of its own quick decline. The mall was to be the last best hope. It would begin with the Buffums building in the east and end with the six-story Home Savings and Loan in the west. In between there would be landscaped pedestrian lanes, sparkling foun-tains, broad murals. The mall was the first of its kind west of the Mississippi River and Dean could still remember standing in the Pomona Public Library with Carl and Alice, staring through a huge glass bubble at some artist's three-dimensional conception of the final product—the pristine facades, the manicured shrub-bery. The mall opened in 1963 and sure enough there were fountains. There were murals and guys in three-piece suits with smiles on their faces. Balloons drifted before smog-choked skies. Within six months, how-ever, the weeds had already begun to sprout among the shrubbery. The hidden speakers had begun to pump their Muzak for the benefit of a dwindling num-ber of shoppers. The first graffiti had begun to appear on the storefronts. The first businesses had begun to fold. Another six months and it was over. There was plywood in the windows of half the stores. The guys in suits had made for the hills.

The Muzak played on, however. As far as Dean knew, it played on still—the Mormon Tabernacle Choir singing "Don't Think Twice, It's All right" from the depths of weed-infested planters. Eventually the only shoppers in sight were the winos lined up in the early morning liquor line in front of the Thrifty's drugstore. The only full-time residents were the inhabitants of the old Pomona Hotel, with its billiard parlor down the stairs, its view of the bus and train stations, its ragged curtains blowing from open windows. Parking places had become like the jackrabbits that once infested the San Fernando Valley. They were a dime a dozen.

And that had pretty much been it for the town. One more broken promise. One more plan gone sour. The land would only stand so many. One could look back on it now, all those folks with their big plans, the Spaniards with their herds, the gentlemen farmers from the East with their dreams of citrus empires and pastoral life styles, the hungry realtors and land developers. One could speculate, with the advantage of hindsight, upon the causes of it all. In fact, if one were so inclined, one could find evidence of the virus on every hand—the power virus as real-estate bug, the insatiable self as the death seed, the shadow at the base of the skull. . . . There was an equation there somewhere. Either that or it was just people fucking up. Perhaps that was how history was best understood. Dean himself was of two minds on the subject. There had been talk at one time, when it was clear the groves were on their way out, of hanging on to some of what had made the town beautiful. There would still be trees, green belts, parks, golf courses. . . . None of it had materialized of course. Developers had milked the place for every dollar they could, gone to war for smaller lot sizes, then squeezed in their jerrybuilt homes tighter than a virgin's ass. Pass me the K-Y jelly, Homer, I think we can work in one more. . . . The big Victorians that had once stood close to downtown were lost in the zoning wars as city councilmen moonlighting as realtors turned them for a profit. Lose a Victorian, gain a MacDonald's. The odd part was that for Dean, there had been a time when all this had seemed quite right and proper, some external reflection of his own sorry state. His town had been reduced to an eyesore, a compost pit of canceled promises. It was a time when just getting up in the morning and walking outside was like looking in a mirror. It was time to move on.

He thought of that time now, driving along Main Street once again, past what was left of the planters, past the murals with their sappy depictions of life on the old hacienda, Indians in loincloths, Spaniards on horses. . . . Apparently the artist in question had not read Brackett on the subject of the Indians of the valley. It was Dean's considered opinion that the artist had obviously bought into some hippie vision of the pastoral, that the proper subject matter for the Pomona Mall murals should have been that series of nearly Biblical catastrophes that marked the beginning of the end for the Spanish ranchers along about 1861. The floods had come first, in unprecedented fashion, effectively turning the entire valley into a great inland sea into which sodden adobes had turned once more to mud, taking their unfortunate occupants with them—returned unto the bosom of mother earth. The floods had been followed by two years of uninterrupted drought. The grass had died, the stock had starved. It was later said that the valley was filled in those days with the hideous bellowing of starving animals. Many of the cattle died in efforts to forage the remaining irrigated enclosures, their horns caught in the woven fence rails. Others were slaughtered by the score for the trifling amounts their hides and horns would bring on a depressed market. And just as in some apocalyptic vision, their whitening bones had covered the arid hillsides while the earth turned hard as iron, and the sky, darkened by desert winds and plagues of grasshoppers, had gone to the color of old brass. And finally, so as to render the devastation complete, there was the smallpox. It took the life of Palomares's daughter. It effectively wiped out much of what was left of those original inhabitants, the squat and unattractive local savages. They died by the score, buried in a mass grave beneath what was now Ganesha Park, lest their bones join those of the cattle bleaching on the hillsides.

Such were the ferocious scenes with which Dean would have entertained the shoppers had anyone commissioned him for the job. He should have chosen for his theme "Canceled Promises and Fuck the Pastoral." As it was, Dean had been asked to participate in the opening festivities. His band had played on a make-shift stage before the walls of Buffums. They'd sipped the beers they'd kept stashed in back of the amps. Someone had passed around a couple of joints and the sunlight had come down off the blue-tiled walls and caught itself in Rayann's hair as it flew away from her shoulders and when he saw her now he seemed to see her most often in just that attitude of concentration. He saw her with her head cocked above an aging violin. He saw for her a halo as well—all red hair and broken bow strings and flying rosin. He saw her in a flowered dress and cowboy boots, a fresh-cut wood stage jumping with the music beneath her feet. But it was more than just seeing her, he thought. Too often now it was where he made his home, in that slant of sunlight as it played upon the polished wood of an old violin, in the spray of dust and hair. . . . The images followed him down dead streets. They ambushed him in the shadows. "You pay or get nothing," they seemed to say, though it seemed to him as if Rayann had managed both. She'd paid and still got nothing. Dean's pain lay in the knowledge that she had paid alone. He had slipped out the back somehow, or tried to, while his girl picked up the tab. He knew not everyone would see it that way. There were times when he tried to see it differently himself. Just not tonight, not in the dead heart of his old hometown, the very capital of welchdom . . . Sneak out the back down here and this is what you got. . . . You met yourself trying to get back in, in an alley full of sad ghosts and one of them was you. It was what became of those who lived too long and too passionately in some past. The present got funky. The roots rotted in the ground. The limbs turned brown. It was enough, he imagined, to make a grown man puke, an aging theologian of hope bawl like a baby and so caught up in the whole thing had he become that if the child at his side had not said something, he undoubtedly would have driven right by the Alibi. The man was bound for another time zone and the Club Alibi wasn't on the charts.

Fortunately, however, or unfortunately, depending upon your point of view, the girl really did say something and Dean really did hit the breaks. Unfortunately he hit them too hard. Or rather, he brought his foot up too high, hit the loose wires beneath the dashboard with his knee, and shorted something out, broke a connection. . . . Who could say? The upshot was, the Falcon ceased to run. It had not exactly been part of the plan and afterward it seemed to him as if several things were happening simultaneously. It was hard to say. The situation was clearly slipping beyond his grasp. The deal was, they had arrived and the girl was getting out of the car. Dean was not sure why these things were happening. He supposed he was not the best of company. He was aware of the blank face of the club, of music loud enough to cause a vibration in the glass at his ear, of the absence of parking places, of Diana Brown looking at him over one white shoulder as she made an exit. He heard her voice, issuing from the back of the Falcon where she had apparently gone to retrieve the Cyclone Air Purifier they'd stashed there for her, together with yet another complimentary dollhouse. Her words were a kind warning. "Listen," the girl told him, "I don't know what your trip is, but if I was you, I would get out of here. And I wouldn't come back." He heard her slam the rear door and then he heard something else as well. He heard her curse beneath her breath and in the next moment she was by his window, pressed against the vibrating glass. "Fuck me in the ass," she said. "That's Chuck's truck. They're here already." And then she was gone. She had apparently forgotten, or failed to notice, that Dean wasn't going anywhere, that his wiring had come unglued, that all systems were down. He was dead in the water on the Pomona Mall where, in the absence of anything more rational, about all he could come up with, by way of an idea, was that really, at another time, another place, in another life perhaps, one could do worse than to fuck Diana Brown in the ass. It was of course a ludicrously idle speculation for a man in his position.

TEN

A number of outstanding figures who were here before the Santa Fé, may well be mentioned. One of these was Frank Slanker, for thirty-three years now the efficient and faithful constable.... When Captain Hutchinson was boring the first artesian wells ... Slanker was foreman ... and Bill Mullholland, Los Angeles' great engineer was working for him at $2.25 a day ... when one day J. E. MacComas came to the shop and said, "We are going to make you constable," and would listen to no refusal.... "We want someone to clean up the town," for there were fourteen saloons in the place.... The streets were filled with drunken Mexicans, sheepherders and miners....

—F. P. Brackett

Dean sat in the dim light that issued from the mall. The girl's words had fallen upon him like a blow. His first impulse was to go for the wiring. It was an odd moment. On the one hand, it was clear to him what had happened. The wiring he had braided in front of Dan Brown's house had worked itself loose. He had hit it with his knee and broken what was left of the connection. The solution was equally simple, one had only to twist the wires back together, touch them to the third. On the other hand, there were already shadowy figures advancing on him out of the night. The chances were there would not be time even for this simple act. The speed with which his plans had broken upon the hard rock of reality was almost dazzling. With a part of himself he seemed to stand back, admiring the way these things had come to pass, the girl scaring him like that, the loose wiring, his own clumsiness. "I don't know what your trip is," the girl had told him.

"Look to your own trip, child," Dean said, though by now of course she was long gone and Dean was alone, his fingers fumbling with the wiring, which seemed suddenly too fine, or to be made of taffy that clung to his skin. Footsteps could be heard in the darkness, booted feet upon the Pomona Mall. . . . Who, he wondered, could he possibly have imagined himself to be? Thinking that his luck would hold, or run any better than the old man's, here, of all places. McCaulys withered and died here. The climate was wrong, the magnetic vibrations askew. At which point it seemed to him there was a voice in the darkness, that of the devil no doubt, loosed for a little season upon the remains of the town. "Yo, magic man," the voice said. The words rang among the empty buildings and Dean, much to his discredit, ran one more time. He had, it would seem, no shame. His sword maiden was on her own after all. The wiring fell from his fingertips. He crawled on his stomach across the front seat and went out the passenger door.

The breath of the mall hit him full in the face. He could feel it cooling the sweat on the back of his neck. The effect was somewhat sobering. He ran with a cold pain high in his chest, the taste of bile in his mouth. Remarkably, he was not without a plan. He cut between two dark buildings, thinking to make for the train station, which lay due north, a scant half mile. He imagined there would be some sort of armed security at the station. The difficult part would be the open stretch of tracks and gravel, fifty yards of no-man's-land separating the back side of the town from the station itself. A wind sprint across steel rails and loose rock.

*   *   *

Dean ran from the backs of the buildings and across a parking lot. The no-man's-land loomed in front of him. Beyond it he saw light. He could hear them behind him and he did not hesitate. He was two-thirds of the way across, leaping rails, sliding in loose rock, before he saw the fence. Eight feet of chain link, invisible from any distance in the darkness, and beyond it, a deserted station. Boarded windows. Boarded doors. The lights he had glimpsed were spotlights trained on the bare asphalt that ringed the old station. There were no trains. There were no buses. No armed security. Earl Dean was quite alone. For some reason, he continued to run. There was little point in it. He could hear them quite well, coming for him across the gravel. At last there was a voice.

"Train done been here and gone, Sonny. You missed it, by about five years." The words were followed by a peal of unpleasant laughter.

Dean turned to face them, the fence at his back. He found them crossing the last of the rails—Dan Brown and Chuck.

"I don't get it," Dan Brown said. "I figured you to be on your way back to the tall pines."

"That girl in the band didn't kill your brother," Dean said.

Dan Brown closed without saying a word and hit Dean with the back of his hand. It was not exactly that Dean had not expected it. Still, it was dark; the punch was difficult to see. It caught Dean flush on the jaw and knocked him into the fence. In receiving it, Dean understood something else as well, that Dan Brown had no more interest in viewing what was on the end of the fork than the average citizen. In fact, and he saw this with a degree of clarity that was somewhat startling, the man had known it all along. He had known it on the lot at the side of the Mid-Dump. Perhaps he had known it before that, even when he was cuffing his daughter on the back of the head and inviting Earl Dean into his house. The girl of course had said so herself, had whispered to the glass of Dean's car what everyone in the valley with the possible exception of Dean had known from the beginning. 'Twas not the truth Dan Brown sought tonight, but rather some way around it, a fantasy he could shape to his own ends, then dare anyone to call bullshit on it. In time, one could see how it would work, how this tale of vengeance would take its place in the greater canon of Dan Brown tales. "Don't fuck with him, honey," the blonde had warned, and who would ever want to? The story would hold. "He's gone just a little bit nuts," she had added and it was, Dean thought, no doubt one of the understatements of the age. Of course the man had gone just a little bit nuts. He'd seen his own blood turn round to bite the hand that feeds, seen his own empire, such as it was, come down as handily as that of William Tacompsy McCauly.

Dean might have laughed out loud had it not occurred to him he was about to die. A silver blade flashed momentarily, a spark from the heat as Dan Brown's arm moved in a fluid arc across the front of his body. There was the soft click as the wrist action set the blade and Dean could feel the cold steel beneath his chin, a point of pain somewhere high against his throat. He thought that was how it would end. It was so fast. And it was only when the end did not come that he realized something was amiss, the absence of pain, the rush of blood held back. It was then he had time to be afraid. It was then that he fainted.

He was vaguely aware of a pain in the back of his head, of the bearded man standing over him, of the cold sweat on his brow. The man pulled him into an upright position. "Jesus, man . . ." Chuck said. "Couldn't see anything but the whites of your eyes, dude."

Chuck seemed to find in this some cause for amusement. Dean didn't say anything. He sat up slowly. The back of his head began to throb. Touching it, he found his fingers sticky with blood. He blinked into the night. They were still at the fence, the deserted station languishing behind them in the midst of the empty lots. Dan Brown was taking a few tokes off whatever it was he kept in the little green bottle.

"All is not lost," he said when he noticed Dean looking in his direction. "I have a plan."

Earl Dean puked in his lap.

"Jesus fucking Christ!" Chuck said. He jumped back to escape the spray.

Dean managed to get to his knees. He crawled as far as the first railroad track and deposited about four cans of Old English 800 between the ties. When he was finished Dan Brown pulled him to his feet once more and began alternately pushing and pulling him back toward the mall. "You know, you're still entertaining, Magic. I got to admit it." Stumbling over loose rock, Dean was aware of the man laughing at his side. "What would you say," Dan Brown asked him, "if I told you there was a slim chance you just might see the sun come up?"

There was a drinking fountain on the mall and Dean went for it. When he had finished with his face and hair, he did what he could for the soiled jeans. When that was done he walked somewhat unsteadily toward a primer-gray Chevy pickup against whose side Dan Brown now leaned. He assumed it was the truck the girl had spoken of. His running days over, he guessed it was time to hear the plan.

Dan Brown straightened as Dean approached him.

"Check this out," he said. He said it very matter-of-factly, as if Dean had not just been puking his guts all over the north end of town, as if all of this was perfectly within the bounds of ordinary behavior. Dan Brown was now wearing some kind of old army jacket, a size too big maybe, the kind of thing one would pick up at an army surplus store. As Dean approached him he pulled the knife from a vest pocket. This time, however, there was no flick of the wrist. The blade remained within the handle. Dan Brown held the knife with his right hand. With his left he reached for Dean's wrist. The man had a grip like a plumber's wrench and Dean felt his fingers go numb. Dan turned Dean's hand so that the palm was turned upward and it was here that he placed the knife.

"I have chosen you," Dan Brown said, "to avenge the death of my brother. I hope you appreciate that this is a great honor. I also hope you appreciate that if you fuck up, I will personally see to it that you never see the sun come up again."

Dean looked at the knife. It was a cheap Tijuana switchblade. The instrument sported a white plastic handle, a red dragon. He stared down at it as an anemic and unforgiving moon reached the zenith of its ascent, bathing the mall in a withering splendor. "A good night for planting oranges," he said. He realized he could say anything to Dan Brown. The man had gone over. "Good night for cutting pussy is what you mean," was Dan's reply. He smiled as he said it, his silver tooth flashing in the light of the moon.

With the knife passed to Dean, Dan Brown now took something from behind one of the front seats of the truck. Dean could not see it clearly. He put it under his jacket and came back around to where Chuck and Dean waited. Dean was once more within a block of the Alibi. It occurred to him that he might have done better had he tried for the club instead of the empty

station, though it would have meant running past Dan
Brown instead of away from him. But then he might
have died at birth as well and been spared the whole
thing. As it was, it appeared he would see the girl
after all.

They walked down the middle of the mall, the
empty storefronts gaping at them in the darkness.
Dean walked in the middle, the cheap switchblade still
in the hand into which it had been placed. He had no
idea of how this would end. It was not unlikely, he
thought, that he would die on the streets of Pomona,
within half a mile of Buffums, half a mile from
Chinatown.

Dean could hear the music from the club once again.
It occurred to him that it was not even close to what
the builders of the mall had had in mind when they
installed the speakers in the planters. The music, however, was not out of place here in the dead mall, at
the heart of a dead town, in the bowels of a dead
valley. It would play well too with the murals as Dean
had imagined them—shopping music in the age of the
Quick Decline.

Dan Brown seemed to be hearing the music for the
first time. He held up a hand, motioning for them to
stop. He removed his jacket and gave it to the bearded
man to hold. "Listen to that," Dan Brown said. He
nodded in the direction of the club. "Is that pitiful shit
or is that pitiful shit?" The question appeared rhetori-
cal, as Dan Brown was looking neither at Dean nor
Chuck, but rather had begun to fool with whatever it
was he'd taken out of the truck and stashed beneath
his jacket. It was a weapon of sorts. There was a flat,
wooden stake, a second knife. As Dean and Chuck
watched, Dan taped the knife to the stake and the
stake to his arm. He was using what looked like black
electrician's tape, using lots of it, and pulling it tight.

When he was finished the knife was flat against the stick and parallel with his forearm. He then raised his arm and made a fist. With his free hand he pushed something on the knife. The thing was a stiletto, the blade coming straight out, a good eight inches and well beyond the knuckles of his closed hand.

Dan tried the blade twice more, then took his jacket from his partner and put it back on. With the jacket in place, the jailhouse weaponry was out of sight. You could see then how it would work. With the blade retracted, there was nothing to be seen beyond the cuff, which fell well below Dan's wrist. Extend the blade, however, make a fist, throw a punch . . . You could see where, if one was good at it, one's opponent would never see the blade until it was too late. Dean drew a hand over his head. If called upon to make a wager, he would wager that Dan Brown was good at it. The thought did little to lift his spirits.

"We shouldn't go after her in the club," Chuck said suddenly. Dean stared at the man in amazement. Could it be that a voice of reason would yet be heard? "Police station is about a mile away down here, man," he continued. The man spoke calmly, as if he had given the matter a good deal of thought. Dan Brown did not look up but continued to make minor adjustments to his invention. "This is your big chance," Dan Brown told Dean. "Don't blow it."

Dean stared at Chuck. The man was not looking at Dan Brown. He appeared to be staring toward the dark roofs of the buildings that lined the opposite side of the mall. Dan Brown fooled with the cuff of his jacket a moment longer. When he was satisfied, he turned once more toward the club. The bearded man fell in at his side, forcing Dean to walk in the middle.

"That's the beauty of this thing," Dan Brown said at last. "We don't go after her. It's Johnny Magic here goes after the bitch. We're just along to back the man's play." After that they walked in silence. It was not far. Chuck, having spoken his piece, was apparently content. Dean realized there was of course little point in hoping for more, or in trying to figure the logic behind any of it. Dan Brown was the kind of guy invented his own logic as he went along; nor did he do so unaided. He had apparently hit upon the correct combination of alcohol and drugs. Dean supposed they lit the old valley for him just so—a landscape more vivid than any that had gone before it, more vivid even than that which had once bloomed for the eyes of the Spanish caballeros. Perhaps the ancient locals, high on some indigenous herb, now extinct . . . But then that was another story. God only knew what jailhouse fantasies played upon the visualization screens of the old mind—grade B horrors never before imagined. The Flying Leathernecks Dine on Bloody Pussy. Captain Blood Fucks the World. A Fistful of Testicles.

Dean stumbled on a curb. Dan Brown caught him by the back of the neck and held him upright. A line Dean had read somewhere sprang suddenly to mind. He believed it to be from Beckett, though he could not recall the work. He felt, however, the compulsion to utter it aloud: "In such a place, in such a world, that's all I can manage, more than I could." Dan Brown never missed a beat. "Don't fall apart on me tonight, Johnny," is what he said, and Dean was, at just that moment, afforded a glimpse of the man at his side, his face suddenly illuminated in one of the streetlights that lingered above the corpse of the mall—the silver smile, the deranged eyes. And one might, Dean thought, just as well appeal to the sea for mercy.

Ahead of them stood the Club Alibi. The door was black. The stucco appeared to have been painted pink. Given the light, it was hard to say. On the door was tacked a poster and approaching it, Dean saw that it was the same speed-metal rendition of his great-grand-father's orange-crate label that had appeared in the paper. The effect was such that for some indeterminate period of time, it all seemed to hang there before him—the label, the girl, the whole silly thing that had, on the evening in question, managed to get the old juices flowing once more. And in the second or so it took Dan Brown to shove him through the door the thing appeared to him as a kind of coat of arms, a symbol of his foolishness, of misspent energies, and he was granted a kind of epiphany: He saw what became of his kind. They came at last upon the hard rock of reality. And they ate shit. At which point the door swung away from him and he was propelled into darkness.

Dean was immediately aware of two things, the stench peculiar to such establishments—the residue of bodies, booze, and stale smoke; and he was aware of the noise—the triple bass line, the bar chords, the speed-metal guitar riffs frying like worms on hot pavement. It was all cranked decibels above what was safe for the human ear and as he walked the first few feet into the club he was aware of nothing but the assault upon his senses. In time his field of vision widened to include the rest of it. His eye was drawn to the blur of light that marked a stage. Presently, he saw the girl.

She was standing on a rectangular chunk of plywood someone had covered with red shag carpet. Dean knew the stage was made of plywood because the carpeting was worn down to the bone in a number of places. Some of them had been patched with silver duct tape. Others had not. The girl herself was, more or less, the girl from the poster. Except that in person she was more impressive and it occurred to him that Stench the bartender had not lied. For here was certainly a five-foot, ten-inch amazon with blond dreadlocks and tattooed arms. A pair of black fishnet stockings exited from a black metal monster T-shirt and found their way into a pair of black-and-red cowboy boots. Her hair swung about her face in sync with the music and at times fanned out and flew before the flat black walls and caught the stage lighting like the mist blown back from the lip of a wave when the wind is from the desert and the sun is low in the sky.

He was aware of Dan Brown and the bearded one pressing against either side of him. There was a girl with blue-black hair and the skin coloring of a corpse coming toward them, out of the darkness and smoke, out of the sound. Dan Brown ordered a pitcher and pushed Dean toward a table. The Club Alibi consisted of one long rectangular room. There were a handful of tables at one end, the stage at the other. Other tables had been pushed aside to form a dance floor upon which several young people in various stages of undress slammed into one another. They seemed to go about this rather sullenly, without real interest, as if it were something demanded of them. A number of the dancers sported shaved heads or colored mohawks but their costumes seemed to Dean as obvious and sad as their dance beneath these smoky lights. In fact they seemed little more than sophomoric contrivances to ward off what, in the end, would not be denied—the unspeakable future.

Most of the club's occupants were young. An exception to this was a pair of fat, aging biker types occupying a table near the stage. Their table was a litter of empty pitchers. They sat watching the girl on the stage, mute with sexual frustration or dumb with drink—it was difficult to say which. Dean wondered if they might not be bouncers. If they were he did not imagine they would be of much help to him. Neither looked quite up for anything in Dan Brown's league—the league of the criminally insane. At Dean's side,

Dan Brown pulled out his little bottle and did his thing with the cigarette. Dean was aware of the ghostly brunette watching him.

He began to look for Dan Brown's daughter. He found her near the stage, kneeling in the shadows at the edge of the dance floor. At least he believed it to be her. He could see only the top of her head, the dark hair, the faded bandanna. She moved in time to the music.

At his side, Dan Brown sat with eyes riveted on the stage, his face a mask of white flesh. Above them, the girl continued to wail, throwing fat, grimy chords off bare cement walls. Dan Brown seemed to watch the girl without blinking. The waitress brought a pitcher. Chuck paid and poured. Dean never had been able to make much of the hair-of-the-dog theory. On the evening in question, however, he went for the glass before him like a dog would a bone. His shirt still stuck to his back. His soiled jeans clung to the insides of his thighs. He still held the switchblade, which seemed to have warmed to his touch, a branding iron on his moist palm. He tried to imagine facing Dan Brown with it. He tried to imagine making the first move, the blind thrust, the desperate lunge. . . . Surely, he thought, it was like the man had said. We are dreamers, shouting out in our sleep, pilgrims lost in a forest of symbols where no man can say with certainty who he is. Who, for instance, Dean wondered, did the man at his side believe himself to be? Jesse James? Joe the Dead? But then one did have his or her front. You had your Theologian of Hope, your Mistress of the Deadly Decibels. . . . Dean made an effort to focus upon the girl. Her voice, by this point in the evening, was little more than a hoarse scream, out of which an occasional discernible phrase would now and then emerge. "I'm gonna take you down," she sang, "to a place you never knew existed. I'm gonna take you down, to a place that's gonna sound real different. . . ."

He was at the point of wondering how long she would go on, when quite suddenly, and to his great horror, Dean realized that she had stopped, that the set was ending, that in approaching the microphone she had begun to issue thanks, to name names. It took a moment for Dean to realize the names were the names of clubs, of future dates, the Anti-Club, Lichtesternuim, Scream. . . . The music was over. It had happened so soon, he thought, there had been so little time. Already the bassist was pulling plugs. Dan Brown put a hand on the back of Dean's neck. "She goes outside, we're right behind her." Dean felt himself nod, as if the whole thing made perfect sense. Dan Brown tightened his grip. "This chick killed my brother, dude. You knew him. You were there. Stand tall, Magic. Make it plain."

And then the girl was moving off stage, exiting not out the front, but out a side door, and Dan Brown was on his feet and pulling Dean to his, then pushing him ahead as the three of them, Dean, Dan Brown, and Chuck, began moving along the western wall of the club.

Others were leaving now as well. Dean saw their faces, streaked with sweat in the dim colored lights, flushed with drink, clouded in smoke. Propelled by Dan Brown's momentum, he pushed past them. Occasionally he would bump into someone; a bare shoulder would slam against his chest. Some young stud would turn on him in anger. One would have thought something might have come of it, but it didn't. He could see how it worked. They would look at Dean but he would be past them almost at once and they would be left looking at the man hard on his heels and the anger would die on the vine. Amazing what the right

light in the old eyes could do to a prospective opponent's resolve. A beefy kid sporting a knotted mohawk
and tattooed shoulders slammed against him, looked
wildly around, first at Dean, then at Dan Brown,
before allowing himself to be pushed aside. Not
tonight. Dean fancied he could hear the kid muttering
to a friend, even as he passed—some disclaimer no
doubt. "Got to work in the morning, dude. . . . Penis
stud giving me trouble, man. . . . Leastwise I would
have put the hurt on that aging motherfucker."

Dean might have laughed out loud, had there been
time. Not tonight indeed. Not in this life, junior. He
saw the fat bikers looking from their table, their asses
glued to their chairs. He saw a side door, the night
yawning beyond it. From the corner of his eye he
caught a flash of white flesh, of purple cloth. Briefly
it seemed to him that a small white face stared back
at him, floating there before the abyss beyond the
door. But it was only for a moment, like some image
caught in the light of a strobe, and then she was gone
and there was only the soiled black curtain, which
marked a kind of backstage boundary, and in the next
instant he was aware of two new faces he had not
seen before. The waitress with the blue-black hair
parted the curtain and two men moved out from
behind it and into his path. They moved to block him
and he saw at once that these in fact were the club's
muscle. It made perfect sense. This was a rough part
of town, kind of place bound to have trouble, and the
pale brunette had known it when she'd seen it. She'd
been hip to Dan Brown since he'd come through the
door. And unlike the two bikers Dean had at first
taken for possible bouncers, these looked more up to
the task—a pair of rangy blacks in black T-shirts. Each
carried what looked to be a slightly shortened pick
handle. They had faces that said all business and Dean
experienced a momentary sense of relief. This was fol-

lowed by the realization that as far as the blacks were concerned, he was with Dan Brown, and Dan Brown was behind him, pushing him forward. The fact of the matter was, they were closing fast, and Dean was out on point.

He heard the voice of Dan Brown behind him. "Bogey, Chuck, ten o'clock." And then to Dean, an urgent hoarse whisper. "Hit the deck, partner. Go for his ankles, then roll clear. Leave him to me." Dean had about two seconds to make some kind of move. The expression on the black guy's face helped him make it. There was a light in the guy's eyes and he was clearly ready to take off Dean's head with the pick handle, so that Dean's shoulder roll was as much self-preservation as strategy. Still, and this was the weird part, the part he would think about later—there was this moment—this split second before he took his dive, in which some new thing jumped within his heart. One could not call it the joy of battle exactly. The truth was he was scared shitless. It was something else. In fact, it had to do with what Dan Brown had said to him. The man had called him partner, and the man was going to save his ass. Now it was true of course that the man had also gotten him into this, that he still held a knife with which he was expected to do something unspeakable, that he had been kept against his will, punched, humiliated, and threatened with castration. And yet for all of that, there was an instant in which it was all forgiven, or at least forgotten, in which Earl Dean, for the first time in his life, was part of something. He had compadres and they were dangerous men, men not to be trifled with. The bouncer was clearly more than he could handle and Dan Brown was going to look out for his ass. He was going to flat put it on the line. Dean was not sure he had ever seen anyone do that, at least not a partner. And so there was this beat—a microsecond, say—in which Earl

Dean really did want to stand tall, to take them just as Randolph Scott and Joel MacCrea had taken them in *Ride the High Country*, straight up and straight on. They would take them like men, by God. And for a moment the image held, frames in a halting film strip, exposed to the light. And then it was gone, the tape broken, the image swallowed in darkness as Dean did what Dan Brown had asked, that is he hit the deck and rolled clear, which meant rolling into the legs of the chairs and tables and it was from there that he saw what went down above him.

The bouncer would have done better to ignore Dean. He had no way of knowing this, of course, no way of knowing the balding cat in the wet T-shirt was in fact the only sane one of the bunch, that the real danger lay in those crazed black eyes coming along behind him. The man misread the situation. He stepped over Dean easily enough. His major mistake was taking the time to punch Dean in a kidney with his pick handle. It was a luxury for which there simply was not time. Perhaps he misinterpreted Dean's going down so easily, believing the whole deal was going to be a piece of cake. Perhaps he was seeking an intimidation factor. Maybe he just liked to hurt people. Whatever the reason, it was a bad move. It cost him time and when next he looked, in that instant before the knife took out an eye, maybe more, he no doubt saw the error of his way, saw it in that onslaught of white-trash fury bearing down suddenly upon him.

Dean supposed, from his position on the floor, it was a vision akin to what those Yankee soldiers must have seen in the eyes of the first of Pickett's men to reach their lines, not yet knowing anything about the backup that had failed to materialize, knowing only one thing, and fear and mercy weren't part of it. Dan Brown closed with a wicked hook, the blade concealed until the very end, at which point it did its work, ripping off what appeared to be about half the bouncer's face, up around his left eye.

Chuck meanwhile had picked up a chair and commenced to do battle with the second bouncer. The ghostly brunette had the wits to go to a phone. Dean saw her there, at the front of the club, a receiver pressed to one ear. If Dan Brown had seen her, he might have killed her, might have sent Earl Dean to do the job, but he had other things on his mind. He was through the first line of defense and his course was set. The man had after all never turned back yet and he wasn't starting now. One might as well have tried to keep a hungry predator from its prey. The highly unfortunate part was that Johnny Magic was still there too. The man was sort of moving Dean along as a wave might move a piece of wood, alternately kicking, dragging, and pushing, extolling and cursing. You wanted to talk about the joy of battle. The man had drawn first blood and he was after the rest. He was way out there somewhere and he was taking Dean with him, through the soiled black curtain and into the night where already the wail of a siren was beginning to echo in the dead heart of the Pomona Mall, where a battered Tradesman van sat, doors open, upon a ravaged parking lot above which a meager handful of stars soiled an otherwise perfect abyss. Dean heard the siren. He doubted that Dan Brown did. He was past all of that now. That shit belonged to the world. At which point, Dean saw the girl once again.

She was at the back of the van. Dean saw her turn toward the commotion spilling from the club. He saw her even as Dan Brown pulled him to his feet once more. "Cut the bitch," the man said. "Cut her." He shoved Earl Dean in the small of the back. Dean stumbled toward the blond, the knife still in his hand, the blade still closed. He heard the siren once more. Too far away, however, to save him now. He stopped short of the van, wobbling like a fighter whose legs are gone.

The girl was not five feet from him, her dreadlocks brilliant before the roofline of the truck. She held to the top edge of the van's door with one arm. The other hung at her side. She looked at Earl Dean with an open mouth. He was aware of some commotion then, of voices coming from the dark interior of the van, but he saw no point in prolonging any of it. In fact, he was convinced, standing before the aging Dodge, in the parking lot of the Club Alibi, that his time had come. There really was nowhere left to run. He would not go for the girl, not even clumsily. Perhaps the sight of her there, openmouthed, alone before the night, his for the taking had, in the end, shamed him into something other than flight.

Earl Dean drew his breath and turned to face Dan Brown. He squeezed at the knife in his hand. The blade snapped open and locked with a soft mechanical click he could feel in his wrist, though there seemed to be little strength left in his hand, as if the resolve he had felt in his heart had not yet reached it, was perhaps incapable of traversing such distances, being of some inferior strain. All he could say for certain was that his eyes met Dan Brown's and he was, in the space of a heartbeat, witness to a remarkable display. For even as the man was taking note of Dean's treachery, his expression changing from one of surprise to cold anger touched with some obscene sense of amusement, there blossomed something else, some new expression Dean had not seen there in the course of the night. Perhaps it had never been seen there at all, in some forty-five years. For even as the familiar sneer had begun to form, it died before Dean's eyes, and its death was somehow difficult to behold. At which point Dean perceived that he was no longer the sole object of Dan Brown's attention. The man's gaze had been turned away, or caught and pulled, as if by some force, and then Dean turned as well and what he saw was Diana Brown. She had at some point, while Dean was turning to face Dan Brown, taken the place of the blond on the running board at the side of the van, and she was there now, her knife in her hand, and when she spoke, she spoke to her father. "She's mine," she said. "You can't have her. I'll kill you just like I killed your retarded brother."

Dean turned once more toward Dan Brown. The play of emotion he had witnessed seemed to have run its course and the man's face was suddenly slack, as if something had been let out of it. And for a moment Dan Brown stood there, possibly for the first time in a short life of sorrow, unable to choose. He was after all facing the fruit of his own loins risen up to oppose him, betrayed by blood, by the stars, by what remains. . . . It was difficult of course to know what thoughts passed through that big triangular head in those few dark seconds on the Pomona Mall, what unspeakable visions of death and destruction, blood and betrayal. No doubt, had things been allowed to continue, some course of action would have presented itself, great violence would have been done, quite possibly to Dean himself, who was still occupying that no-man's-land between father and daughter, standing approximately where he had been pushed, gaping back in the direction of the club so that he was in a position to see one of the bouncers stumble into the night, pick handle raised. And Dean shouted. Who could say why? Perhaps, in that moment, it seemed to him that Dan Brown stood alone, betrayed and outnumbered. Stand tall, the man had told him. Stand tall indeed. And Dean had shouted and Dan Brown had turned, but already he had hesitated, facing his daughter, and the hesitation, Dean supposed, had cost him in the end. It was the girl in the band after all who brought him down. She had come around through the van and out the back and off the rear bumper, swinging the telecaster as she came, like some sort of battle-axe, the full weight of her not-unimpressive body behind it, and catching Dan Brown cleanly across the back of the neck. Dean could hear something crack even from where he stood. He saw Dan Brown go down and then lie where he fell, in a painfully unnatural position, and it was, Dean thought, just like the Duke had called it. It was how the great ones went. No gun battles and no blazes of glory for Dan Brown. He would go as so many legends had gone before him—too big to take head-on—back shot by a sodbuster. In Dan Brown's case, the situation had reached grotesque new heights, probably, at least in the mind of the Duke, never before imagined. For the sodbuster in question was possessed of blond dreadlocks and there were purple circles beneath her eyes.

Chuck stumbled into the lot on the heels of the bouncer. His balding head was streaming blood. The bouncer must have thought he'd finished him inside. For he never looked back. He went straight for Dan Brown, pick handle raised. He was about to bring it down when Chuck threw a body block that cut the bouncer's legs out from under him, buckling a knee at a bad angle. Both men slid toward Dan Brown. When they bumped against him, Dean saw him move. He saw his eyes blink but he remained on the ground, in the bad position. The pallid brunette was next out the door and there were two uniformed cops on her tail. Pomona cops were famous as world-class weight lifters. The two who arrived at the Club Alibi looked like cartoons, thick red necks bulging out of dark blue shirts that looked about five sizes too small. They wore helmets and carried nightsticks and the moonlight glanced off their gold shields and helmets. In a more orderly universe they were what Dan Brown should have had to throw himself against. As it was, they stood around viewing the carnage, their only real task that of separating Chuck and the bouncer—which, by this stage of the game, was not much of a job, certainly less than what all those hours in the gym had prepared them for. In fact, they had been cheated too, and they looked like they knew it.

Dean looked toward the interior of the club but he did not see the other bouncer again. When he looked for the Mistress of the Deadly Decibels, he found her gone. The van was still there, its doors open to the night. The band was there too, the bass player and the drummer. Dean had scarcely noticed them on the stage. Now he saw why. They were simply scaled-down replicas of their guitarist. They were very young, he thought. Perhaps they were college girls after all. They appeared to him altogether frail and miserable. In fact, without their leader they were, it seemed to Dean, barely there at all. At which point he noticed that Diana Brown had vanished as well. Sharing the lot with him, there were only the children from the band, the pallid brunette, Chuck, the bouncer, the two cops, and Dan Brown. One of the fat bikers he had seen earlier put in a brief appearance at the rear door. The man said something. It sounded like, "What the fuck?" And then he was gone.

At last a couple of paramedics showed up and found their way to Dan Brown and Dean moved a few steps closer himself and chanced to look into the man's eyes. It was something he had till now avoided and he knew at once that he should have put it off altogether. For he saw them blink and then hold him with an expression he knew he would carry to his grave. It was a look of such righteous indignation, of such mute, impotent fury, that he was at once forced to reevaluate his surroundings. The night was an illusion after all. A trick done with mirrors in which the terrifying immensity of the heavenly abyss was nothing more than some pale, external reflection of what was in fact the abyss of the soul. And it seemed to Dean, peering into the windows of Dan Brown's, as if the gravitational pull would surely claim them all. In fact, it seemed to him that in the end it would have to claim even that vague reproduction—the illusive night, with its faint stars, its black holes and nuclear engines, its hidden patterns, the whole righteous mess of things— the mysterious disposition of the Profundity as it were, sucked right down into that infinite waste of impotent rage, at which point Dean remembered his sales pitch.

It's not the suction, Ms. Finkbinder. Any piece of shit can generate suction. Airflow is the thing. You lose your airflow, all the goddamn suction in the world's not going to buy you a pot to piss in.

ELEVEN

As constable, Slanker saw much of Tonner . . . taking him home literally hundreds of times. At such times Tonner often talked of the hereafter, and so earnestly that Slanker once said to him . . . "You do not talk of the things sober that you do when drunk. . . ."

—F. P. Brackett

In the land of the quick decline, the cops knew trouble when they saw it. They also knew when a game was up. The pair that answered the brunette's call knew Dan Brown as well. They were not compassionate men. Perhaps their hearts had been removed to make way for larger and deeper pectoral muscles. Or perhaps they knew the stories, knew about the cop who'd lost his nightstick, then managed to get himself beaten to death with it one long-ago summer's evening. Though perhaps, Dean thought, they were too young for that. The cops were younger than he was. Everyone, it seemed, was younger than Earl Dean. The cops did not seem particularly interested in asking anybody anything. There appeared to be something vaguely flirtatious going on between them and the pale brunette and together they stood around cracking jokes in the poor light as the two paramedics worked at strapping Dan Brown to a stretcher. Dean could hear a second siren now, echoing among the empty buildings, but he saw no need to hang around. He'd had enough of these cops with their bulging necks. He'd seen enough of the pallid brunette. He might have gone to Dan Brown but did not think he was quite up to meeting that stare. Once had been enough. As he started back through the doorway and into the club it seemed to him that one of the cops said something to him, or perhaps only about him. At any rate he did not stop and no one moved to intercept him. He made it quickly through the front door and fairly stumbled into the cool breeze that brushed the empty storefronts of the Pomona Mall.

The fact of the matter was, Earl Dean didn't feel well. Johnny feels low were the words that came to mind. They seemed to spill from the empty buildings, a haunting refrain. He was headed, for reasons not precisely clear to him, particularly when one considered that his car was to the west, in an easterly direction. Ahead of him the lights of Buffums cast a pale, faintly phosphorescent glow before which the trees twisted themselves in a variety of gaunt, black shapes like so many impaled saviors.

For a while, all he heard were the sounds of his own footsteps, the rush of his own blood, the distant wail of a siren. Then he heard something else. Voices. Clearly female. Raised in heated debate. Fairly screaming as a matter of fact. The voices came from somewhere on the mall, back among the trees, from a building perhaps, or an alley beyond. Dean stopped to listen. He might have walked on. The problem was, he was reasonably certain one of the voices belonged to Dan Brown's daughter. As for the other . . . he could only guess.

He found them near the entrance of a narrow alley. Diana Brown stood facing the taller blond. Between them, on the ground, still in the box, sat Earl Dean's Cyclone Air Purifier. For a moment it appeared to him as if Diana was trying to make some sort of deal involving the unit. This was only for a moment, however, and the first words he was able to distinguish clearly had nothing to do with the machine. "I want my money," he heard Diana say. "I want it now, that or the jacket." The blond said something Dean could not hear. She made a move as if to turn away. Diana caught her by the arm, or rather tried too. What she got was a fist full of leather. At which point the larger girl came back around with a short, straight right that seemed to catch the smaller girl cleanly in the mouth. Diana took a step backward, tripped over the boxed Cyclone, and landed hard on her ass. The blond then pulled off the jacket, and it must, Dean thought, have been the jacket Diana had spoken of, and threw it in Diana's face. She did this with considerable force. And Dean heard her voice, clearly, for the first time.

"Go, goddamn it," the girl shouted. "Take your fucking jacket. Take your fucking family. And get the fuck out of my fucking life." Diana Brown pulled herself off the ground. It occurred to Dean that the girl's family was already in a state of swift decline, so there was really not much left to take. It occurred to him as well that given the girl's proclivity for pulling knives, now was the time. As it was, she never had the chance. Perhaps the blond girl shared Dean's concern, for even before Diana could fully set herself, the girl from the band began to run.

She was headed back down the alley in the direction of the club when quite suddenly she was caught in a shower of light, momentarily displayed in full silhouette before some approaching vehicle. Dean heard her voice for the second time. He heard the whine of brakes and saw that the vehicle in question was the battered Tradesman van he had seen at the club. The lights stopped. The girl moved out of their glare and into the darkness. A door swung open on creaking hinges, then slammed shut. The lights began to move once more. Dean looked toward the van. It was a full two seconds before he realized that Diana Brown had taken a position squarely in the center of the alley, at the side of the Cyclone, that she was holding her ground before the approaching lights and looking for all the world as if she meant to stay there.

Dean would never know for sure. He reached her, he felt, in that instant before the van could take her upon its horns. He had thought to pull her back but had moved too quickly in order to reach her in time, and his momentum carried them forward instead. He believed the van swerved as well because he could hear the grinding of metal, the tinkle of breaking glass—what he took to be the van sideswiping a building and then hitting something else. There was a sharp cracking sound, an explosion of glass and plastic, as the lumbering pile of Detroit steel encountered one Cyclone Air Purifier, ground it beneath its wheels, and was gone. At which point it occurred to Dean that his sword maiden had made good her escape once more, that in all probability his path would not cross hers again. Pity there had been no time to ask her about the name of her band. She was, it seemed, to remain an enigma. The night had given. And the night had taken away.

What he was left with was Diana Brown. They were alone in the alley, still locked in a somewhat awkward embrace before an ancient brick wall streaked with graffiti. There was no one to hold but each other, nothing to remind them of their ax mistress save the sharp sweet scent of exhaust and burning oil—enough to suggest the van that had taken her was in need of a valve job.

It seemed to Dean at that moment as if the girl in his arms had begun to cry. He felt her shudder against his chest. He might have held her for some time. Anyone would have. But then she seemed to pull away rather abruptly and he released her. Her lip was badly split and there was blood on her top. Her eyes, however, were quite dry and her face was lit with a dark light he did not believe he had seen before, even when she had appeared at the back of the club, holding her ground before her father. She had lost her bandanna. Her hair was loose and wild about her shoulders. He found it longer than he would have guessed, richer as well. In fact, the young woman now before him bore scant resemblance to the girl with whom he had once argued on the porch of a tract home in the heart of Clear Lake.

They did not leave the alley right away. The girl did not seem inclined to do so. Dean waited in silence as she poked through what was left of the Cyclone Air Purifier. It was not clear to him what she was looking for. Perhaps it was not clear to her. She seemed rather pitiful, he thought, alone there, the twisted remains of some attachment dangling from her hand, her dark hair catching some bit of light that snaked its way from the mall, along the backsides of the empty buildings with their broken rain gutters, their rusted pipes.

At last she dropped the attachment and picked up the leather jacket. She pulled it on. It was much too big for her. Without looking at Dean she began to walk away. When he caught up to her, they walked together in silence. He was not sure where they were going. They cut between a pair of buildings and back to the mall. In the distance Dean could see the Falcon, a pale metal ghost in the shadows.

"I'm sorry," Dean said at last. His voice sounded hollow, absurd in this emptiness. The girl continued to walk. Dean felt compelled to say more. "Can I take you anywhere?" he asked. He thought maybe he should take her home, or to a hospital. He thought suddenly of the mother she had mentioned. He put a hand on her shoulder. "Listen to me," he said. "I'll make you a deal. Let me give you a ride someplace. I'll teach you how to hot-wire a car." He could not bring himself to leave her, alone at the Pomona Mall.

The girl watched him with great interest. He explained each step as he went along, showing where the two wires went, one from the engine to the dash, the other from the dash back to the engine, the third to the solenoid. When it came time to make the connection she wanted to do it. Dean let her. He saw her smile as the car's headlights found their way into the shadows. He assumed it was because she was pleased with her work. "You know something?" Diana Brown asked him. "You should stick to hot-wiring cars and forget the knife fights." Dean was given to understand that she was smiling at him. He did not, however, take her words as an insult. Her smile was without malice.

"I suppose," Dean said to her, "you're gonna tell me I was holding the knife incorrectly." Diana Brown laughed out loud. The sound was like the call of a night bird, sudden and sweet.

"You were all fucked up," she told him. "Danny would have killed you for sure."

The girl was silent after that and with nothing else to go on, Dean drove her home. She did not speak again until they had started down her street in Clear Lake and come within sight of the house, at which point Dean felt her stir at his side. When he looked at her, he found her staring straight ahead, her hands tucked tightly beneath her arms, pinned to her ribs. "So why did they call you Johnny Magic?" she asked.

Dean was a moment in replying. "Actually," he said, "not too many people did." He parked in front of the house. "I had a band for a while. I did most of the vocals. The name was sort of a joke."

Diana continued to stare into the street. Her face was stern and white. He saw one of her arms tremble slightly, as if she had taken a chill. He was moved by the sudden inclination to put his arms around her once more, as he had in the alley in back of the mall. He stayed where he was. "A friend of mine started calling me that," he said at length. "She thought it was funny." Diana Brown turned to face him.

"Buddy shouldn't have ripped off my mom," she said at last. "The guy was really an asshole." Dean nodded. He had never doubted it.

The house was quite empty. There seemed to be some lag time here, as it took Dean a moment or two to realize he had come in. It had happened, it would seem, of its own accord. He had simply gotten out of the car and followed her to the door without really thinking much about it. But this wasn't quite right. He had thought about it, if the truth were to be known. In fact he had prayed, or come as close to it as any member of his order might, that this girl would not send him on his way, that he would not have to drive these streets alone in these last hours of darkness. Anything, he thought, was preferable to that. But then that wasn't quite right either. Or it was only partly right. He didn't want to leave the girl. He told himself it was because she had no more business being alone than he did. But he lied. He just didn't want to leave her. It had come to seem to him as if there was something wrong with the darkness and he found that he didn't like it, or was afraid of it, whatever it was. He believed as well that she was what stood between him and it.

*   *   *

They wandered for a time in the empty house, turning on lights as if to rid themselves of something. The crippled chandelier cast once more its sorry shadow across marred drywall, a soiled mustard-colored carpet. When he asked her about the blond, meaning the woman who had first answered the door, she only shrugged. "She lives in Chino," she said, as if that were the end of her, and he suspected it was.

Dean took a chair by the overturned table, in the light of the chandelier. Diana continued to roam the house. At last she came back out into the living room and lay down on the couch. She lay for some time on her back, staring into the ceiling. And then she seemed to go to sleep. Dean sat for a time, listening to her breathing, watching the rise and fall of her delicate ribs. Finally he decided to turn off some of the lights.

He was wandering somewhere at the back of the house when he found the girl's room. The bed was covered with clothes neatly folded and arranged in piles—as if she were planning a move. There was a small desk cluttered with papers, an artist's drawing pad, several photographs. Dean poked through some of the stuff. A photograph caught his eye. It was, he saw, a photograph of Dan Brown in front of the Clear Lake house. He was standing at the side of his panel with a young, dark-haired woman. The resemblance was unmistakable. The woman was Diana Brown's mother, the light, if one were to believe Chuck, of Dan Brown's sorry life. The photograph was bright with color. Things looked newer in it, the grass, the stucco, the colored rock roof. The woman was smiling into the sun. Dan Brown, Dean thought, looked about as he had remembered him, younger, thinner, slightly crazed.

There were also, among the clutter, several news clippings that pertained to the band, Pomona Queen, together with a pair of posters, the likes of which Dean had seen at the Club Alibi. He pushed aside the clippings and lifted the cover of the sketch pad with his thumb. The page was covered with writing, what he took at first to be a poem. Upon reading it, however, he came upon some lines that were familiar to him: "Yeah sure I hear voices / yeah sure I see lights / I think it's okay, if you don't cross the line." He recognized them as lines he had heard at the club, sung by the girl in the band. At the top of the page was a title: "Love Crash" by Diana Brown. Dean stood looking at the lyrics for some time. They suggested, he thought, a universe.

Dean had the feeling that he was on to something here, and he might have gone on snooping about the room indefinitely had not the sound of an engine in front of the house stopped him. He closed the sketch pad and walked to the kitchen. He had, on his way to Diana's room, turned off most of the lights so that the house was quite dark. He now stood in a dark kitchen and looked from the window above the sink. There was a white pickup truck parked in the driveway. He was trying to see if there was anyone in it when he heard someone at the front door.

He turned to face the interior of the house, the sink at his back. It was the position in which the woman saw him for the first time. He had the advantage on her. The porch light had been left on. She had left the door open behind her and he could see her fairly well by the light that issued from the porch. He, on the other hand, was standing in the shadows. When she caught sight of him he knew he had scared her. He could hear the sharp intake of her breath. He stepped away from the sink, giving her a better look at him. For a moment they stood in silence, regarding one another across the kitchen. He did not, however, have to study her for long to know who she was. The resemblance was still quite obvious—the slight, angular frame, the straight, black hair. There was even something about the way she stood, one leg straight, a hip thrown slightly out and away. She wore a pair of tight jeans and a black motorcycle jacket. There was no question about who she was.

The woman got to a light before he did. His first impulse, upon seeing her clearly, was to believe that she was not well. Her hair had none of the sheen of her daughter's. Her skin was pale and there were faint circles beneath her eyes. "I'm with Diana," Dean said. It was, given the circumstances, about the best he could come up with.

"Where is she?" the woman asked.

Dean told her. The woman went past him and into the house. Dean followed as far as the living room. He found her kneeling there at the side of the couch. She had taken off the jacket and covered Diana. Her arms were slender and white, like her daughter's. As he watched, the woman turned off the light. She continued, however, to kneel at the side of the couch. Dean turned away and walked to the porch. He was wanting a breath of fresh air.

The truck was a battered Toyota. Upon approaching it, Dean could see that the back was filled with white plastic buckets. There were even, he saw—he couldn't quite help himself—a few crushed petals. He was still looking at them when the woman walked out of the house. He heard her boots on the driveway and turned to face her.

She stopped near the front fender and produced a cigarette. "I hear you drew down on Danny," the woman said. She said this as she fumbled with the cigarette, first getting it between her lips, then getting it lit. She had left her jacket in the house and even with the poor light, Dean could see the tracks on her arms. When she had the cigarette going she looked at him and smiled. Somehow hers was more difficult to read than her daughter's. Dean said nothing.

"He's finished," the woman said quite suddenly. "I got a call. He's finished whether he lives or dies." She looked away, into the street. "Not that it makes any difference," she added. "Not now."

She took a long, hard drag on the cigarette, held the smoke in for some time, then let it out slowly.

"So fucking bizarre," she said. Dean found it difficult to tell whether she was talking to him or to herself. She looked at the house. Dean waited, but she said nothing more.

"She works for you?" he asked. He was thinking about the buckets in the truck. The woman nodded. "I have a route," she said. "I let her off up on Foothill tonight. When I went back to pick her up, I couldn't find her. . . ."

The woman looked toward the street. She looked younger, Dean thought, out of the light. At last she shook her head. "Debbie told me about Buddy," she said. "I couldn't fucking believe it. . . ." Her voice grew faint. Beyond the grass a light flickered in the window of a neighboring house and went out. "Do you even know who I am?" the woman asked suddenly.

"I've assumed you are her mother."

The woman made no response.

"There's a resemblance," Dean said.

"She and I just recently got to know one another," the woman told him. It appeared to him as if she was trying to decide how much of it she wanted to lay on Dean. "It's a long fucking story," she said at last, then added, "I slam a little dope." She continued to look directly at him when she said it. Dean took it for the abridged version of the long story. "She's been trying to help me out," she said. At which point she shook

214

her head, dropped her cigarette in the drive, and ground it out with the toe of a boot. When she had done this, she turned toward the truck.

"You're not staying?" Dean asked. He found that he was thinking suddenly of those clothes covering Diana's bed, as if she were planning a move, he had thought.

"I have to do a couple of things," The woman told him. "Someone has to ID Buddy." She seemed to add this as a kind of afterthought.

"Then you'll be back?"

The woman was standing closer to him now, and not looking quite so young as she had only moments before. Up close one saw the road burn. It hung in the air like a scent. Dean found himself trying to guess her age. Early thirties, perhaps. She would have been a teenager when her life became entangled with Dan Brown's, when she bore him a child.

"She'll be all right," Diana's mother told him. "Kid's like a cat. Always lands on her feet. Besides"—she was already opening a door—"she has you."

"What's that supposed to mean?" Dean asked her. He felt unclear as to whether this was being offered as accusation or commendation. The woman produced a wan smile and climbed behind the wheel of her truck.

Dean could hear the white plastic buckets, empty in the bed, rolling against one another as she backed out of the driveway. She turned into the street and drove away without looking back. Dean watched her go. He waited until the sound of her engine had faded into the night, then went back into the house.

He found Diana Brown on the couch. She was still sleeping. The jacket her mother had placed over her had fallen to the floor. Dean picked it up. He had in mind covering her with it, then he did something else instead. The shoulder facing him was the one with the tattoo. He felt compelled to touch it and so he did, tracing the raised purple scars with his fingers. The flesh was cool and soft. It seemed to him that he could feel her pulse, though perhaps it was only his own that he felt, in the tips of his fingers. And then he covered her with the jacket and seated himself on the floor, his back against the couch, and from time to time he would turn to look at her. There was a light on somewhere in the back of the house and he could see her profile quite clearly, the long lashes, the dark brow. He thought about what she had said to her father, in the back of the bar. "She's mine," she had said. "You can't have her." He was wondering suddenly just who she was talking about—the girl in the band, as would have seemed obvious, or could it have been someone else? Could it have been a reference to something only her father would have understood? In short, he wondered if the words could have referred to her mother. He thought of something Diana had said in the car, that her mother couldn't let Danny know where she was. One could see how that might have played. One could see how walking out on Dan Brown might not be the easiest thing to do, not when one was the light of the great man's life. One could see how the rest of it might have worked as well, how Buddy might have found her, maybe even decided on some brand of low-rent extortion. But then Diana had found her as well. The dance had begun. It had ended in the parking lot of the Club Alibi, at the Pomona Mall.

Dean could not say of course if this was how it had actually gone down and yet he found there was something about it that suited him, just as it suited him to believe there had been more to her pursuit of the girl in the band than what was suggested by Fall Down Debbie. He thought of the songs he had found written in the pad. Perhaps even those had something to do with this woman she had set out to win back. Perhaps she had thought, you write a few songs, you find someone to do them. . . . Who knows? Maybe you even make a few bucks someday, get a new life, then find out down the road somewhere—he was thinking now of the woman in the driveway, of the speed with which she had made her exit—that the object of your affections is only marginally interested, that in fact you have only invented another's need out of your own.

There really should be a way, he thought, a mark perhaps, as in the Revelation, of telling the good ones from the bad. At which point he thought of the scar on the girl's shoulder. And he thought maybe there was.

The golden days in the canyon had ended badly. Lots of things had ended badly about that time and there was, Dean supposed, enough blame to go around. Still, when Dean thought of all that had soured, the image that came most readily to mind was that of the good engineer—perched there on his hillside, at the side of his invention, wrapped in that autumnal light beneath the sycamores, having assumed the lotus position, a jug of Gallo Hearty Burgundy on his knee, his bald pate delicately aglow in some state, Dean would guess now, after all that had transpired, of sexual arousal. For certainly the man had gone after all the young pussy he could get, and he'd gotten, as near as Dean could tell, quite a lot. In the end he'd even gotten Rayann, and Dean had lost her. Or so it seemed to him then. He had been told otherwise. One was supposed to be cool about that sort of thing then. Rayann, it seems, had expected as much out of him. In short, Dean had failed the hipness test. Later, when it became clear Rayann was going to New Mexico, she had invited Dean to go with her.

Engineer Bill was going too, of course. There would be another canyon, another swing. There would also be more privacy, greater risks and explorations. In the end it was jealousy that kept him from it. Sharing had its limits and he had seen her go without him. At least he had told himself that sharing had its limits, that jealousy had kept him from it. For jealousy, he thought, was something he could live with. He thought it preferable to fear. And in the years that followed, thinking was something he had done a lot of.

He had been back at Carl's for a month when on a summer's night a phone call had come from Rayann's mother. Something, it seems, had gone awry in the land of enchantment. There had been a phone call from Bill. There was something wrong with Rayann. Rayann's mother was going to fetch her daughter home and she had wanted to know if Dean would come with her.

The engineer had met them at the airport and whatever serenity he'd possessed in the canyon seemed to have deserted him in the desert's hard, white light. He looked old and tired and it was hard to tell if he was pissed off or maybe just a little bit scared. Rayann, it seems, had begun to have, he had faltered here. Dean would always remember that, how he had faltered. Episodes, the man had said. She'd had several episodes . . . had in short become a bit more than the engineer could handle. In fact, he'd looked just a little bit relieved to be rid of her, and Dean to this day regretted not swinging on the fucker. Dan Brown was what the man had deserved. What he had gotten was something less.

Rayann had come to them that morning on the arm of a nurse, a large straw purse in her hand. The purse seemed uncharacteristic of her at the time. He did not yet understand the extent to which her character had been taken from her. Later, in a cab, in a moment of lucidity, she had held his arm and told him that she was afraid. And well she should have been. For what was to come were a string of mental hospitals, a merry-go-round of drugs and doctors, of visions and humiliations, a long and bitter retreat. Dean had gone along for the ride, as much, at any rate, as one could. He always knew where she was. And occasionally there would be one of those moments, like that time a couple of years ago when, calling from a bar in Prescott, he had, for a golden hour or more, gotten her back, and they had talked about the old times and about the music. They'd talked about the house in the canyon. They had even gone so far as to laugh at the expense of Engineer Bill. And Dean had undertaken the drive down, only to look once more into lifeless eyes, to be told, and this by Rayann herself, that she could not see him without an appointment. He'd gone north after that. It was the direction of choice for a good number of his generation. Dean had simply followed suit, though certainly with none of the optimism with which he imagined his great-grandfather heading west. That West was long gone, the West of the imagination. What was left was the road north, the march into colder climates, the chilly retreat.

Dean had gotten as far as the Owens Valley, where he bused tables, washed windows, turned what creative talents as were left him to the production of cowboy art and in general did his best to think of it as an alternative life style. There had of course been other women in his life, but none to judge his heart and on a bad night he would still make his call. Rayann Kellington died on the fifth of May, 1987, of peritonitis in a mental hospital in Phoenix, Arizona. There were no phone calls left to make.

*   *   *

At some point, Dean must have drifted into sleep because the next thing he knew a pale light had found its way into the room and the girl was gone. Dean went to the kitchen window. His car was gone as well. It had been a mistake, he supposed, teaching her to hot-wire it.

He was still standing at the window when the phone began to ring. He would have hoped to remain calm. Unfortunately his heart fluttered wildly against his breast bone. He expected Diana Brown, or perhaps her mother. When he said hello, however, there was only a long pause on the line, a faint mechanical hum. At last a man's voice, faintly familiar said, "What the fuck," half to itself, then to Dean, "Who is this?"

Dean recognized the voice as Ardath's. "How's the arm?" he asked. He made the unfortunate discovery that he was feeling slightly giddy.

"The fuck . . ." the voice said again. "If this is who I think it is," the voice continued, "you are dead meat. Do you hear me you useless fuck . . . You are dead . . ."

Dean hung up. He was just about to remove the phone from the hook when it rang once more. "Yes," Dean said. He guessed it would be Ardath. There was a moment's pause and then the voice of a rather official-sounding woman somewhere who wanted someone to come somewhere to identify the remains of a certain Buddy Brown. The voice sounded constipated and Dean hung up. One would have to assume that Diana Brown's mother had not kept her appointment, that something had come up. Well, things had a way of doing that. This time he did remove the phone from the hook. He could hear it buzzing at his back as he went once more to the sink. The hangover he'd been anticipating had come with the first light. It was everything one might have hoped for. Dean drew water in a pan and set it on the stove. There would be time at least for a cup of coffee, waiting out a ride from the office—at which point he found Diana's note.

It was on the bar where, hours before, Dan Brown had planted his knife. In full, it read:

> Yo, Magic Man—
>   Had to make use of your wheels, dude.
>   I'll bring them back.
>
>   D—

Dean decided that the office could wait. When he had finished making the coffee he poured himself a cup and went into the backyard to greet the sunrise.

William Tacompsy McCauly had kept no diaries. None of his letters had been saved. In the absence of such, his family had been left to cling to just about any recollection that involved him, much as a dying man clings to hope. Dean was no different. Milly was his source and what stories she could deliver seemed to him an endless source of mystery and fascination. One of his favorites came from the time shortly before his great-grandfather's death and after the loss of his leg. It seems he had gone to the bank one morning and had taken his youngest daughter with him. He was using crutches then, forcing them to walk slowly, with Milly opening doors. They had finished with their banking and were on their way outside when a curious thing happened. Milly was holding the door as her father came through, when she noticed a man near the entrance who had lost both of his legs. He was sitting on a little sled on the sidewalk and selling pencils. There was a second man, with just one leg, leaning on crutches talking to him and, just as William McCauly came out of the bank, two other men, each of whom had lost a limb, stopped to talk to the pencil vendor. The sight had struck Milly as quite odd and fifty years later she could recall wondering what her father's reaction would be. He had only been home from the hospital a short time then and was a man given to long silences. On the morning in question, however, he went straight up to the men and he said: "Boys, let's have a convention." The men laughed, as did William, at which point he had given each of them a dollar and passed on, and Milly had followed. But it was, she had said, a singular sight, her father, together with four other men all of whom had lost something, standing together like that, in the sunlight at the side of the street, laughing at her father's joke. A week later and the man was dead, shot on the streets of Chinatown.

They buried William McCauly in the big cemetery south of town, just off the Phillips Ranch Road. He had gone there with his new wooden leg and his secrets and he was there still, somewhere, beneath ragged grass and smoggy skies. Dean had visited the place once upon his return to the valley. The office, however, had been closed and he had been unable to find the plot, the cemetery being rather large, and in the end he had been driven off by a stray dog which he took to be rabid. Still, it seemed to him just now that he could sense the old man's presence somewhere in this hazy morning light. In fact, none of the old ones had gone far. Palomares and Vejar were buried north of town in what amounted to a vacant lot. Tonner lay with the Spaniards. He supposed that in any other community the place would be of some significance. Here it had been reduced to little more than a weed patch, the tombstones vandalized beyond recognition. Even the Indians buried at the foot of Ganesha Hills, beneath the park, had lost their monument, the work no doubt of a Brackett scholar. . . . Motherfuckers too short, fat, and unattractive for no stone, Jack. Piss on 'em. They were like that here. They were hard on history. At which point it occurred to Dean that there was an engine somewhere off the alley. Again, he would have hoped to remain calm. Again he failed. He went rather unsteadily to the fence and was treated to the sight of one of Pomona's blue-and-yellow trash trucks making its way slowly though the thickening yellow light, and he returned to his seat. He read Diana Brown's message several more times. Given its brevity, this was easily done.

He had taken a post at the edge of the patio, in a fading metal lawn chair with plastic webbing. The webbing was sun-bleached and frayed. Having finished with the note, he began to think about Ardath and the man's threat. They were not, he supposed, items to be taken lightly. He began to think that perhaps he should go into the house and look for a weapon. He then discovered that he was still in possession of one, that resting against the flesh of his leg was the cheap Tijuana switchblade Dan Brown had pressed into his hand. Granted, it was not much of a weapon and he would no doubt hold it incorrectly, but then Ardath, should he come alone, would be operating with only one arm.

Dean took the knife out and looked at it, opening and closing the blade several times in the morning light. For some grotesque reason he had begun to think about what it had been like, making those calls to Rayann. It was like calling on God, he thought suddenly; you dropped your dime, you entered your code, and then you waited in the empty electronic silence, your heart in your throat, and he considered afresh one of the tenets of his faith, that no man could say with certainty who he was, or what he had come into the world to do. Dean knew he could not. He'd come home to claim his inheritance. To all intents and purposes, it would seem that this was within his grasp. He'd seen Carl driven to the breaking point.

He'd seen his Cyclones returned. One would have thought it enough. But of course it wasn't, not now, in this rotting chair, surrounded by these old bones, before this valley of promise. Dean opened and closed the knife one more time. The sun would be above the mountains soon, he thought. It would be hot. Though that scarcely mattered. He would await the coming of Pomona Queen.